# Praise for *Cold Snap*

"Angela Sylvaine knocks it out of the park with this fantastic sequel to her beloved *Frost Bite.* Fun, fearsome, and nostalgic, *Cold Snap* is everything you could want in a horror novel and more. Put this book at the top of your reading pile immediately."

—Gwendolyn Kiste, four-time Bram Stoker Award-winning author of *The Haunting of Velkwood* and *Reluctant Immortals*

"Angela Sylvaine gleefully fills the *Stranger Things* void with infectious sci-fi horror fun! *Cold Snap* is an epically bingeable sequel that left me hungry for more wormy mayhem!"

—Brian McAuley, *USA Today*-bestselling author of *Breathe In, Bleed Out*

"The spirit of '80s Amblin films and *X-Files* paranoia spread through these pages like a cold front. In this sequel, Sylvaine builds on the genre-bending thrills of *Frost Bite* with a wider scope, higher stakes, and new layered characters while maintaining the heart of the series. Readers will want to follow Realene and Nate to ends of the earth."

—Joey Powell, author of *Squirming All the Way Up*

# Praise for *Frost Bite*

"*Frost Bite* is propulsive, wonderfully weird and joyously nostalgic. Loved this coming of age, speculative novel!"

—Erika T. Wurth, author of *The Haunting of Room 204* and *White Horse*

"A gleeful romp through blood-drenched snow. Sylvaine's debut is both bone-chilling and heart-warming at once, equal parts nostalgia and fresh spins on classic tropes—a coming-of-age horror perfect for readers of any age."

—Lindy Ryan, Bram Stoker Award-nominated author of *Bless Your Heart* and *Dollface*

"*Frost Bite* is a welcome skittering slice of another time. Sylvaine deftly brings grit-your-teeth hopefulness, heart, and a meteorite with a mean streak in this love letter to '80s/'90s creature features. Endearing and beastly."

—Hailey Piper, Bram Stoker Award-winning author of *Queen of Teeth* and *A Game in Yellow*

# Cold Snap

Book Two in the *Frost Bite Series*

## Content Warnings

Death, Death of a Parent, Death of a Child, Animal Death (no domestic animals harmed), Graphic Imagery, Violence, Dementia, References to Domestic Violence, Profanity, Religious Extremism.

**Reader note: No dogs or cats are harmed in this novel.**

**Reader discretion is advised.**



Edited by Rob Carroll
Book Design and Layout by Rob Carroll
Cover Art by Eric Hibbeler
Cover Design by Rob Carroll

Library of Congress Control Number: 2026934327

ISBN 978-1-958598-55-9 (paperback)
ISBN 978-1-958598-88-7 (eBook)

darkmatter-ink.com

# Cold Snap

Angela Sylvaine

DARK MATTER INK

***Other Books in the Frost Bite Series***

*Frost Bite*

***Other Books by Angela Sylvaine***

*Chopping Spree*

*The Dead Spot: Stories of Lost Girls*

*For Loki,*
*my desk buddy during the drafting of this novel*
*and Pumpkin to my Realene*

# One

**CALVIN PULLED THE** auger from the newly drilled hole in the iced-over lake, releasing a burst of frigid water that splashed his duck boots. Sweat dripped from beneath his fur hat, one he'd made himself from several of those prairie dog vermin. Normal ones, not the wormy kind that he'd been told gave him the scar on his left hand and took ten goddamn years of his memories. Last thing he recalled now was Martha leaving him on Thanksgiving Day 1988. Three sheets to the wind, he'd eaten the whole damn turkey himself before smashing her commemorative thimble collection with a hammer. A real kick-in-the-nuts memory, those buggers left him with.

Setting the auger down beside his folding chair, he dropped his line in the hole and set his rod in the metal holder, completing the picture of an old man out fishing. He genuinely liked fishing, ice and otherwise, but couldn't do it in Demise. Their hyper-salinated lake didn't freeze and nothing could live in it. Wasn't natural. Plus, he'd grown up on the Lakota reserve in Manitoba, which was about an hour west of here, and he tried to visit the area a few times a year. Lizard Lake held a lot of good memories for him, some of which he could still recall.

This trip across the border wasn't about catching anything, though, except maybe for some military types up to no good. Slumping into the folding chair, his breath rasped in white puffs. He considered lighting up a smoke, but he promised Realene he'd try to quit. *Never too old,* she'd said. Calvin felt a twinge of guilt at keeping the truth about his trip from her, but Colonel Harmon was all she had left after losing her ma and her dad before that. He couldn't accuse Realene's father figure and hero of some serious wrongdoing without first being sure.

When Calvin's crackpot nephew insisted he had photographic proof of the search for an alien ship in the Canadian wilderness near the family's hunting cabin, Calvin expected some *National Enquirer*-style blurry images of discs and orbs, but what he'd gotten were close-up shots of what may have been hunter or farmer types traipsing through the snow with something like metal detectors. And one of the men looked an awful lot like Harmon. After that, Calvin figured a "fishing trip" was in order.

He lifted his binoculars to his eyes and scanned the treeline. Just past a copse of spruce at the edge of the lake, someone had erected a steel frame and begun enclosing it with corrugated sheets painted white to match the surrounding snow. Only the side closest to Calvin was still uncovered, offering a view inside.

Two men clad in hooded Carhartt jackets stood atop the ridge, facing away from him. He got up for a better look and adjusted the binoculars to zoom in. The structure was being built around a circular crater much like the one that had been blasted into the earth behind his trailer only three months back.

Another goddamn meteor strike.

He let the binoculars dangle against his chest while he crouched down to dig through his tackle bag. He pulled out a boxy, green satellite phone he'd picked up at the army surplus store and dialed the only person in the world he still trusted: Realene.

She beat those wormy little bastards once; she would do it again.

Today was the day of the big funeral back in Demise, but the timing couldn't be helped. Realene had to know the worms may be back, and she had to know now.

The line rang and rang.

A beep sounded and a voice came over the line. "You've reached the Gustafson's," she said on the recording. "Me and Ma can't take your call right now, but if you leave a message, we'll call ya back." *Beep.*

"Realene, girlie, we got trouble." His fishing line twitched, tugging at the pole as something took the bait. "I'm up at

Lizard Lake near Winnipeg. There's another one. A crater. A crash site."

Something splashed in the water, yanking his rod from the holder and sucking it beneath the ice. He lowered the phone and peered into the murky depths, saw a shadow flit past. Helluva fish.

But the shadow was not a fish. It was furry and brown, and when it burst from the hole in the ice, it bit down onto Calvin's gloved pinky with its teeth. The satellite phone fell from his grip and landed on the ice with a *crack!*

Teeth sliced through fabric, skin, and muscle. Calvin shrieked and flung his arm back and forth in an attempt to free his finger from the demonic little beast, but the creature, *a goddamn beaver,* only clamped down on his finger tighter, with huge incisors built to gnaw through bark and wood. They hit bone and threatened to keep going.

Calvin spun in a circle, whirling and pinwheeling across the ice like Nancy Kerrigan at the 1994 Winter Olympics. He tripped over the very same hole he bored and stumbled head-first into his folding chair, becoming entangled. The damn critter remained, though, and those teeth clamped even tighter while Calvin thrashed wildly to free himself of icy canvas and metal.

Now crouched on his hands and knees, he raised the arm from which the beaver hung and smacked it down on the ice, leaving a splatter of blood not from the creature, but from his own hand. Wailing in excruciating pain, he slammed the thing onto the frozen surface over and over again until finally it came free, taking his finger with it as it skittered across the ice.

He sat back on his knees and clutched his wrist with his good hand, staring at the tiny stump where his pinky had once been. A steady flow of blood pumped from the mangled digit, drenching his glove and dripping all over the ice.

A good twenty-five yards away, the beaver had regained its footing and stood on hind legs, tail braced flat behind it. The creature stared at him with black, beady eyes, then spit Calvin's severed finger onto the ice, where it bounced once, twice, then slid slowly to stop. That little mouth pulled back, displaying buck teeth colored red.

Calvin's anger turned to fear, recalling Realene's description of the colony of alien-infested prairie dogs standing tall and bloody mouthed before they'd attacked.

"Well, shit."

Beavers were vegetarians, or "herbivores" as Nate would say, just like prairie dogs. It took something mighty sinister to drive them to crave flesh and blood. Something like those goddamn alien worms. And beavers lived in family units, meaning there were likely more of these infected buggers nearby.

Calvin stood, ready to run like hell.

Raised voices sounded behind him, and he turned. The two guys he'd spied atop the ridge now raced toward him across the lake with guns drawn. From this angle and distance, he saw they wore some sort of black, rubbery masks that covered their necks and faces. Not an inch of skin showed.

The beaver gave a high whine and charged the men, galloping across the ice with mouth opened wide, sharp teeth gleaming. One of them aimed and fired two quick shots, dropping the critter. Calvin glanced at his duffel bag, wondered how fast he could grab the hunting rifle tucked inside.

Not fast enough.

Without warning, his vision blurred, and his body started to sway. His legs gave out beneath him, and he dropped first to his knees, then flat on his face, only vaguely feeling the cold surface against his skin before everything went black.

# Two

**REALENE CLIPPED ON** a pair of earrings from Ma's massive collection, butterflies dotted with a rainbow of gems. A gift from Dad for no particular reason other than to make his wife smile. They'd tangle in Realene's curls, the metal prongs snagging when she tried to remove the things later, but maybe the physical pain would be a relief from the overwhelming ache building in her chest.

On the living room TV, a WDIZ reporter in a black trench coat spoke into the camera. "It's a sad day for the people of Demise, North Dakota. Three months ago, a meteor landing triggered the cult leader known as Reverend Zebediah to poison the town's water supply with lead in an attempt to usher in a judgment day that would spare only his followers. More than three hundred people died in what is now being referred to as the Meteor Murders. Among the dead was WDIZ's own Shelley Schraeder, who was brutally murdered by one of Zebediah's lieutenants for bravely attempting to report from inside the congregation's stronghold."

The reporter continued: "In addition to those whose lives were lost, hundreds more were left with dementia-like memory loss as a result of the poisoning. Demise will feel the effects of that day for generations to come, and today we gather to mourn those we lost."

Realene flipped off the TV, leaving the trailer in silence, and went into the entryway. A box labeled "Mementos" sat on the floor at the base of the shelves on the far wall. She'd pulled it out to look through some of the items Ma had treasured, stuff from when her and Dad were dating, from when Realene was a kid.

Just love notes and craft supplies and the terrible artwork kids make.

She put on her duck boots and coat. They looked ridiculous with her long black dress. Her graduation dress. Ma had encouraged her to get it, said the color and style were versatile, perfect for all kinds of occasions.

Realene pulled a piece of paper from her coat pocket and unfolded it, staring at the words. The eulogy was short. She assumed there would be many others who wanted to speak on behalf of their family members and friends, and she wasn't sure she could get out more than a few sentences anyway. Probably should've attended the community planning meetings for the service so she knew what to expect, but she hadn't really wanted to think about the funeral, about Ma's death.

The therapist she'd seen once and never gone back to called it denial, but Realene didn't see the point of dwelling on the past. She was focused on her work at the hospital and preparing for school in the fall so she could move forward and forget about that whole nightmare. Forget about Ma dying when it should have been Realene.

Her tabby cat, Pumpkin, walked up, arching his back. She gave him a little scratch. "You be good while I'm gone, Punky. No parties." He didn't laugh, because he was cat. Besides, it was a stolen joke from her dad, one of his favorites. Too bad he wasn't around to hear it.

She put the eulogy back in her pocket, and instead of crawling back into bed like she wanted to, forced herself to walk out the front door. The little plastic thermometer that hung from the railing on the deck showed it was thirty degrees. The sun shone down, not a cloud in the sky. The storm-of-the-century Realene had so desperately prayed for apparently wasn't happening.

Descending her front steps, she looked across the street to the field where the meteor had crashed three months ago. The crater there would soon be filled in and the plot of land turned into a memorial park. A shape emerged from the sunken hole, climbing over the lip, and she took a few steps forward, her boots squelching in the mix of grass and mud that had emerged from beneath the partially melted snow.

The prairie dogs, and every other infected animal, were gone. Eradicated. This was a person. A big one, with his dark hair tied back in a ponytail. Calvin's nephew, Big Kev. *Of course it was Big Kev.*

A second person emerged from the hole, this one wearing a cowboy hat. Kev's buddy, Flint. Big Kev picked up the section of crushed chain link fence in their path and chucked it a good ten feet out of their way when they easily could have gone around it. *Show-off.*

The two men crossed the street, heading toward her.

"Find any little green men down there?" she asked when they reached her, having to look not *at* but *up* at Big Kev the closer he got. He wore a T-shirt proclaiming "*The Truth is Out There*" beneath his open coat. Hard to believe he and his dad, who looked very much alike, were related to scrawny little Calvin.

"Little green men are a product of science fiction." He crossed his arms over his broad chest. "Eyewitness accounts suggest they're actually gray."

Realene smirked. He was obsessed with the meteor landing, had spent hours examining the site for proof of what he thought was the cover-up of a UFO crash.

"Okay. Find any little gray men down there?"

Flint gave a small smile that raised the corners of his bushy mustache. "No, but that doesn't mean we're wrong. That crater over there is definitely a landing site of some sort. I can feel it."

"Flint here's one of the foremost experts on the topic of all things UFO," Big Kev said. "Comes from the Roswell area. Maybe you've heard of it."

Realene resisted rolling her eyes. As if anyone hadn't seen that episode of *Unsolved Mysteries*. "This was actually a meteor. I saw it myself. Giant rock. Not a ship."

"No offense, but you can't be trusted," Big Kev said. "Might have had your mind tampered with, like Uncle Cal. Memory loss and difficulty recalling events is common among those involved in alien sightings and abductions."

"Calm down, Agent Mulder," she said.

Flint chuckled, earning a glare from Big Kev.

"Or you could be in on the government-orchestrated cover-up of alien life," Big Kev added. "I hear you're pretty friendly with that Colonel Harmon."

"Yeah, I am. You got a problem with that?" After many city leaders and police were infected or killed, the colonel was the one who made sure the town's residents had food, medical care, and housing. He was a hero.

"Uncle Cal doesn't like him either, eh?" Big Kev said. "Says he can't be trusted."

Realene was well aware of Calvin's feelings about the "government bastards" who'd kept them quarantined and swore them all to secrecy about what really transpired in Demise, under the threat of treason charges, but she didn't have time to fight with Big Kev about it. Not today, at least. "Whatever, dude. Where's Calvin? Did he already leave?"

"Why should I tell you?" Big Kev asked, the muscle in his jaw twitching.

Flint cleared his throat. "I'm guessing from this little lady's attire, she's heading over to the funeral."

"Oh." Big Kev scuffed his boots in the melting snow. "Sorry. I, uh, forgot that was… Sorry. Uncle Cal left yesterday. Drove to our cabin up north to go ice fishing."

"He went fishing?" Her voice rose in pitch, seemed to echo around them.

"Yeah. Never really understood the appeal myself. Kinda boring."

Calvin knew how tough today was going to be for Realene, and he'd just left.

To go fishing.

Big Kev shoved his hands in his coat pockets. "You okay?"

"I gotta go." She stomped toward Ma's van parked in the driveway. The slushy snow splattered beneath her feet, marring the hem of her ankle-length dress.

Big Kev said something more about being sorry, but she missed most of it. The beat of her own angry pulse in her ears drowned out his words.

**REALENE BLEW OUT** a breath as she approached the overpass that rose over the railroad tracks, trying to let go of her anger at Calvin abandoning her when she needed him. Someone had spray painted the green and white sign proclaiming she was now entering Demise city limits, population 4,944. A red -327 had been added below the number.

One of those 327 was Ma, and this day was about honoring her memory.

Realene slowed. A mass of black-clad pedestrians in winter coats and snow boots clogged the road, all of them heading toward the city's lone cemetery. Following the instructions of an officer with orange lighted batons, she pulled into the entrance for the Snack Station as she had a hundred times for work. The gas station itself was no more, destroyed during the alien invasion. The lot and surrounding open land were being used as a makeshift parking lot since it was directly across the street from the cemetery.

She turned the car off and removed the keys from the ignition but didn't dare get out. Not yet at least. She had forced herself to eat a toaster strudel before leaving the house, and her stomach was threatening to throw it back up. After taking several deep breaths to calm herself, she pulled on her gloves and stepped out into the afternoon chill. It was a typical Midwestern spring: warm enough to dig the graves, but still cold enough for piles of dirt-crusted snow leftover from the harsh winter to line the berms and curbs. It would take months for them to melt completely. Realene joined the crowd of mourners and crossed the street to the cemetery, the front gates of which were located at the corner of Olson and Main. She didn't bother to look both ways before crossing since the surrounding roads had been closed to thru traffic for the day.

People talked quietly with one another as they walked but were otherwise mostly reserved. The loudest voices belonged to a group of rowdy protesters that had gathered in the park across the street. They were shouting something about government conspiracies and alien cover-ups. Everything about the protest was in bad taste. Big Kev probably would have loved it.

State troopers had started to move the protesters away so they couldn't be heard once the service started, but Realene was unimpressed by their apparent lack of resolve. They had no connection to the deceased either. This was just another day's work for them, and it showed. She scanned the group for any sign of the Revelation cult members but didn't see any faces she recognized. She guessed they knew better than to show up today, especially when everyone in town still blamed them.

A wall of people had gathered at the cemetery gates and were preventing her from seeing inside.

"Family members of the deceased, this way," a voice called over a bullhorn.

Realene followed the voice's instructions and snaked her way through the crowd until she came to a chain link fence guarded by two men in military uniforms, one of whom wielded the bullhorn. The other man held a clipboard.

"I'm family," she said to the man with the clipboard. "My mom is...*was*...Marion Gustafson."

"Realene Gustafson?" the man asked after finding her name on the guest list.

She nodded.

He checked her name off the list and handed her a program before stepping aside to allow her entry. "I'm very sorry for your loss, ma'am."

"Thank you." She looked down at the program. It said "In Loving Memory of Our Lost" on the cover, and she flipped it open to find a list of names and birthdates. Seeing her mom's name among the rest still didn't feel real.

Someone bumped her from behind and she mumbled "Sorry" before looking up to find she had breached the human wall and was now inside the cemetery proper, a field of frost-covered gravestones stretching out before her. Excluding the existing family plots, most of the coffins awaiting burial were lined up in the farthest corner of the recently expanded cemetery, the earth there exhumed en mass to accommodate all the needed new graves. Some of the waiting coffins were black, others white. Some big, others small.

*So small,* Realene lamented, choking back a surge of emotion.

She scanned the rows, trying to find Ma, who'd be buried beside Dad. The coffin seemed nice when Realene chose it, a lovely mahogany with silver accents, but 'nice' didn't help it stand out from the rest.

The crowd pushed her from behind, forcing her toward several sets of bleachers erected at the edge of the cemetery. Realene climbed the steps and was herded into a row near the top, stuck between two people she recognized but wouldn't call friends: a cashier at Blockbuster and a guy who'd been a year ahead of her in school.

Nate was burying his dad today, too, and had wanted her to come with him, his mom, and his new girlfriend, Trish, but Realene said no, thinking privacy would be better while she processed her emotions. Now she wished she had him next to her, wished to hold his hand. He knew Ma, loved her. She craned her neck, tried to find him in the stands but couldn't.

Realene once again searched the cemetery, looking this time for Dad's headstone in hopes of finding Ma. Bodies pressed in from both sides, and she breathed faster, feeling claustrophobic even in the open air.

A familiar voice came on loudspeakers that had been set-up for the ceremony. "Attention, everyone. Attention." It was Colonel Harmon. He wore his dress uniform and stood at a podium atop the small dais that faced the bleachers, speaking calmly into the microphone there. Realene almost cried out in relief from seeing someone who knew Ma, cared about her. He'd called to check in on Realene that morning, in fact, and hadn't judged her when she started bawling.

"We'll get started with the service here momentarily, but I hope you'll allow me a few words first." He scanned the crowd.

Realene raised her hand a bit, hoping to catch his attention, but his gaze skated over her. "We have all been through more these last few months than any town should, but the kindness and resilience you have all demonstrated has been an inspiration. While we'll never be the same, will always be scarred by the tragic events that took place here, we *will* carry on."

No one applauded, but many nodded and turned to one another in agreement.

"Senator," he said, stepping aside for a man in a suit, an expensive looking peacoat, and leather gloves. Realene recognized the man as Senator Schmidt, a Republican who'd won largely on his platform in support of the armed forces, though he'd never served himself.

"I stand here truly humbled and inspired by the strength of this community in the face of unspeakable evil," he began. "Matthew 5:4 says, 'Blessed are those who mourn, for they will be comforted.'" He carried on like this for a while, his words more fitting for a campaign speech, until the people in bleachers started to get restless.

Sensing the shift in mood, Harmon stepped up and placed a hand on the Senator's shoulder as a signal for him to wrap things up.

Senator Schmidt finished his speech saying, "Please accept my condolences for your loss and know that we at the state level remain committed to helping your community rebuild. May God be with you today and every day." He gestured toward the man behind him, clad in a white robe and purple sash. "Pastor Haagenson."

Realene frowned, wondering why Pastor Brent from Bethel Lutheran wasn't doing the service. He was the one Ma would've wanted.

Harmon and Schmidt descended the short set of stairs off the dais and took two reserved seats in the front row of the bleachers. Realene stood, thinking maybe she could go sit beside the colonel for the service, but someone behind her shoved her back into her seat.

Pastor Haagenson said, "Let us pray."

Realene bowed her head, a bitter wind whipping through the air to sting her face.

"Heavenly Father, we thank you for your presence today and ask that you give us strength. We give thanks for the time we had with our loved ones and rejoice that they are now free, that they are now in a better place."

She gripped her hands together in her lap and prayed harder than she ever had that Ma was with Dad now, that they were together forever in Heaven.

"Help us carry our sorrow without bitterness, to look ahead and push forward one day at a time. Heavenly Father, we ask that you grant us comfort and peace, that you ease our pain, that you inspire us to provide one another comfort and support. Amen."

"Amen," she said with the crowd, her voice no more than a rasp.

"Thank you all for coming. Today will not be easy, but I hope that we will all find strength in community."

The sentiment, while nice, didn't make Realene feel any better. Despite being huddled amongst a crowd of people she'd know her entire life, she'd never felt more alone.

"We have a short program of music and prayer, after which families and friends of the deceased will be invited to visit the grave sites to place flowers or mementos, and to offer silent prayer."

Realene retrieved the paper from her pocket and stared down at the eulogy no one would hear. Ma was just another name on a list now, with hundreds of others, and nothing more. Tears dripped down her face and landed on the paper, forming water stains on the ink.

The pastor called a choir of children to the stage, all of whom were clad in white choral robes topped with winter coats. A woman Realene assumed was their music teacher stood before them and blew a pitch pipe, then signaled the children to begin. Their little voices sang of the greatness of God, and Realene wondered if she was supposed to look at them and think of angels.

Ma's eulogy slipped from Realene's hand, settling on the slushy, metal step. Her resolve, any strength she might have had, shattered, leaving her hollow. More than anything, she wanted her dad, wanted him to wrap her in a hug and tell her everything would be okay.

A low hum filled her ears, drowning out the rest of the service. When the others around her got up and finally began to file down the bleachers toward the graves, she shoved past them down the stairs.

She wanted, no, *needed*, to talk to Colonel Harmon.

As she approached, she watched him shake the pastor's hand, thanking him, when a soldier rushed up. The man pulled Schmidt and Harmon aside, speaking to them quietly, then ushering them away.

"Wait," she called, but the colonel had already disappeared into the throng of people.

Gone.

Realene pushed through the crowd, out the gate, past the rings of people surrounding the cemetery. She glimpsed other faces she knew, but no one acknowledged her, too caught up in their own grief to care about hers.

She ran to her van—Ma's van—which she'd nicknamed Barbara Eden in honor of Ma's love of *I Dream of Jeannie*. If only it could grant wishes like she did.

Realene drove home in silence. The trailer was empty except for Pumpkin, who sat in Ma's recliner. From behind him, atop the rickety, plywood bookshelf, the answering machine flashed, signifying a message. Whoever it was, she didn't want to talk to them, didn't care what they were selling.

Eyes blurred by tears, Realene rushed through the living room, through the kitchen, shedding her coat and boots as she went, until finally reaching her bed. She crawled beneath the covers and burrowed her face into her pillow, the butterfly earrings she wore cutting sharply into her skin.

# Three

**THE PHONE RANG** from Realene's nightstand. She pulled her Oma's colorful handmade afghan over her head and waited for the answering machine in the living room to pick up, but another disturbance cut through her knit shroud.

Pumpkin.

He meowed again and again, changing pitch and frequency, even raising himself up to perch on his front paws, positioning himself right beside her ear.

"Fine, I'm up." She threw off the blanket and swung her long-john-clad legs over the side of her twin bed.

A chill seeped into her bedroom through the trailer's thin, corrugated steel exterior and wood-paneled walls. In most places, mid-March meant the beginning of spring, but not in Demise. She glanced out the bay window at the sea of white drifts from the storm that hit the day after the funeral, the bright white snow reflecting the sun and causing her to squint.

Realene grabbed her dad's favorite old flannel from her bed post, catching a whiff of motor oil and Marlboros, and slipped it on over her T-shirt. The smell was at once comforting and heart-wrenching, the hug she desperately needed but would never have again. She'd been thinking a lot about him, remembering things she hadn't thought about for a long time.

There were a couple tough years before he got sick when he'd drink too much and talk to her like she wasn't a kid. Tell her things she didn't want to know. He confessed he regretted joining the military, regretted things he'd taken part in. But he couldn't find a way out. She assumed he was talking about his time in Vietnam, but he never went into detail.

She wondered if being in a cult was like that sometimes, where you couldn't find a way out.

Pumpkin twined around her ankles, and she tore her gaze away from the window, trudging from her room and down the narrow hallway, past the washer and dryer piled with dirty clothes. Sunshine spilled into the kitchen window, highlighting the mess of the kitchen, almost as bad as when Ma was alive. Realene had since cleaned up the church programs and other junk mail Ma wouldn't part with, but discarded Swanson TV-dinner trays and Pop-Tart wrappers took their place. The only thing Realene seemed capable of lately was sleeping and eating.

She grabbed the bag of Whiskas from the cupboard and bent to fill Pumpkin's bowl, which had been licked clean. "Okay, you were right, I'm sorry." She gave his head a little scratch as he chomped on his kibble.

Did Pumpkin miss Ma and Dad, too?

Of course he did. They were a hundred times better companions than Realene, never would have forgotten to feed him.

Realene put the food back in the cupboard and shuffled toward the living room, her hip bumping the kitchen table. The funeral program fluttered to the yellowing linoleum floor, and she picked it up, staring at the cover. No picture of Ma or special Bible verse chosen just for her written in script below her name, no heartfelt words inside or details of Ma's life.

She set the program down and continued into the living room, where she slumped into the recliner.

The phone attached to the wall behind the chair gave a shrill ring, and she winced. It rang again and again, and she barely suppressed the urge to tear the thing from the wall and smash it.

"Leave me alone." She pressed her hands over her ears as the answering machine beeped. The tape was already half-full with messages from Nate, of his too-soft voice saying he was worried about her. And a couple were from the Colonel, who just wanted to make sure she was okay.

She wasn't, but they'd forget about her soon and move on.

Nate had his precious girlfriend and his mom, didn't need Realene anymore. Calvin didn't need her either. He had actual family to care for him now. Probably why he went fishing without even saying goodbye, without saying he was sorry for missing Ma's funeral.

She dropped her hands from her head, heard only blessed silence. *Good.* She grabbed the remote and flipped on the TV. The screen showed Senator Schmidt doing a press conference at the state capital. He was positioned at a podium flanked by the U.S. and North Dakota state flags.

"This tragedy only reinforces the need for a strong military presence. Thanks to the immediate response of our brave men and women in uniform" —he gestured behind him, where Colonel Harmon stood wearing his dress uniform— "more loss of life was prevented. The Democrats would have Steele Air Force Base closed—"

She flipped the channel to Turner Classic Movies, which was playing *My Fair Lady*, one of Ma's favorites. Realene had seen enough of the senator trying to use their tragedy for his own purposes. But what was Colonel Harmon doing there? She'd thought better of him. Never thought he would allow himself to be used as a political prop.

The phone gave another shrill ring, and she chucked the remote at the handset, knocking it from the cradle. Pumpkin eyed her warily from the floor beside the chair but finally jumped into her lap. She pulled the lever to lay back in the recliner and allowed him to tenderize her body with his front paws before curling up on her chest, his purrs reverberating through her rib cage.

"Just you and me now, Punky." She wrapped her arms around him and squeezed him tight. Tears dripped down her cheeks to soak his fur.

**NATE DROVE DOWN** a slushy Main Street, the Pixies' "Wave of Mutilation" blasting from his truck's speakers. He still wasn't used to all the empty lots and boarded-up buildings that now dominated Demise. A few businesses had reopened quickly, like the Blockbuster and Valley Dairy, but many had Closed signs or were damaged beyond repair.

He pulled into the lot of the rainbow-striped building that used to be the Skateway roller rink and had recently reopened as a gym after the owner was killed during the Meteor Murders. While he had a lot of good memories at the rink with Realene, he figured change was a good thing. It was time for all of them to move on.

Trish appeared in the open door to the building, waving as she ran toward the car with her blonde ponytail bouncing behind her. She wore teal leggings that he knew had a sexy matching crop top, but it was hidden under her oversized sweatshirt and coat.

Nate flipped the radio to the pop station, Trish's favorite.

She hopped in the passenger side of the truck, throwing her duffel bag at her feet before leaning over to plant a kiss on his cheek. "Hi, baby."

"Hi, muffin. How was class?" He took in her sweet face. "Fantasy" by Mariah Carey played on the radio.

He still couldn't believe Trish was his girlfriend. They'd gone to the same high school, but she was a year ahead of him, and they'd never even spoken back then. No reason for a cheerleader to talk to a stoner like him.

"It was okay."

"Just okay?" He glanced her way as he looped around the parking lot, heading toward the exit. "What happened?"

She lowered the volume on the radio. "Nothing. It's just, well, there's a position open for an instructor. It'd just be two classes a week, Step Aerobics and Tae Bo. I was, like, thinking about applying."

"You totally should. You'd be awesome." He didn't know much about the workout scene, but he did know she looked adorable in her brightly colored leotards and leggings. "They'd be lucky to have you, seriously. You even got me hooked on aerobics."

"That's true." She grinned. "I think I'll do it. Apply, I mean. Yeah. I'm gonna go for it."

"They'd be crazy not to hire you." He pulled onto Main, passing by the boarded-up McDonald's.

His mouth twitched at the memory of a car crashing into the very same McDonald's PlayPlace back during the alien invasion and how the exploded ball pit distracted the zombified children that were chasing them just long enough for he and Realene to get away. It wasn't funny then, but Nate found it somewhat funny now.

"What are you smiling about?" Trish asked.

"Just thinking about those zombie kids I told you about. The ones from the McDonald's."

She stared straight ahead, hands clasped tight in her lap. "Oh."

"Shit," Nate blurted, realizing his mistake. "I mean, shoot." He reached over to squeeze her knee. "That was a stupid thing to say. I'm sorry."

Trish's little sister Mindy had been infected, but unlike a lot of the other kids, she didn't make it. Trish tried to find help, but by the time she got back, her little sister was gone. They'd had to bury an empty coffin, Mindy one of dozens who were missing and presumed dead.

"Forgive me, muffin?" he said.

She narrowed her eyes, then gave a small smile. "I guess so."

They passed the cemetery and both went quiet. The new burial mounds were visible even beneath a fresh blanket of snow. The cemetery was almost full now, which is why a new site was being planned on the east side of town.

He couldn't help but zero in on the section of the cemetery that held his dad's plot. Trish had been forced to kill her father in self-defense just like Nate had. It was what bonded them early on in the survivor's support group. But unlike his dad, hers had been a good man.

Nate pulled through the intersection and past the empty space where the Snack Station had been. Everywhere he looked, there were reminders of the tragedy and everything they'd lost.

"I can't wait to get out of here for a few days," Trish said, reading his thoughts. "Never thought I'd be excited to go to Canada for spring break, but it'll do."

"Totally." He'd always laughed at the idiots on TV partying it up at MTV *Spring Break*, but Trish had changed his whole outlook on things like that, showed him that being so judgmental all the time wasn't healthy.

"Except I look so pale, and I can't even tan before we go because of that truck crashing into the Tan-a-Rama."

"I'm sure they have tanning salons in Winnipeg." Nate guided the truck down the overpass that crested the railroad tracks.

"Oh yeah, totally, they're everywhere." Trish paused, then said, "So, um, you're still totally set on inviting Realene?"

His grip tightened on the steering wheel. "I think a change of scenery would be good for her."

"It's a little weird how close you two are. Like, why doesn't she have any female friends?"

It was an old argument, one he was sick of having. "She's been my best friend since we were kids."

Trish turned toward him, her mouth pursed in a pout. "I'm sorry, baby. I know, I get it. It's just, I don't think she likes me much."

"She hardly knows you," Nate said. "And this trip will be the perfect chance for you to spend some time together."

"You're right." She grinned. "I'll make her like me, even if it kills me."

He frowned. Realene couldn't be *made* to do anything, and she'd be totally okay if Trish died trying. "I should talk to her first. I'll drop you off at my mom's."

"Uh-uh. We're a package deal, a power couple. I'm coming with."

Nate kind of liked the feeling of someone being so possessive of him. He knew she'd never have anything to worry about with Realene, but it was the thought that counted. "Power couple, huh?

"Totally. Like Britney Spears and Justin Timberlake."

Nate pictured himself with bleach-blond hair and suppressed a laugh as he turned into Plainview Trailer Park. Pulling up to the curb, he noted the snow still piled around the van's tires. Realene hadn't returned any of his calls, and it looked like she hadn't left the house since the funeral. "Maybe I should go in alone, scope things—"

The passenger-side door slammed shut. Trish was already outside and trudging through the snow.

Nate rushed to catch up to her. "Listen, I need you to take a back seat on this, okay? I'm not sure how she's going to react to us just showing up here."

Trish stopped. "I lost my mom when I was twelve, remember?"

"Well, yeah, I know. I mean, I remember."

"And I lost my dad to those worm things. That reverend may not have shot him, but he was still a victim of all of it, just like Realene's mom."

"You can't talk about that," he said. "I wasn't supposed to tell you." Harmon made them sign some serious paperwork, basically saying they'd be indicted for treason if they ever shared what really happened in Demise.

"You know what I mean. I understand what she's going through. That's what allowed you and me to connect, right?" She continued up the walkway, stomping through the snow in her Reebok high-tops.

Nate followed, hoping that Realene wouldn't just punch Trish in the face the moment she saw her. Trish knocked politely on the front door.

Nate climbed the porch steps and stepped in front of her. "Might be better if she sees me first."

Trish moved aside and they waited. No response.

Nate knocked this time, louder, and glimpsed a shadow move behind the gauzy curtains covering the kitchen window. "Dude, you know we can see you in there, right?" He shouted.

Still no answer.

He pulled his keys from his pocket and inserted his emergency copy of Realene's trailer key into the lock. This would give her one more thing to be pissed about, but he had to do it; she'd left him no choice. He opened the door and Trish followed him inside.

"We're coming in," Nate called, leading the way into the living room. "Hope you're decent."

The recliner sat empty except for Pumpkin, who raised his head and gave Nate a slow blink.

Pain spiked in Nate's chest.

Ma had been like a second mother to him, and he'd failed her, hadn't been there with Realene the night she died. He shook the thought from his head. *No.* He wouldn't let himself get stuck in the past.

Nate scratched Pumpkin's back, earning a purr.

"Hi, kitty, kitty," Trish said, reaching out to pet Pumpkin.

His purr cut off, but he allowed her to scratch his back. Not full approval, but not a rebuke, either.

Nate crossed the darkened living room, coming to a halt at the edge of the kitchen. Ma's piles of junk mail and church programs were gone, not thrown away but packed up. He'd helped Realene with the task, which took several days and resulted in plenty of tears and laughter.

Now instead of paper, the counters were cluttered with old food containers and other trash.

Trish pushed past him. "Oh my gosh, it's a mess in here." She took off her winter coat and hung it on the back of a chair, revealing a Guess-brand sweatshirt. "I don't care if it's too cold outside for ants, this kind of filth still brings bugs, spiders, and all kinds of other critters." She pulled on a pair of kitchen gloves and grabbed an empty garbage bag from the box to start throwing away the debris. "See? It's good I came. We'll have this place spiffed up in no time. 'Clean house, clean mind,' my mom always used to say, and it's so true."

"Thanks, muffin." Nate gave her a peck on the cheek as he passed, glad she had something to occupy her so he could try to talk to Realene in private. "I'm gonna check her bedroom, see if she's there."

Nate grimaced at the mounds of dirty clothes piled high in the hallway. He knocked on her bedroom door. "Rea? You in there?"

Nothing.

"You have company or something? Girl, maybe? A guy? Some rando you picked up at the truck stop?"

"You're not funny," Realene said, her voice muffled behind the door.

Nate opened the door a crack. "What was that? I thought I heard you say, 'Come in.'"

Realene furrowed her brow. "Yeah, fine, I guess."

Nate entered her bedroom and closed the door behind him.

Realene sat up against her headboard. "I didn't give you that key so you could break in, or throw a party, or do whatever it is you're doing."

Nate forced himself not to laugh at her hair, which was matted and messy as a bird's nest. "This all could have been avoided if you'd just called me back."

He took a seat at the foot of the bed and looked around at the room he'd basically grown up in. Nirvana posters and anatomy diagrams plastered the wood paneled walls, and the framed photo of her mom and dad that she loved so much—the one from their family road trip to the Grand Canyon—still stood on the nightstand but was now half-hidden behind a pile of discarded Snapple bottles and candy wrappers.

"How you doing?" he asked.

"I'm alive." She crossed her arms. "So, are we good? You going now?"

"Nope." He stood. "Come on, get up."

She slumped, shaking her head.

"You think Ma would want to see you like this?"

Her face flushed red, and she jumped from bed, getting in his face. "Screw you."

"My girlfriend wouldn't like that much."

Realene rolled her eyes, and they quickly filled with tears.

Nate wrapped his arms around her and pulled her in close. Her body was stiff at first, but after a minute she hugged him back, and they just stood like that. He wasn't sure for how long.

There was a light knock on the door, then it opened. Trish peeked her head in.

"Realene, hi, are you okay?" she asked. "Nate was just so worried about you. And I was, too. I lost my mom when I was young, so I totally know what you're going through. It's just so hard."

She came up and placed one lime-green rubber-gloved hand on Realene's arm.

Realene looked at Nate, staring daggers at him.

Catching Realene's drift, he pulled Trish away, putting a little distance between the two. "Privacy, remember?" he whispered to her.

She gave a pout. "I just wanted to say, you know, what works great for me when I'm feeling crummy is exercise. Moving your body." She looked back to Realene. "Have you ever tried Tae Bo? It's really the best. It's like dancing mixed with fighting. Never mind, it's decided: I'm totally taking you."

"I wouldn't mind punching something right now," Realene's said, her hand curling into a fist.

"That's the spirit," Trish exclaimed, then frowned. "Those clothes, though. They just won't do. But no worries. I'll lend you one of my outfits, something cute to workout in."

With a nervous laugh, Nate hustled Trish from the room, hoping to stave off an attack. "Let's go, babe." He nudged her down the hallway and into the kitchen, which actually looked a lot better after just a few minutes of Trish cleaning it up. She'd managed to collect most of the trash in that short time, filling a trash bag that now sat against the fridge.

Realene followed them in silence. When she saw the state of the kitchen, she opened her mouth to say something that Nate doubted would be a thank-you, but she was cut short when a loud thump smacked the side of the trailer outside the living room, causing Pumpkin to bolt from the recliner. "Why can't everyone just leave me alone?" She shoved past Nate on her way to the front door.

Nate went after her, watched as she put on her boots, threw on her coat, and grabbed the baseball bat leaning against the wall, still stained with blood from their epic battle against the alien-infested creatures.

"What are you planning to do with that?" he asked.

She didn't respond, just threw open the front door.

# Four

**A GUST OF** icy wind hit Realene, and she stopped to zip up her coat and tug her hood over her head. Being outside was the last thing she wanted, but she wouldn't let those psycho cultists keep harassing her. They'd gotten worse since the funeral, not only screaming curses but lobbing various fruits and vegetables at the trailer, as if it was her fault their madman leader had gotten killed.

Nate called out behind her, but she ignored him. Holding the bat under one arm while making her way down the steps and onto the path, she pulled her gloves from her pockets and tugged them on.

She stopped.

Their bus, which she hadn't seen since that day at the lake, was parked at the bottom of her driveway. The metal tire spikes had been removed, and the strange septumnox symbols that combined the cross and a seven to symbolize the plagues of God's wrath had been painted over with white paint and then painted over again with slogans proclaiming:

*Reverend Zebediah was framed*

*Don't trust the government*

*Colonel Harmon = Satan's Minion*

Atop the slogans, counter messages were spray painted by vandals:

*You're not welcome here*

*Get out of Demise*

*Go to hell, murderers*

Someone she didn't recognize—a young guy of about twenty-five—popped out of the top hatch of the bus and lobbed a potato at the trailer, which hit the trailer's metal siding and plopped into the snow.

"Seriously, guys? I mean, this is just a waste," she said. "That potato might have grown up to become tater tots someday."

Nate walked up behind her, Trish close behind him. "What are they doing here?"

"Harassing me, as usual." She raised her voice so the cultists could hear: "Seriously, I'm calling the cops if you guys don't knock this crap off." She'd called the police before, but the cop who responded had used more force than she was comfortable with, probably looking for an excuse to rough up the cult members. So, she was hesitant to call them again, but the threat itself was still effective.

"Get the hell out of here, you psychos!" Nate said.

The bus door opened with a hiss, and Irene appeared in the doorway looking much older than she had just a few months ago. Her once perfectly styled curls were now grown out and showing their gray roots, making her look a lot like Cruella de Vil.

"How dare you show your face here," Realene yelled. Irene was supposed to be Ma's best friend and watched her die at the hands of Irene's idiot Messiah.

The back door to Calvin's trailer banged open to reveal Big Kev wearing just a hockey jersey and boxer shorts. "Hey, what're you all shoutin' about?" he asked.

"We know you're in league with those government devils," Irene said. "Spewing their lies, tarnishing the name of the divine Reverend Zebediah."

Realene took a defiant step closer to the bus. "You mean Jeff Hozak? He was a psychopath."

"He wanted everyone in town to die," Nate said. "All so you assholes could secure your place in heaven…as if that's where you'd end up."

Trish stepped up beside Realene.

"He never poisoned anyone, and you know it!" Irene shrieked.

"Hey, yeah, that's what I've been saying," Big Kev said.

"This is none of your business," Realene said to Kev. She knew Big Kev was right, but there wasn't anything she could do about it. Besides, the cult deserved to take the blame.

She rested her bat on her shoulder and strode through the snow. "I've always wanted another crack at you. Looks like today might finally be the day."

Nate grabbed her by the sleeve. "Easy, killer," he whispered.

"Should I call the police?" Trish interjected. "I think I should call the police. I mean, clearly she's a psycho, but she's, like, also an old lady. You know what I mean?"

Realene gave Trish a death glare.

"What? We're supposed to respect our elders," Trish said. "I just don't think beating her up is the best idea. That's all."

Realene pulled the bat from her shoulder and tapped Trish on the chest with the barrel. "Did I ask you what you thought?"

"Hey now," Nate said, stepping between Realene and Trish and pushing the bat away.

Irene continued her ranting from the bus's steps. "Harmon is in league with the devil. We won't allow him to tarnish the name of Reverend Zebediah."

"I think he did a fine job tarnishing his own name," Realene said. "Like when he shot Ma, and you helped him. Remember that?"

The young guy who had lobbed a perfectly good potato at the trailer appeared beside Irene. His hair was buzzed short, and he wore a pristine dress shirt buttoned all the way to the top. "Everyone calm down."

"Who the hell are you?"

"This is Birdie, my new second in command," Irene said. "He's only been with us a few weeks and already he's my most trusted lieutenant." She beamed at the young man.

"Your name is *Birdie*?" Realene asked. She started to laugh but stopped. "Wait. What do you mean 'second in command?'"

Irene stood taller. "That's right, I've taken on the mantle of leadership here on Earth, while Reverend Zebediah looks on from Heaven above, as was his plan should he ascend early."

"We're just trying to restore the good reverend's name," Birdie said, sounding more bored than zealous. "And we know you're both working with Harmon, helping him hide the truth."

"The colonel is a hero. You should be thanking him for everything he's done to help Demise survive," Realene said. Harmon made sure everyone had food, housing, and support. He even met with the president and got a state of emergency declared so that the town could receive federal funds.

"I don't know, man," Big Kev said. "I don't trust that guy."

Realene turned to stare at him. "Seriously, dude, get lost."

He stomped back inside, slamming the door behind him.

Realene loosened her grip on the bat and allowed it to fall limp at her side. She was so damn tired of all this bullshit. Big Kev was questioning the one man who'd gotten Demise through the past few months, and Irene was actually picking up new recruits. What was the point of even fighting anymore?

She started to head back inside.

"You get back here. Confess the truth to save your soul!" Irene yelled.

Realene turned back around but didn't raise her voice, kept a tight hold on the rage that wanted to break free. "Don't you ever come back here, Irene. If you do, I will kill you. Literally. I'll smash your face in with this bat and watch you die. You understand?"

Irene's mouth dropped open.

Realene trudged back up the walk, exhaustion pulling at her limbs. Nate and Trish followed.

"That was crazy," Trish whispered. "I mean, I thought you were really going to bash her brains or something. Not that she doesn't deserve it, but you can't, like, threaten to kill people."

"Do you ever shut the hell up?" Realene asked.

Trish huffed and turned to Nate, but he just shrugged and raised his hands in surrender.

"I'm going back to bed." Realene climbed the steps and pushed inside the trailer. She started to shut the door behind her, but Nate stopped the door before it could close completely.

"Wait, we need to talk," he said, forcing his way in behind her. "It's important."

Realene shucked her coat and boots onto the floor in the entry, then proceeded to plop down in the recliner. Grabbing the remote, she switched on the TV and started flipping the channels. "Fine. Talk."

Trish scurried past, eyes averted, and resumed her cleaning of the kitchen. Realene opened her mouth to protest, then closed it. Maybe if the girl kept busy she would at least be quiet.

Realene stopped on MTV, where *Spring Break* was in full swing. A bikini-clad Carmen Electra was hosting some kind of swimsuit fashion show on the beach. Because she was *sooo* compelling in *Baywatch.*

Nate gestured toward the TV screen. "Um, that's actually what we wanted to talk to you about."

The Backstreet Boys came out on the stage and started playing "Everybody" while drunk coed's shook their asses on the catwalk.

"Oh my gosh… I love this song," Trish exclaimed from the kitchen. She dropped her garbage bag to dance along with the band. She clearly had their routine memorized.

Realene snickered, glancing at Nate.

He wasn't laughing, though. A little smile tugged at his lips as he watched his girlfriend dance to a song Realene knew he hated.

She hit mute on the TV. "You wanna talk to me about The Backstreet Boys?"

"Kind of. Spring break, actually. Trish and I are going, and we want you to come with us."

Realene grimaced. "Like, to Florida?"

"I wish. Winnipeg."

"Canada?" Realene let out a loud snort. She was certain Nate was joking now.

"The Colonel is doing some kind of research up there, and he said we should come visit, so we're taking him up on the offer. He got us a free room at the Holiday Inn."

"It's a Holidome," Trish added. "It's got a pool and a mini golf course and an arcade. And, like, the drinking age is eighteen, so we won't even need fake IDs. It's going to be so totally awesome."

"Totally," Realene said, mocking Trish's enthusiasm.

Nate pulled his car keys from his pocket and handed them to Trish. "Can you do me a favor and go warm up the truck?"

She looked between the two of them, then said, "Okay, baby." She took off the kitchen gloves and laid them on the table, then gave Realene a forced smile. "Oh, and don't think I forgot about Tae Bo. We'll go after break. You're gonna absolutely love it."

Realene would rather eat a pound of raw Brussel sprouts than be trapped in a room with Trish for an hour. "We'll see," she said flatly.

Once Trish had gone, Nate turned to glare at Realene. "You're a real asshole, you know that?"

"Me? You're being ridiculous, *baby*. What, you like the Backstreet Boys now?" She motioned to the boy band still dancing silently on her TV. "We used to make fun of all the idiots who like this crap."

"Yeah, and we were being jerks. I mean, who cares what other people like if it makes 'em happy."

"So, I'm an asshole *and* a jerk now. Wow, Nate. Tell me again why I should go to Canada with you?"

Nate shoved his hands in his jeans pockets, like he always did when he was starting to clam up. "Because it'll be fun. And because I miss you."

Realene sighed. "If you really wanted me there, you wouldn't have waited to invite me until the day before you left."

"Dude, like I said already, I've been trying to call you. Have you even listened your messages?" He gestured toward the answering machine, whose message light was flashing. "Seriously, you're in a funk. Come with us."

Realene's stomach twisted. "It's only been a week since the funeral."

"Ma died three months ago, and you think she'd want you just wallowing like this? You need to move on."

"That's easy for you to say. You're probably glad your dad's dead." She stood. "So just go on up to spring break and get hammered with a bunch of morons to celebrate."

"What's your problem? I'm trying to help you, you know."

"I don't want your help. I want to be left alone."

"No." He stepped closer, so their faces were just a few inches apart. "You're my biff, remember? I'm not gonna let you wallow."

"Best friends forever." She scoffed. "Maybe you're the one that needs to move on, accept we don't need each other anymore."

He swallowed heavily. "You don't mean that."

"You have Trish now, and I'm just a jerk who's dragging you down." She sat back down in the recliner and grabbed the remote.

"So… That's what this is *really* about. You'd probably like her, you know, if you'd just give her a chance."

"Would I, though?"

"She makes me happy. I thought that would be enough for you."

Realene unmuted the TV. "Bye," she said.

He stared at her, dumbfounded, but she kept her focus on the TV.

"Fine," Nate finally said. "Have a nice life." He strode from the room and slammed the front door behind him.

Reacting to the noise, Pumpkin came slinking out from under the couch and peeked into the entry way, somehow judgmentally.

"Don't you look at me like that," Realene said to him. Her eyes burned with tears, and the dancing co-eds on the TV screen blurred.

# Five

**NATE TROMPED THROUGH** the snow, refusing to look back at Realene's trailer as he made his way to his truck. He hopped into the driver's seat, and with breath puffing out in white clouds, said to Trish, "She's not coming."

"Oh, baby. I'm sorry." Trish unbuckled her seatbelt and scooted over, wrapping one arm around his back and laying her head on his shoulder.

He focused on breathing in and out, in and out. Realene treated Trish like crap, didn't even try to get to know her, and now she was acting like their friendship meant nothing to her. "You were right. I don't know why I even invited her."

Trish pulled back. "She's your best friend."

"Maybe not anymore." He was sick of trying to make Realene feel better when she didn't seem to care about him. "She's kind of an asshole."

Trish gave a surprised laugh. "Yeah, kind of."

"Sorry about that. I mean, the way she treated you."

"I know I can be a lot to handle. I, like, get on people's nerves, I guess." She fiddled with her coat's zipper, tugging it up and down again. "But I don't really care what other people think about me. I like who I am."

"I like who you are too, muffin. You're perfect."

She planted a strawberry lip gloss flavored kiss on his lips, then buckled back in.

His chest ached with the realization of how lucky he was to have her. Screw Realene. Trish was more than enough, and she wasn't obsessed with the past. She knew how to live in the moment. "I'm really glad it's going to be just us. I know it's only Winnipeg, but it's going to be awesome."

"*Just* Winnipeg? That's better than Florida, like *way* better. I've always wanted to stay at the Holidome. Wait, do you have a bathing suit?"

He guided the truck toward the trailer park's entrance. "Nope." He couldn't even remember the last time he'd gone swimming. Elementary school swim lessons? He wondered if they had swim trunks out at Scheels yet.

"Oh, we should swing by your mom's and tell her we'll be out of town," Trish said. "Just so she doesn't worry."

"You just want to say hi to Trout." He turned onto the main road. After Walt died in the Meteor Murders, Nate's mom took his dog, Trout, in. The company was good for both of them.

She giggled, the sound easing the tightness in his chest. "Busted. But I mean, I like your mom too."

He turned into a residential neighborhood of older ranch-style homes and parked across from the house where he grew up. Seeing it still put a knot in his stomach. Too many memories tied to his dad.

The street was icy, and he took Trish's hand as they made their way up to the house. His gaze strayed to the path that snaked around the garage, where he'd been attacked by the infected buck that ultimately killed his dad. Well, *almost* killed.

Nate and Trish climbed the couple steps onto the porch, which still boasted a plastic, holiday nativity scene despite it being March, and knocked on the door. A horn honked, and he glanced behind him. The Revelation cult bus was parked on the side street, exhaust pluming from the tail pipe.

"Isn't that—" Trish started, when the door opened.

There, in the doorway, standing beside Nate's mom was Irene.

"What are you doing here?" he asked.

Trout pushed past the two women and ran out into the front yard to do a lap through the snow, then dashed back up to Trish, his whole butt wagging as she stooped to pet him "Who's a good boy? Yes, it's you. You're such a sweet baby."

Nate's mom's face was pinched. "Nathan. You should've told me you'd be coming by. I would've made a hotdish."

"It's okay, Mom." He watched Irene. She smiled her old smile, the one of a harmless old lady, but he knew it was a mask.

"We were just catching up." She grasped both of his mom's hands in hers. "You think about what I said."

She stepped through the door and both he and Trish instinctually backed away, as if touching her might stain them. Even Trout took a step back, his tail going still as he watched her pass.

"Come in, I'll put on some coffee," Nate's mom said, going back inside and leaving the door cracked for Nate and Trish to follow.

Seeing Irene come down the front steps, Birdie jumped from the bus and jogged over to take Irene's arm and guide her across the ice-slicked road. He had a hold of Irene's elbow when he lost his footing, his feet slipping out from under him, causing him to fly up in the air and land hard on this back. Because he was gripping Irene's arm, he took her with him, yanking her down hard.

She cried out, her legs sticking up in the air, flailing.

Trish moved toward the edge of the porch. "Should we help them?"

Birdie stood and reached down to help Irene, who was now on all fours. She grasped his hand, and he fell again, also ending up on all fours. He swore and crawled toward the bus, leaving Irene to crawl after him.

Trish let out a giggle, quickly raising her hand to cover her mouth. Nate's shoulders shook as he tried to hold in his laughter. Soon, they were busting up. That earned them glares from Irene and Birdie, who finally made it to the bus and pulled themselves to a standing position, using the vehicle as a brace to guide them to the door.

"You're letting in the cold," Nate's mom called from inside the house.

Nate and Trish went inside and stamped their feet to knock the snow from their boots before removing them. He hung up his coat and noticed the photo display on the wall had changed. Once upon a time, it held family photos, which later transitioned to photos of just his mom and dad after Nate'd been disowned. Now it was a shrine.

A large photo of his dad in his early twenties, wearing his Army mechanics uniform, was hung at the center. He'd served under Realene's dad, Louie, who'd advanced to Staff Sergeant. Nate's dad never moved up, insisting Louie was out to get him. Other photos of Nate's dad surrounded the larger one, all featuring that same stoic face.

His mom emerged from the kitchen, saw where he was looking. "Such a handsome young man, wasn't he? You take after him."

Nate would never understand how she still loved his dad after all the physical and mental pain he'd caused her, but it would be a waste of breath to question her about it. The ceiling fan spun overhead, creating a soft whir. His mom ran it no matter the temperature outside, a habit Nate had picked up himself. They both had a fear of total silence.

Trish pulled a plastic baggie of bone-shaped dog treats from her coat pocket. "Here, Mrs. Haugen. They're homemade with peanut butter, oats, and some other stuff. My dad taught me how to make 'em. We used to take a batch to the animal shelter every Saturday. I hope Trout likes them."

"I'm sure he will love them, dear." Nate's mom took the treats and placed one hand on the girl's cheek in a display of affection more tender than she'd shown Nate in months. "And what a lovely memory of your father. It's so important we keep them alive in our hearts."

"What did Irene want?" Nate asked, moving into the living room. The piles of survivalist literature and discarded peanut shells that had littered the room when his father was alive were gone, but a Bible and religious study workbook were stacked on the coffee table.

The TV was muted, but televangelist Jimmy Swaggart filled the screen, preaching to a stadium full of people. Nate remembered the guy saying something about how Christians are supposed to be the most forgiving people in the world, but as Realene had pointed out, that may have been after his multiple prostitution scandals. Nate's mom had replaced one charlatan with another. "I hope you're not sending this guy any money."

She perched on the armchair. "It was Reverend Zebediah that poisoned everyone, wasn't it?" Trout trotted over, sitting dutifully at her side.

Nate clenched his teeth, taking a seat on the couch. Trish joined him, staying quiet. "That's what Colonel Harmon says."

"Is it true?"

Trish shifted, straightening the hem of her sweatshirt.

"I don't want to keep talking about this. Can't you just let it go, Mom?"

"Is. It. True?"

Nate sighed. "Jeff Hozak was a bad guy. People were hurt and died because of him." He stared at the wood grain of the coffee table, pockmarked with small burns from his dad's cigarettes. Another bad guy. His mom seemed to have a thing for them.

"Nathan." She reached for her Bible, held it up. "Lying is a sin."

"I'm not lying." And he wasn't… Not exactly.

"You aren't telling the truth either."

"Is that why Irene was here? To convince you the reverend was some kind of martyr?"

"I know he wasn't a good man." She placed the Bible on her lap, rested her hand on the cover. "He hurt people, killed people. I saw that with my own eyes."

Nate relaxed back into the couch, some of the tension leaving his body.

"But if he didn't poison everyone, what *did* happen?"

"I can't say."

"A false witness will not go unpunished."

Nate stood and took Trish's hand, leading her from the room. His patience was already too thin from the morning's events; he couldn't tolerate a Bible lesson from his mom. "We should go. We need to pack."

"We actually stopped by to tell you we're going to Winnipeg for few days," Trish said. "The colonel's there, and he got us a room at the Holidome so we can have a little getaway. Isn't that nice?"

Nate's mom followed them to the door, clutching the Bible to her chest. "He's in Winnipeg? Why?"

"I don't know, Mom. Some kind of research or something. He didn't say." He put on his coat. "We probably won't even see him."

"We're going for spring break," Trish said, taking her coat from Nate's outstretched hand.

"Why would he give you this gift? What does he want?" his mom asked.

"Nothing. Jesus. He's just being nice."

"Do not take the Lord's name in vain."

Heat crept up his neck. "Why do you want to know? So you can report back to Irene?"

She clutched the Bible to her chest like some kind of shield. "Beware of false prophets who come to you in sheep's clothing but inside are ravenous wolves."

Like Jimmy Swaggart? he wanted to ask but didn't.

"Bye, Mom. Love you." The words spilled from his mouth, and he wanted to suck them back in, knowing she wouldn't say she loved him back.

He was right. She didn't make any move to hug him either.

"You be careful with that man," she said, then closed the door behind them.

# Six

**THE TEMPERATURES THREATENED** to hit freezing again, despite it technically being spring. To stay warm, Realene wore long johns under her sweats and her dad's heavy flannel over her T-shirt. His pension came to her now that Ma was gone, but it wasn't a lot of money, and since Realene had quit her job at the hospital, she couldn't afford to turn up the thermostat beyond what was needed to keep the pipes from freezing.

She stuck a Hot Pocket in its crisping sleeve and popped it in the microwave, setting the timer for one minute and fifty seconds. Nate once made her do a blindfolded taste test with and without the crisping sleeve to see if it actually made any difference. It did.

Tears stung her eyes, and she slumped into one of the dining room chairs. She'd really screwed up, taking her anger over what happened to Ma out on Nate. Maybe lost him forever. The mood ring on her finger, her last gift from Ma, was a bottomless black.

She inhaled the scent of her dad from his flannel, imagined asking him for his advice while he sat in his recliner smoking a cigarette. Like the time she'd borrowed the girl across the street's brand-new Strawberry Shortcake doll, without permission, and accidentally snapped off its head. He'd pulled her onto his lap and said, "Everyone makes mistakes. The important part is admitting it, saying you're sorry, and making it right if you can." Realene had done that, including paying her one-dollar weekly allowance to the girl for six months after, which had put a major dent in her candy budget. She had to do the same thing now with Nate. Not the dollar part, the apology part.

The microwave beeped, signaling her Hot Pocket was ready. She grabbed it and walked over to the answering machine, hoping Nate had tried to call at some point in the three days since he'd left for Winnipeg. It would be just like him to forgive her before she'd even admitted to being wrong.

She hit the button, and the machine began to play, starting with the most recent messages first. The robotic voice stated the date and time, then played the message. There was nothing new from Nate, just his old messages asking her to pick up, saying he had something fun planned for them for spring break.

But that was okay. She'd call him, call that hotel they were staying at, and apologize. And when they got back, she'd take them to dinner, make an effort to not hate Trish.

She took a bite of the Hot Pocket as the messages kept playing, the cheese scalding her mouth.

A telemarketer offered HBO and Cinemax as an add-on to her current cable package for the low price of $9.99 per month, but she didn't have an extra ten bucks.

Colonel Harmon checked in a few times, wanting to make sure she was okay, asking her to call him.

Her throat tightened. Her dad may be gone, but she still had Harmon, who'd once said she was like the daughter he'd never had.

Then Calvin's voice blared over the speaker.

"Realene, girlie, we got trouble. I'm up at Lizard Lake near Winnipeg. There's another one. A crater. A crash site."

The Hot Pocket slipped from her hand to splat on the floor.

In the recording there was a splash, then a sound like something rubbing against the phone, fabric maybe, followed by a loud crack.

The machine beeped, indicating the end of the messages.

"Oh, God." She struggled to control her breathing.

Another crater. Another crash site.

They were back. "Thousands of ordinary meteors hit every year," she mumbled. "Maybe this one doesn't have worms."

She checked the date of Calvin's message. He'd sent it the morning of the funeral. It had been on her machine for more than a week, and Calvin hadn't called again after he got cut off. He might be hurt, or worse.

She rushed into the entryway and shoved on her boots, ran across the yard and banged on the back door to Calvin's trailer.

Big Kev answered, wearing his typical hockey jersey and sweats. "What do you want?"

"Is Calvin home?" she asked, frantic breaths misting the air.

"No. He's still fishing up at—"

"Have you heard from him lately?"

He scrubbed a hand over his face as if he'd just woken up. "Sorry, what's this about?"

Realene pushed past him through the door. Her eyes struggled to adjust from the white snow to the dark interior of the trailer. "I need to know if Calvin's called you recently, like within the last week. It's important."

Big Kev walked toward the kitchen, and she followed. The hulking figures of Calvin's taxidermied animals lined the tops of the cabinets and every available wall in the living room, though many of those were missing limbs, eyeballs, and patches of fur from their taxidermy fight.

"No, he hasn't called. Why?"

"I think something's wrong. I was listening to some old messages on my machine, and he said there's another meteor site up near there."

With those magic words, Big Kev was wide awake. "I knew it." He sat down at the kitchen table, where two PC monitors sat side by side, along with a printer and a stack of those AOL CD-ROMs that promised free internet access. "It's another UFO retrieval and cover-up." He clicked away on the keyboard and brought up a folder containing several files. "The Alien Alliance saw some strange activity up there—guys with Geiger counters not too far from our family's hunting cabin. Real *Men in Black* stuff. They sent me the photos."

A picture popped up on screen of a snowy landscape near some trees and a lake. She squinted at the man in the foreground and sucked in a breath. The face was a little blurry, but it looked a lot like Harmon.

"Did you show these to Calvin?"

He scoffed. "Sure did. He didn't care, though. Thinks all this 'alien stuff' is a joke."

Realene sat back in her chair, staring at the screen. "When did you show him these?"

"I don't know, like the day before he decided to go fishing."

Calvin hadn't been going fishing. He saw the photo of what could be Harmon and wanted to check it out.

"What was on the message he sent you?"

Realene ignored the question. "I gotta call Colonel Harmon." She stood and rounded Big Kev, grabbed the phone sitting on the table behind the computer. The dial-up internet screeched from the handset, and she pulled it away from her ear. "Dude, turn that off."

"No way. I don't trust that guy. Neither did Calvin."

"Look, I think that's him in the photo. That's Harmon. I have to see if he knows what's going on." She raised her eyebrows, but Big Kev didn't move. "Have it your way. I'll just call from my place."

Before Realene could act on her threat, Big Kev brought up the internet connection window on the computer screen and clicked it off, then sat back in his chair with a huff. "No. If you're gonna call him, I'm want to hear what you have to say."

She dialed Harmon's number, turning her back to Big Kev as it rang so she wouldn't have to see his judgmental face.

"Sergeant Nance," a brusque woman's voice said.

"I need to speak with Colonel Harmon. This is Realene Gustafson. It's an emergency."

"The colonel isn't available," the women said. "Can I take a message?"

"I have to talk to him now."

"Ma'am, he isn't available. I can tell him you—"

"Is he in Winnipeg?"

"Ma'am, I can't—"

"Look, I know he went up to Canada and there's another meteor. I need to talk to him about what's happening."

"I will relay to him that you called."

"Just put me through to colonel," she yelled. But before she could take a breath, the line on the other end went dead. Realene looked at the handset in disbelief, then slammed it back on the cradle. "Shit."

She picked up the phone again and dialed 4-1-1.

"What did they say? Who are you calling now?" Big Kev asked.

The phone operator picked up, and Realene said, "I need to make an international call to the Holiday Inn Holidome in Winnipeg, Manitoba, please."

"One moment," the operator said.

"Seriously, are you going to tell me what's going on?" Big Kev asked.

"Shh." She twisted the phone cord round and round her finger until it cut off the circulation and turned the tip purple. Nate and Trish were probably having the time of their lives lounging in a hot tub right now, blissfully unaware of the danger they were in. Realene had to warn them.

Several clicks sounded, and the line finally rang. "Holiday Inn and Holidome Fun Center, this is Chrissy. How may I help you?"

"I'm looking for a guest, Nate Haugen."

"Room number?"

"I don't have his room number. Can you look it up?"

"No, ma'am."

"Well, can you at least tell me if he's checked in?"

"I'm sorry, ma'am, we can't give out information on our guests."

"Please, this is an emergency."

"I'm sorry, ma'am, I can't do that. Can I help you with anything else?"

Realene hung up the phone. Her vision blurred, and she leaned forward, bracing her arms on her knees as she stared at the linoleum floor.

"You okay?" Big Kev asked.

If she hadn't been such a bitch to Nate, she'd be up there with him. She'd be able to help.

"Hey, you're kind of freaking me out," Big Kev said.

She paced back and forth across the kitchen, the glass eyes of the taxidermied prairie dogs following her. *We're baaack* they seemed to say.

Nate had been gone for three days, Calvin for more than a week. Harmon probably had it under control, but she couldn't be sure. And he wouldn't know to look for Calvin.

"I have to go up there. See if they're okay."

"I'm in." Big Kev stood from his chair.

Realene grimaced. "Who said you're invited?"

"If they found another ship, I need to know. Besides, you're gonna need a guide, and I know the area better than anyone."

She rubbed her throbbing temples with her fingertips. "First of all, there was never a ship. It's a meteor. And second… You're right. It'll be easier if I have your help."

"Wait here while I go pack a bag." But before heading to his room, he stopped. "You gotta drive, though. I don't have a car."

"Crap. My van's almost out of gas, and I'm too broke to fill it." She held out her palm. "Pay up. This ride ain't free."

"No problem. Calvin's got a stash." Big Kev reached above the fridge to pull an old Folgers can from the cupboard. He removed the plastic lid to reveal a roll of twenties.

"What did he do? Rob a bank or something."

"Nah, it's his cigarette money. Two packs a day adds up, and he's been putting it aside." Big Kev pulled out the cash and returned the can, now empty. "Seems right to use it for this, take down whatever cigarette smoking man he's caught up with."

"Okay, yeah. Get packed. Meet you at my car in ten."

He wrinkled his nose. "Let's make it twenty so you can shower first. You kinda stink."

She resisted the urge to punch him, knowing he was right.

# Seven

**TWENTY MINUTES LATER,** Realene and Big Kev met back at her car and together shoveled the vehicle out of the frozen slush it was stuck in. He swore the whole time. If her dad was looking down on her, he'd be very disappointed; the first rule of North Dakota winters was to shovel snow while it was still fresh.

She pulled her knit cap from her head and stuffed it in her coat pocket, exposing her still damp hair to the cold air. Big Kev snickered, she assumed because of her rogue curls that were quickly turning into crunchy locks. Another rule she'd violated: never go outside with a wet head in winter.

Realene unplugged the extension cord that connected to the block heater beneath the car's hood, necessary to prevent the engine from freezing in subzero temperatures, started the car to let it warm up, then went back inside. Pumpkin sat in his carrier, yowling at her through the caged door. She'd considered taking him with her, but she wouldn't put him in danger again. He'd already used several of his lives surviving the worms and facing off with Murray the tiger.

"Sorry, Punky, but I'm not sure how long I'll be gone."

She tried not to think about what may have already happened to Nate, telling herself that if he had been badly hurt, or worse, she would somehow know. She rubbed her thumb over the jagged scar that marred her palm, the mirror image of Nate's, then checked her front pocket for her pocketknife, the one she and Nate had used to become blood siblings. Finding the knife right where it should be, she slung her packed duffel bag over her shoulder and grabbed the cat carrier before locking the door and trudging back outside. The sky was clear for the moment, but the Weather Channel said a storm would be rolling in by evening. They should make it the two and a half hours north to Winnipeg well before the snow hit.

Big Kev, crouched behind the van, stood as she walked up. He'd already opened the back hatch and thrown his own bag inside. "I instant messaged Flint. He should be back in town tomorrow to keep an eye on things, keep us informed of any funny business."

"Your cowboy buddy?" She put her duffel bag in the trunk.

"He's the president of the Alien Alliance, knows more about what the government is capable of than anyone. Said he can keep an eye on the message boards and what's going on around Demise." He pointed at the portable defibrillator encased in plastic and red leather that Realene always kept in her car beside a jug of ice melt and a Super Soaker filled with salt water. "Is that one of those things they use to shock people?"

"In case of emergency." *Or alien infection.* After she had to resuscitate Nate with the defibrillator, they'd learned electricity killed the worms, so she kept the device in her car. She hoped she never needed it again.

"And the water gun?"

"In case of emergency," she repeated, ignoring his confused expression.

Pumpkin clawed at his cage.

"It's okay, bud." She tugged open the sliding door and placed him in the back before hopping in the driver's seat.

When the passenger door opened, Realene expected to see Ma's petite figure, bundled up and ready for bingo. But it was Big Kev, his body taking up twice the space Ma would've.

"Something wrong?" he asked.

She didn't answer, just shifted the van into reverse and pulled onto the road. "You get ahold of the hotel?" While she'd been showering and packing, he'd called the Holidome.

"Same answers as before. Refused to give me any info on Nate. But I was able to book us their last room."

"Room? As in singular?"

"I was lucky to get that. It's spring break, remember?"

She turned from the trailer park onto the main road. "If there's only one bed, you're sleeping in the bathtub."

"I'm bankrolling this, remember? You're sleeping in the tub."

"Uh-huh. I'm the one who got Calvin to stop smoking. Plus, you live in Winnipeg, just stay at your house."

"What if I want to play mini golf?"

Big Kev tuned the radio to 97.5 The Rock right as Realene crested the overpass and continued through the four-way stop and down Main. "Sunday Morning" by No Doubt played, and she felt a twinge of guilt for not being at church. A little extra help from God today wouldn't be a bad thing.

She glanced at the cemetery as they passed, which had been blanketed in snow since the funeral, making her parents graves even harder to distinguish from the rest.

Realene pulled into the parking lot of the strip mall that sat across the street from Revelation Evangelical. The church was now surrounded by a barbed wire fence and locked gate, but that hadn't stopped people from plastering the brick exterior with graffiti to match what had been spray painted on the bus. In Realene's opinion, the building should've been torn down.

She pulled up to the Happy Paws Vet and Pet Hotel at the end of the strip mall. At one time, there were five other businesses in the strip, but the one at the opposite end was smashed up during the Meteor Murders and two others were vacant. Plenty of businesses had been damaged that night, and even more closed later because the owners or their family members had died or were suffering from permanent memory loss. There was one other business still open and boasting several cars out front: Demise Liquor Depot.

"I'll be right back," Realene said, but Big Kev hopped out of the car to follow. She grabbed Pumpkin, who growled and hissed from inside the carrier, clearly recognizing their destination.

A blonde woman wearing scrubs dotted with puppies and kittens manned the reception desk, a toothy smile on her face. "Checking in?"

She froze and so did Realene. Somehow she had completely forgotten that Brooke's mom worked at the vet.

"Realene Gustafson, is that you?" She rounded the desk, her perfectly white nurse shoes squeaking on the tile floor, and wrapped Realene in a hug, smothering her in jasmine perfume.

"Hi, Mrs. Spicer," Realene said, her voice muffled.

The woman pulled back, holding Realene at arm's length. "I was so sorry to hear about your mom, honey."

"Thanks."

She pointed to a flier on the wall that featured a picture of Brooke's face, and the words *Have You Seen Me?* "My Brooke was never found. They said she was probably one of those who were too, well, damaged to identify." She cleared her throat, blinked rapidly. "But, I'm still hoping, well, maybe she got that dementia and just wandered off. She could still be out there somewhere, right?"

"Sure," Realene lied. She had no idea what had happened to Brooke's body, but she was certain the girl was dead since Realene had been the one who killed her after she had attacked her and Ma in a worm-infested rage.

"I wake up and just expect her to come down for breakfast, you know?" Mrs. Spicer fanned her face and blew out a breath.

"I know. Me, too. With my ma, I mean." Realene felt a pang of guilt for being so self-centered lately. There were hundreds of people in Demise who'd experienced loss and trauma, and they managed to drag themselves from bed each day.

Mrs. Spicer turned to Big Kev and held out a manicured hand to greet him. "And you are?"

"Uh, Big…er… Kevin." He shook her hand.

She leaned in close to Realene and with her eyes still on Big Kev, whispered, "He's cute."

"Oh, we're not—I mean, he's just a friend."

"Right." She winked and walked back around the desk, pulling out a file folder from the shelves lining the wall behind the desk. "All right then. Let's get you checked in." She smiled at Pumpkin in his carrier. "And this must be Pumpkin."

Realene lugged the carrier up to set it on the counter, stretching her fingers in relief. She might have to cut back on Punky's Temptations. "Yep."

Pumpkin hissed and swatted at the bars.

"Oh, what a tough a guy you are." Mrs. Spicer giggled, clearly used to feisty cats. "I see we have him booked for one week. You kids going somewhere on vacation?"

"Winnipeg. For spring break." Big Kev grinned.

"Oh. Well, that sounds…lovely. My late husband and I met at spring break. In Cancun. But I'm sure Winnipeg is nice, too."

The dot matrix printer behind the desk whirred to life. Mrs. Spicer tore off a printed sheet and placed it in front of Realene, had her sign the bottom.

"You call me when you get back, and we'll have dinner. It's so nice to reminisce with Brooke's friends, you know?"

"Sure, yeah. Thank you." Realene scurried from the office and out to the car, hopping inside. "Jesus."

Big Kev got in, eyeing her. "What the hell was that? You gotta pee or something?"

"I just had to get out of there, is all. I don't like talking about that stuff, the murders, I mean. Makes me kind of sick to even think about it."

Big Kev nodded knowingly. "PTSD. Got it."

Realene's face grew hot. She hated being diagnosed by professionals, let alone idiots like Big Kev, but in this instance, playing along was a better alternative than admitting to murder. "Yeah," she grumbled. "That."

Several people were now standing out front of the Revelation church across the street, one of whom was Nate's mom, Sophia.

Realene's anger returned.

"Uh, hello? Are you gonna drive or what?" Big Kev asked.

Realene gritted her teeth and drove out onto Main Street. She wanted to drive through the barbed wire fence and punch Sophia right in the face for rejoining with those people, but she had to put Calvin and Nate first. She couldn't waste any more time.

**ABOUT AN HOUR** into the drive, Realene once again found herself flipping through radio stations, and eventually settled on a station playing "Unbelievable" by EMF. She turned the volume up to discourage Big Kev from sharing anymore of his alien conspiracy crap.

In the passenger seat, he had the Rand McNally Atlas open on his lap, examining the map of Lizard Lake. The photos his Alien Alliance friends sent were a half-mile from his family's cabin and right near the lake Calvin had called from. He slapped the atlas closed. "I think it's time you tell me truth about what's going on here. Uncle Cal would only say that the poisoning in Demise was a false flag operation, but I know there's more to it than that, and I'm pretty sure it's the reason we're heading north."

Realene turned down the volume. "He didn't say anything else?"

"Just that he was going fishing. Didn't even mention seeing Harmon in those photos." He crossed his arms. "Can you believe that?"

She *could* believe it. He was trying to protect her. He wanted to investigate before he said anything.

"Whatever's happening here, it's dangerous, isn't it?" he said. "Life or death stuff."

Realene hesitated, then nodded.

"Then I have the right to know the truth. My life could depend on it."

"I can go to jail just for telling you."

"Not my problem."

"I'm serious. If it's ever found out I said anything, I'd be found guilty of treason. You can't tell anyone else what I tell you; not your family, not the Alien Alliance, no one. Okay?"

Big Kev thought about it for a minute. "Okay."

Realene recounted the events of those two terrible days in Demise with more detail than she knew she remembered, as if the full story had been lying dormant inside her subconscious, just waiting to be exorcised. Big Kev let her talk, didn't ask any questions or interrupt, even when she got to the part about Ma taking that bullet from the Reverend.

She finished, and the vehicle fell into silence.

The whole story sounded so outlandish, so ridiculous, she was sure Big Kev would think she was making it up.

Big Kev took a moment to ponder things. "Worms in a meteor, huh?"

"Yep."

He leaned his head back against the seat, looking thoughtful. "Rad. This doesn't disprove UFOs, though. It's likely there are many alien races of varying intelligences and technological capabilities. Star people can take many forms."

"Star people?"

"Think of it as the Lakota term for aliens. But a more accurate translation would be 'spiritual ancestors not from earth.'"

Realene thought of all the times she'd laid in her backyard with Nate, the two of them looking up at the stars together, guessing which of the little white dots held life. "So, you believe me?"

"Of course." He went quiet for a moment. "Also, I'm sorry about your mom. She sounds pretty awesome."

"She was a hero," Realene said. Telling her Ma's story felt good, actually. The NDA Realene signed had made it impossible to honor Ma's bravery in public, but now at least one person had heard the truth.

"Apple doesn't fall far from the tree, apparently."

"What do you mean?"

"Uncle Cal is always talking about how brave you were during that time. Even said you saved his life. That true?"

Keeping her eyes on the road, Realene shrugged. "I guess you can say that, yeah."

"You don't sound convinced."

"Calvin didn't die that day, but he'll never be the same. I didn't save his life. I saved the parts of it I could."

Big Kev whistled. "Wow. I thought I was the skeptical one."

She glanced at him in disbelief. "Skeptical? You're the most believing person I've ever met."

"You make me sound gullible."

"Aren't you?"

Big Kev shrugged, and the pair fell into silence until the next mile marker.

Realene was the first to speak again. "So… What got you into UFOs?"

Big Kev, who was now flipping randomly through the pages of his atlas, paused. "I don't know," he mumbled, then returned to flipping pages. Her remark about him being gullible had obviously struck a nerve.

Feeling guilty now, Realene forced a smile onto her face. "Sure, you do. Spill it."

Big Kev closed the atlas and heaved a sigh. "My dad."

"Oh, yeah? Is he part of the Alien Alliance, too?"

Big Kev grimaced. "What's with the twenty questions?"

"Humor me, will you?"

Big Kev looked down at his lap. "He's not just a member. He's the founder. Started the group after a close encounter in the woods. Came across a crashed ship while he was out hunting."

Realene's stomach dropped. Was the Demise meteor not the first? "Oh, yeah?" she said, choking out the words. "And when was this?"

"Eh… Like ten years ago. Long before what happened in Demise."

"What happened to him? Anything? What was the encounter like?"

"He was burned pretty badly on his leg. And when he reported it, he became a joke." Big Kev swallowed heavily. "The media made him out to be a crazy drunk, and after his injury, he wasn't able to work. Uncle Cal would send us a little money when he could, even though he thought my dad was nuts too. My mom left a couple years after it happened, said he wasn't the same man she married."

"I'm sorry." Realene understood now why Kev had such a problem with the reverend being blamed for Demise. It was another example of the military covering up the real story and telling lies.

"But now, with all this, we can get proof. I mean, that would change everything. People would realize Dad was telling the truth."

No wonder he was so dedicated to proving the existence of alien life.

"I hope Uncle Cal is okay. We should head right to the spot where he was fishing, see if we can find any sign of him."

Her heartbeat sped up at the thought of the second crash site. "Um, let's go to the hotel first. We need to check in, and this way we can try to find Nate. Maybe he already knows something."

They passed a sign advertising a gas station, the last exit before the border and the perfect excuse to stop this conversation. "Bathroom-break time," Realene said. She took the exit and pulled into the Loaf n Jug, parking at an empty pump.

"I'll grab snacks," Big Kev said, hopping from the car.

Realene followed him inside and asked the cashier for the bathroom key. The guy handed her a hubcap with a key attached. No way she would forget to return that.

When she rejoined Big Kev, he was standing beside the van with a plastic bag in his hand. He opened it to show her his spoils—two Cherry Cokes and two packs of Hostess cupcakes.

"Nice." They were junk food kindred spirits.

Realene stretched her arms over her head, gearing up for the last leg of the drive. Hopefully they'd find Nate and Trish at the hotel, and everything would be fine. Calvin, too. He might have just forgotten to call back. Could have even called in the time since they left.

"Hey, I'm gonna check my messages real quick," Realene said.

A "Phone" sign on the building pointed around the corner to the far side of the structure. She followed it to the public phone booth, but when she got there, a short man with a buzz cut was already on the phone, his back turned to her.

There was something familiar about him. Realene moved closer, the scrape of her shoes on the snowy ground causing the guy to turn. "Birdie?" she said.

# Eight

**REALENE SPRINTED BACK** to the van and hopped in the driver's seat. "They're here," she said, breathless.

Big Kev looked up from his snacks. "Who's here?"

"The goddamn cult. I don't know if Irene was following us or what." She turned on the car, and the radio played "Satan is My Motor" by Cake. Realene shifted into reverse and hit the gas, throwing Big Kev forward to catch himself on the dash.

"Hey, slow down." He buckled himself in as she peeled from the parking lot, then turned down the volume on the radio.

"Can't, we gotta lose them."

Realene pulled back onto the highway and stomped down on the accelerator to put some distance between them and the bus. They passed semis, a station wagon packed with kids, and an older lady going unbelievably slow in the left lane and blocking any advance. Big Kev leaned over and pressed the horn, something Realene hesitated to do herself, her natural politeness hard to overcome even in an emergency.

In response, the old lady promptly slowed down and moved over but then proceeded to give them the finger when they passed.

Realene thought they might have lost the cult, but when they pulled up to the border crossing, which consisted of four lanes—two allowing cars into Canada and two controlling traffic back into the U.S.—she noticed the bus just a few car lengths behind them in the next lane.

Manned guard booths flanked each lane, and she drummed her fingers on the wheel as both she and the bus advanced.

"Dude, you need to try and act natural," Big Kev said.

She rolled her neck and blew out a breath. Just taking a little trip up north, nothing weird happening here. The lane the bus was in moved much quicker than theirs. It was just her luck she picked the slow lane. Same thing always happened at the Piggly Wiggly.

After an excruciating wait, the car ahead of them pulled away and the guard waved her forward, putting them side by side with the bus. She plastered on a smile as she rolled down her window and shifted the car into park.

"IDs please," the border patrol officer instructed. She wore a blue uniform, not unlike a police officer, and held a clipboard.

Realene fished her driver's license from her wallet, glad they didn't require passports since she didn't have one. She handed Kev's Canadian driver's license and her own North Dakota one to the woman.

"Reason for visit," she asked, writing a note on the clipboard.

"Spring break. Heading up to the Holidome in Winnipeg." Realene tried to look excited.

The woman nodded, likely very used to young people crossing the border due to the lower drinking age.

"What about you, Kevin? Headed back home?"

"Oh, no, not yet. I been looking out for my uncle in Demise. Just going back for a few days for spring break."

"Demise?" The guard frowned looking again at Realene's ID before handing both cards back to her. "Real shame what happened, eh?"

"Oh, yeah, real shame." Realene glanced over at the bus, wondering how close they were to being cleared.

"Nervous about something?" the guard asked. She lowered her clipboard, craning her neck to see in the back seat.

Realene was about to say no when inspiration struck. "Um, yeah, actually. You see that bus there?"

The guard glanced back over her shoulder. "What about it?"

"Well, I don't know how much detail you saw about what happened with the meteor murders…"

The woman waved a hand dismissively. "It was all over CBC."

"Okay, well, that bus, those are the Revelation cult members. The ones that followed Jeff, uh, Reverend Zebediah."

The woman gasped. "The poisoners? They're just…out."

"The reverend died and their lieutenant's in jail, but the rest of them, yeah. I guess they didn't do anything illegal or whatever, at least not that can be proven. But we pretty much steer clear of 'em in town." She dipped her head sheepishly. "I don't know, maybe it's nothing, but they had all kinds of weapons and stuff stockpiled. I just thought you should be aware is all."

"Stay here." The woman stepped away and spoke into the radio clipped to her uniform at the shoulder.

"What the hell, dude?" Big Kev asked.

"I figured if they can't cross the border that's a good thing, right?"

They watched as several more guards approached the lane next to them. The woman came back, her face pinched. "Pop the trunk for me."

"Oh, sure." Realene got out and walked behind the vehicle, tugging the handle to raise the gate.

The guard inspected the bags there, but she kept glancing to the side, where the cultists were filing off the bus.

A couple Realene recognized as the owners of Olson's Candy Shop came down the steps, looking like harmless old folks on an outing from their nursing home to get cheap medications across the border. There was no sign of Sophia.

"Okay, you can close it. You're good to go," the guard said.

Realene got back in the van, buckling her seatbelt.

"You have fun now." The guard waved them forward.

"Thanks. You too." Realene cringed at her faux pas, then realized this probably was fun for the guards to have a little excitement. And who knew what Irene had stashed in that bus. She probably wasn't stupid enough to smuggle weapons across the border, but Realene could hope.

She advanced slowly, taking one last look at the bus, which was now being circled by a guard leading a German Sheppard on a leash. Irene, hair sticking out in every direction like she'd suffered an electric shock, waited near the guard booth. She looked up just as Realene passed, and her eyes widened.

Realene blew her a kiss.

Irene's face went red, and she ran, albeit slowly, toward the van. Shouts rang out from the guards as they rushed her, grabbing her arms and dragging her backward.

Realene couldn't help but giggle as she watched Irene being dragged away in the rear-view mirror.

Big Kev raised his hand for a high five, which Realene gladly gave him. "Dude, did you see her face? That was epic. No way they'll be able to follow us now."

**THE FOUR-LANE HIGHWAY** expanded into six lanes as they got into the heart of Winnipeg, and Realene leaned forward in her seat, clutching the steering wheel tight. She reminded herself to pay attention to her kilometers per hour to ensure they didn't get pulled over for speeding. Or more likely, going too slow. The city was more than a hundred times the size of Demise, and she felt the weight of the buildings towering around her, as if they might topple over and crush her at any moment.

Crusty snow marred the curbs, but the storm hadn't started yet, so at least the roads were dry.

"You, uh, want me to drive?" Big Kev asked. "I'm a pretty good driver, got my CDL and everything."

"Just tell me where to turn for the hotel," Realene said, flinching as a city bus zipped past her on the right.

"I thought we were gonna stop at Timmies."

She'd been all for a pit stop at Tim Horton's for some Timbits and a double double, but now she just wanted to get off the road before she keeled over from a stress-induced heart attack. "Hotel."

"Fine. The turn's just ahead here, right at the stop light."

She reached the intersection and made the turn. They continued another six blocks, and the tall office and apartments gave way to more reasonably sized ones, then to neighborhoods with snow-dusted lawns. She eased back in her seat, taking one hand off the wheel at a time to stretch her fingers.

They passed the airport and reached the edge of town. Big Kev pointed out the neighborhood where he shared an apartment with his dad and older sister, Ana, just a few blocks before Realene finally saw the sign for the hotel atop a tall pole. Beneath the green Holiday Inn logo were pink letters that proclaimed the location a "Holidome Indoor Fun Center."

She pulled into an entrance which led to several businesses, including a bar beside the hotel called the Merry Moose, whose sign featured a cartoon moose wearing flannel and holding a mug of beer. The parking lot was packed with old cars likely driven mostly by teenagers and mounds of plowed snow that had turned gray and slushy—the kind of snow that packed hard and felt like a rock when you threw it. She drove slowly, slamming on her brakes when she spotted Nate's truck, which was pulled into a spot facing the side of the building.

Big Kev jerked forward, his seatbelt stopping him from slamming his head into the windshield. "Would you stop doing that?"

"That's Nate's." They'd at least made it to the hotel and checked in, a good sign.

"Check out the snow underneath." He perched higher in his seat. "Not melted, and I think it snowed Friday. Means that truck hasn't moved in a couple days."

That probably meant they were holed up in the hotel having fun a safe distance from this potential new meteor. She blew out a relieved breath and pulled forward, finding a vacant spot toward the back of the lot.

"Let's go." Realene grabbed her bag, leaving the defibrillator, and started the trek across the parking lot. Not seeing Kev beside her, she looked back to find him crouched down behind the van. "What're you doing?"

"Just knocking off some ice chunks." He stuck his arm under the vehicle.

"It can't wait?" She continued toward the front doors.

Big Kev jogged up beside her as the doors slid open and chattering voices assaulted her ears. The Holidome's atrium was huge, with a swimming pool, hot tub, and miniature golf course beyond the front desk, and a playground with a multicolored curly slide at the back, near what looked to be a video arcade. Thatched roofs and fake palm trees gave the whole space a tiki bar feel, and the air reeked of chlorine. Everything looked a little rundown—the golf course greens were torn in spots, the thatched roofs were missing big chunks of palm, and the decorative wooden trusses above the atrium were cracked and sagging in spots—but the hotel had no reason to fix things. It's not like a bunch of drunk spring breakers were gonna care.

Around the perimeter of the atrium were the hotel rooms, extending upward for six stories. The first-floor rooms backed up to the pool, each boasting a small patio enclosed by a metal fence that had once been painted white but was now mottled with rust. The rooms from the second floor up featured small balconies that overlooked the space.

"Beauty, eh?" Big Kev started to wander away, and she grabbed his elbow.

"Hey, we're on a mission, remember?"

"Right, yeah. Sorry."

Realene led him over to the check-in desk, which was manned by three employees, all of whom were talking to guests. The guy ahead of them, who wore swim trunks and nothing else, complained about the ice machine running out before he could fill his bathtub—which he was planning to use as a cooler for the massive amounts of beer he'd brought. When he left, one of the desk employees, a young woman with curly hair pulled up into a hot-pink scrunchie, called out, "Next."

Big Kev said, "Hi, we're checking in," and pulled out his ID and the roll of cash.

She typed away on her computer, glancing behind them and groaning at the growing line, which didn't appear to be guests checking in. Most of them were in bathing suits and flip flops.

"How many keys?" she asked, chewing a wad of gum the

same color as her scrunchie. Her name tag read "Chrissy," probably the same one they'd spoken to on the phone.

"Two please." He elbowed Realene and raised his eyebrows. "I wonder if Nate and Trish have checked in yet?"

"Oh, right. Um, miss, can you tell us if a Nate Haugen or Trish… Trish…" She squinted, still completely blanking on the last name. "I guess just Trish. Can you tell us if they've checked in? They're our friends, we were supposed to drive in together, but then—"

"Room 107," Chrissy said, sliding the keys cards across the counter. The little paper envelope was labeled 619.

"Oh, great, thank you." Apparently little miss customer service had stopped caring about the rules and would do anything to get rid of them.

Chrissy leaned over to the guy working beside her and said, "Where the hell is Dave? Pauly's waiting for me. He's taking me to see *Cruel Intentions*."

The guy ignored his coworker, calling out, "Next."

Realene pulled Big Kev out of the way. "Let's stop by their room first."

They passed a small room labeled Business Centre, which featured computers and a printer for guest use, and continued down the hallway labeled "Rooms 100-130." She dodged a giggling couple chasing each other and stopped at room 107, where a "Do Not Disturb" sign hung from the door handle. Pounding on the door, she called, "Nate? Trish? Are you in there?"

She waited, heard nothing.

Big Kev stepped up beside her and pounded even louder. "Put on your clothes and answer the door."

Realene grimaced at the mental picture his words conjured.

A petite girl in a tie-dye coverup wandered by, eyeing Big Kev up and down. "Whoa. How tall are you?"

"Six foot five." He puffed out his chest, and Realene resisted rolling her eyes.

"Oh my gosh, you're like more than a foot taller than me. And I love your hair." She tugged on his braid, which hung down his back. "Want to come hang out at the pool with me and my friends?"

"He's with me," Realene said. She crossed her arms and stepped up beside Big Kev, a little irritated that the girl hadn't noticed her at all, even though she was only two feet away.

"Oh, bummer." The girl wandered off, bumping into the wall with one shoulder then meandering toward the other wall.

"Dude. Not cool," Big Kev said.

"We're not here for you to pick up chicks. Let's go put our stuff in the room and try calling them." Nate was probably just hanging out with Trish somewhere around the hotel, but she still wanted to find him and tell him about Calvin and the meteor, if for no other reason than to keep him out of the danger zone.

# Nine

**THANKFULLY, THEIR ROOM** did have two beds. Realene was still tempted to make Big Kev go home but decided that would be rude. Plus, she was starting to like him. She used the phone in the room to try Nate's room, but there was no answer. While Big Kev left a message for his dad and sister, Realene looked out the sliding glass door that opened onto their tiny balcony.

Though it was only lunch time, the spring break festivities had picked up since they'd checked in, likely due to the partiers finally waking up for the day. Their room was one of the ones that overlooked the central atrium of the hotel, giving them a full view of the pool, mini golf course, and playground six stories below. Bathing-suit-clad college kids packed the pool and surrounding lounge chairs, their boisterous voices filling the cavernous space. From above, the disrepair of the hotel was even more obvious. Even the fake palm trees looked tattered, as if they'd been through a real hurricane.

Realene eyed the first-floor rooms, the ones whose mini-patios backed up to the pool, and counted seven spots over to the one that should have been Nate's. From her vantage point, it appeared the curtains on the patio door were mostly, but not all the way, closed.

Big Kev came to stand beside her. "Now can we drive out to Lizard Lake? Try to get answers about Calvin?"

"Not yet." Yes, she was procrastinating going to the lake, but she wasn't ready to face another meteor, especially without Nate to back her up. She pointed to a patio on the first floor. "I think that's their room. I'm gonna go look inside through the back."

Her stomach twisted at the thought of getting caught. How embarrassing. Would she be arrested? She'd never been to jail. Canadian jail was probably a cake walk, but still.

"We should go undercover."

"As what?" She hadn't brought anything close to a disguise. "Hotel staff?"

"Nah, dude. Drunk idiots." He jutted his chin down at the crowd around the pool, at least half of whom were most definitely drunk idiots. "If we're caught we can just pretend we forgot what room we were in or something."

Realene had to admit it was a pretty good idea. "Alright, fine. But I don't have a suit."

"Better figure something out, then."

She grabbed her bag and went into the bathroom, cursing herself for not thinking to bring along something that would have helped her fit in. Her only option was a sports bra and her sleep boxers, so she went with it. After wrapping a towel tight around her chest, she came out to find Big Kev had changed into knee-length swim trunks.

"Dude, you need to get some sun," he said.

"I'd only burn." Her pale legs were a gift from her Nordic ancestors. "Where the hell did you get swim trunks?" There was no reason he would have brought those to Calvin's.

"I'm always prepared for anything." He pulled out a pair of sunglasses and put them on. "Kidding. I paid a guy in the hall a couple toonies."

"Isn't that only four bucks?"

"Drunk idiots, remember?"

She really hoped that guy was not now wandering around naked. "Let's do this."

They rode the packed elevator down to the lobby, and Realene thought she might be getting a little tipsy from the fumes of alcohol permeating from the spring breakers around her. As they exited, she pasted a dopey expression on her face and gripped Big Kev's elbow, as if trying to steady herself. A glance at the front desk showed the staff was still busy and not paying much attention to the partiers. Realene led Big Kev past the mini golf course and toward the pool, weaving through the fake palm trees. The rusted metal fence that circled the pool and separated it from the surrounding room balconies had an open gate to enter through. A white sign with red painted letters proclaimed "No lifeguard on duty. No running. No glass bottles. No alcohol."

Realene snorted. Clearly no one was following the alcohol rule. Many of them carried cans or plastic bottles of soda that were likely spiked, and she watched as one girl took a swig from a bottle of Hawaiian Tropic tanning lotion.

She and Kev entered through the gate, stepping from the AstroTurf surrounding the golf course to the water-splashed cement. A girl in a bikini raced by, a guy chasing her and trying to snap her ass with a towel. Apparently, they hadn't gotten the "no running" memo either.

A guy nearby had plugged in a boom box and cranked up the volume. "Smells Like Teen Spirit" by Nirvana played, but Realene mostly smelled chlorine from the pool, so strong it stung her nose even though she hadn't touched the water.

She counted the patios and headed toward the one that should belong to Nate and Trish. A couple of the other patios they passed had people on them. They lounged in the chairs there or roamed in and out of their rooms through the patio doors. The fences didn't have gates, but she watched as a guy stepped over the fence and took a running jump into the pool, landing cannon-ball-style as his friends cheered. A girl on a chaise pool float shrieked at the wave of water that drenched her.

They reached Nate's room, and Big Kev easily stepped over the fence. Realene, however, eyed the metal barrier, which reached her midsection.

"Need a boost?" Big Kev joked.

Ignoring him, Realene dragged a chair from a nearby table and stepped on the frayed fabric seat, which allowed her to sit atop the fence and swing her legs over. Her natural unathleticism took over, and when she let herself drop the couple of feet to the ground, she lost her footing and fell flat on her face. Heat flaming her cheeks, she popped up, no longer covered by her towel.

To his credit, Big Kev didn't laugh, did a good job holding it in. He did point at her boxers, though, which were patterned with little smiley faces and the words *Don't Worry Be Happy* on the butt. "Nice shorts."

"They were on sale," she mumbled, snatching her towel from the ground.

A guy on the patio for room 106 leaned over the fence separating the two spaces. "Did it hurt?" he asked.

"I'm fine." She willed her blush to fade as he surveyed her up and down.

"When you fell from heaven," he replied with a dopey grin.

"Oh." She cocked her head. The guy was actually cute, kind of alternative looking with tattoos, like he might be in a band or something.

Big Kev strolled over and threw his arm over Realene's shoulder. "She's taken."

"The cute ones always are." He turned back to his friends, who were snickering.

On second thought, she decided to keep her towel off. "Thanks," she said to Big Kev.

"No prob." He dropped his arm. "But to be clear, I have no interest in you."

"Thank God for that." She crossed to the patio door. "Keep a lookout, yeah?"

"Roger." He stood with his back to her, scanning the pool area.

Realene had been right about the curtains, which hung with a foot gap between them, allowing her to peer through the door and into the room. The king bed was sloppily made, and two suitcases sat in the corner. "They're not here."

Big Kev pushed her aside to see for himself. "Yeah, I don't seem 'em either."

"What're we doing? Breaking in?" a voice said.

Realene whipped around to find a girl standing behind them on the patio. "What? No. We—"

"Ana," Big Kev said, picking her up in a bear hug, then setting her back on her feet.

"Hey, little bro." She straightened her coat, which she wore over denim overalls. Like her brother, her dark hair hung in a long braid. "Got your message."

Realene barely recognized the girl she'd met a handful of times as kids, back when she'd come down to visit her uncle Calvin. It must have been ten years since she'd seen Ana, and the sight of her sent Realene's heart beating faster.

"What are you doing here?" The words came out sharper than she intended.

"Kev said there was mini golf and cute girls." She smirked. The long, beaded earring she wore drew Realene's gaze to her neck. "Nice shorts."

"They were on sale," Big Kev said.

Realene quickly wrapped her towel back around her, not meeting Ana's eyes. Heat climbed up her chest and neck. "We're not here to have fun."

"Uncle Cal's missing." Big Kev crossed his arms. "We're gonna head out to Lizard Lake and see what we see."

"That's a forty-five-minute drive," Ana said. "Should be able to make it there and back before the storm rolls in, if we leave now."

"We?" Realene asked. No way were they taking her with them.

"You got a problem with that?" Ana arched an eyebrow.

"Yeah, I do." Realene stalked closer to the girl, who was a few inches taller than her. "You have no idea what you're getting yourself into. It could be dangerous."

"Well, if it's dangerous, then I'm definitely coming." Ana crossed her arms, mimicking Big Kev's pose. "It's my job to look out for my family, eh?"

"Yeah, but this is complicated, okay? You don't know what you're dealing with."

"Okay, so tell me." Ana glanced at her brother.

He winced and raised his hands. "Sorry, I've been sworn to secrecy."

She narrowed her eyes. “Fine. Don’t tell me. I’m still coming with.”

“No, you’re not,” Realene said.

Big Kev gave a choked laugh. “Oooh, you shouldn’t have said that.”

Ana took a step toward Realene, so only a foot of space separated them, and Realene’s stomach did a little flip.

“You gonna stop me?”

Realene gave a frustrated growl. “We don’t have time for this.”

“Then let’s get going. I call shotgun.” Ana turned and gripped the little white fence with one hand, then hopped over it easily.

Realene gave Big Kev a look and he shrugged. “Sorry.” He pulled a deck chair over to their side of the fence, offering her his hand.

Great. She was about to face another meteor site and maybe more alien worms without Nate, and with a girl who had no idea what they were up against.

But they had to go. If Calvin was out there, they had to find him. He’d called Realene for help. She wouldn’t let him down.

“Fine.” She took Big Kev’s hand and climbed over the fence.

# Ten

**REALENE GUIDED THE** minivan down the gravel road that led to the lake, which was clear of snow, as if it had been heavily traveled. Strange, since it wasn't on the map. The road continued along one side of Lizard Lake, but Ana instructed her to turn off on a side road to get to their cabin. The lake was to their left as they drove, just a half mile through the trees, but wasn't visible.

Realene gnawed at her lip, wishing she'd slipped a note under Nate's hotel room door, letting him know about the meteor. His truck had been gone from the parking lot when they left, and she had no idea where he'd gone or when she'd be able to talk to him.

A moose crossed the road ahead of them, and Realene slowed, peering at it for any sign of infection. It swung its head their way, then turned and continued into the trees. Just a normal moose.

"You okay?" Ana asked from the passenger seat.

"Fine," Realene said. "How far's the cabin?" They'd decided to start by checking there for any sign of Calvin. If he wasn't there, they'd look for him in the area where the photos were taken.

"We're almost there." Ana angled to face Realene. "Sure you can't tell me what's happening here?"

"Positive."

They drove in silence until the cabin finally came into view. The log-built structure was small, just a square with a door flanked by two windows and a pitched roof with a chimney. Calvin's truck was parked to one side, tucked between the house and the trees. Snow covered the truck's cab and filled the bed.

"Maybe he's just holed up here," Big Kev said.

Realene hoped so, but it seemed like a stretch. If he was, why hadn't he reached out to anyone since calling her? She parked and hopped from the van, waiting on the simple porch that extended across the front of the cabin. Big Kev pulled out his keys, but the front door was unlocked. He went in first with his sister close behind.

The living room was directly inside, furnished with a couch and rocking chair that faced a fireplace. Past the end of the couch was a wall with two doors, one that led to a bathroom and one to what looked like the only bedroom. The other side of the cabin housed a makeshift kitchen along one wall—just a mini fridge, sink, and short counter, topped with a hot plate. Behind the couch sat a rustic wood table and two chairs.

The decor reminded her of *The Red Green Show*, every wall packed with mounted antlers, stuffed fish, reclaimed road signs, and other random junk.

Ana went toward the bedroom while Big Kev surveyed the kitchen. "Dirty dishes in the sink."

She stuck her head out. "His bag is in here, but he's not."

"Looks like we're going for a hike."

Realene really wished Nate was here.

"You're staying here," Big Kev said to Ana, who opened her mouth to protest. "If anything happens and we, like, don't make it back, we need someone who can go for help."

"Come on, guys. You gotta tell me what's going on." She blocked the door. "What are you afraid happened to Uncle Cal?"

Realene wedged past Ana to get outside, zipping up her coat and pulling on her gloves. Big Kev followed suit.

"Fine, don't tell me, but who the hell am I supposed to call if you don't come back?" Ana stood in the open door, her glare fixed on Realene.

"Get a hold of Flint," Big Kev said.

"From the Alien Alliance?" she asked. "Jesus, is this some kind of UFO hunt? Don't tell me Uncle Cal is caught up now."

Realene chose not to answer that. "We better get going."

The sky was turning dark, the predicted storm brewing on the horizon.

"If you end up in some secret government bunker, I'm going to kick both your asses," Ana said, then returned inside and slammed the door.

Realene met Big Kev's gaze and couldn't help but smile.

"She's kind of protective," he said.

Realene figured growing up without their mom would do that to a person and silently pledged to get Big Kev back safe to his sister. On the plus side, Ana was kind of cute when she was angry.

Opening the van's trunk, Realene pulled out the Super Soaker and slung it across her chest. Kev snickered, and she said, "I took out an infected hawk with one of these, you know."

"Yeah, right." He pointed in the direction of the lake. "The photos were taken on the far side of the lake. We can follow the trees around the edge to stay out of view."

While some of the snow accumulation had melted, the crunchy layer left would be hard to navigate. She'd promised herself after the Meteor Murders to get into better shape and was greatly regretting breaking that promise as she huffed behind Big Kev.

Worry built in her gut with each heavy step. What if Calvin was dead or infected? "You come out here a lot?" she asked, desperate for a distraction from her thoughts.

"Not anymore. Dad used to bring us out when we were kids. You know… Before. He taught us to shoot out here. Rifles, mainly. I was going to learn with the cross bow, but yeah, we never got to that. Now we use the cabin mostly for research. Watch the skies away from the city lights."

"Sounds like you miss it."

"Nah. What Calvin's working on is more important. It was just meant to be, I guess."

They reached the lake and started to go around it.

Realene scanned the frozen surface, noticed some kind of snow-dusted lump a few hundred feet out. "There," she said pointing at the mound but not waiting for him. She ran from the tree cover onto the lake and skated across the snowy ice, her duck boots gliding along as well as any blade. Was the shape a person?

She pushed herself as fast as she could, her breath coming in fast pants. Big Kev kept up, visible in her periphery. As they got closer, she realized the mound was small, too small to be Calvin.

Her foot hit something, a break in the ice, sending her sprawling for the second time today, but much worse. Her knees hit the ice first, and she cried out on impact, managing to catch herself with her hands before her face bashed into the surface.

She groaned and rolled onto her back before sitting up.

Big Kev crouched, brushing his hand through the snow to expose a perfectly circular hole drilled in the ice. "A fishing hole." Something protruded from the hole, and he grabbed the end and pulled.

A pole.

"It's Calvin's." He rotated the handle to show her Calvin's initials carved into the surface.

Realene crawled over to the mound and brushed the snow from it. A collapsed folding chair and a duffel bag. "He wouldn't just leave his stuff out here."

Big Kev looked toward the edge of the lake. "What the hell is that?"

She followed his line of sight to a break in the trees and what looked like some kind of airplane hangar or warehouse that blended in with the surrounding snow. "You tell me."

"That wasn't here a week and a half ago when those pictures were taken." He reeled in the line on the pole and collapsed the rod, sticking it in his pocket.

"Come on, we've got to get closer." She skated back toward the trees and climbed the bank.

Though it wasn't yet 3:00 p.m., the sky darkened as clouds rolled in overhead and a light snow began to fall. The freezing air stung her cheeks.

They hiked through the trees as quickly as they could, coming up behind the warehouse. Realene rushed across the gap in the trees that had allowed them to glimpse the warehouse. The trees provided at least a little cover to get a look at the front of the building. It was constructed of corrugated steel painted white, and there were no windows. Only a roll-up garage door for vehicles and a smaller door for personnel.

She halted at the sight of Nate's plow parked beside a couple of other nondescript looking trucks.

"What?" Big Kev whispered, coming up behind her.

"We've gotta get closer."

"Wait," he said, but she didn't. Couldn't. Had to find out if Nate was okay.

She rushed up the warehouse, pressing her body to the corrugated steel wall. Big Kev joined her, panting.

Realene noticed a seam in the metal where one piece was joined to another by screws and followed it with her gloved hand. Near the bottom, one of the screws was loose. She was able to remove it and wedge her fingers into the gap.

"Help me." She dropped to her knees and pulled on the metal. He removed the fishing pole from his pocket and wedged the handle end in the crack and pulled, levering the metal apart just a few inches, but it was enough.

"Hold it there." She dropped to her stomach and looked through the crack, which offered a view of the large interior. A crater exactly like the one in Demise filled most of the space. In the center where the meteor would be, sat a large, clear plastic box with holes in it. The box held hundreds of bloody and battered rats. They were infected, probably on purpose to contain the worms.

Realene started to breathe faster, hyperventilating.

"Hey, take it easy." Big Kev put his hand on her shoulder, and she focused on the pressure of his hand. Counted down from twenty. She had to calm down, focus.

Nate was in there, might be in danger. She couldn't afford to lose it.

Working to slow her breathing, she said, "I'm okay," and peered through the crack again.

Several cars were parked near the far wall, and at least a dozen people roamed the space, some in civilian clothes and some in white contamination suits and gas masks. Several appeared to be armed. Animal cages and shelves containing what looked like lab equipment spanned the far wall.

She noticed another, much smaller plastic box hanging from a crane hook above the crater. A large black worm squirmed inside, one just like the queen they'd killed at the lake.

A new queen.

"No fucking way." She sat back, trying to calm her heart, which felt like it might explode in her chest.

Big Kev dropped to his knees and looked through the crack in the siding. "Jesus." He stood. "This is a whole new species we've never cataloged before," he said, talking to himself.

Realene looked back through the gap and saw Nate staring at the crater as he backed away. Trish waited off to the side, unmoving, with her arms wrapped around her stomach.

Colonel Harmon walked up wearing a Carhartt jacket like the one in the photo. None of the men wore uniforms, but they had to be U.S. military. He tried to put a hand on Nate's shoulder, but he smacked it away. One of the armed men grabbed Nate's arm, and Nate decked the guy hard in the face.

The guy shoved Nate into the wall of cages, and screeches filled the air. Harmon yelled something, and the man backed away from Nate, who strode over to Trish and grabbed her hand, pulling her toward the exit at the front of the building. His coat was torn, and blood smeared his knuckles from the punch.

Something bumped her foot, and she looked behind her to see Big Kev pacing through the snow, talking to himself. "They'll never be able to cover this up. We've got them, we've finally got those bastards."

From the low angle, she glimpsed a series of barely visible green lasers extending from the building just past where they'd pried away the metal.

"Stop," she said a second too late.

Big Kev's foot crossed the laser's path and an alarm sounded inside, a short repetitive blare, followed by a robotic voice saying. "Perimeter. Perimeter. Perimeter."

Realene looked back through the gap. The colonel and the guy Nate had been fighting ran toward the rear of the building.

Nate and Trish slipped out the front door.

"We've gotta go," Big Kev said, yanking her away from the building.

She glanced behind her, trying to get a glimpse around the building at Nate's truck, but she couldn't see it, couldn't tell if he made it out.

Realene and Big Kev ran back into the woods that surrounded the lake. Sharp branches tore at her coat and scraped her skin as they barreled through the trees. Her shoulder blades itched, expecting to feel the pierce of a bullet at any moment.

A cramp burned in her side, and her legs trembled from exhaustion, but she pushed herself forward. They'd made it almost all the way around the lake when a roar sounded to her right, out on the ice. She looked back.

The snow cleared just enough to reveal a large, dark shape standing on the lake. It opened its mouth and bellowed, the sound echoing through the still winter air. A bear. It began to run straight toward them.

# Eleven

**WITH THE ROAR** of the bear reverberating through her bones, Realene found an untapped reserve of energy and turned to bolt.

"Stop!" Big Kev said and snatched the back of her coat, halting her. "Don't run. It'll just give chase."

"Don't run? Are you kidding me?"

"We have to stand our ground. Make ourselves look threatening." He waved his arms in the air as if trying to draw the animal toward them. "No way we can outrun it anyway."

Frozen in place, Realene watched as the bear loped across the ice, breath puffing from its nostrils. Snow whipped through the air, peppering the bear's fur, but it didn't seem to notice, remained totally fixated on the two of them amid the trees.

"I don't think it's threatened," she said, eyeing the closest trunk. Could they climb to safety? No, bears definitely climbed trees.

The bear let out another roar, opening its mouth wide to show sharp teeth that were a heck of a lot bigger than those of a prairie dog. She'd trade a horde of those little monsters for this big one in a second.

"This isn't right," Kev said, dropping his arm and taking a slow step back. "Bears stalk, they don't attack like this."

"The worms," Realene whispered, creeping backward alongside Kev as she raised her Super Soaker. "It's infected." She flashed back on that buck that almost killed her at Nate's, the one that skewered his dad before charging her.

A razor-sharp shovel would come in very handy about now.

Big Kev motioned to the Super Soaker. "What's the range on that thing?"

The sky darkened further as they were swallowed by the shadows of the trees.

"Not far enough." She'd have to let the animal get close to blast it in the face, and even then the salt water would only slow it down, not stop it.

The bear slowed as it approached the edge of the lake, sniffing the air.

Realene pumped the Super Soaker and braced herself, aiming for the beast. She'd have to try and hit it as soon as it entered the tree line.

Its huge paws sank into the snow along the shore, and she met its glassy black eyes, imagined she saw the shimmer of wiggling worms in their depths. The weapon shook in her hand, her aim wavering. She pressed her elbows to her sides, trying to hold it steady.

A crack split the air, and she flinched. The bear roared again and reared around, its focus torn from Realene and Kev. Another crack, a gunshot, sounded, and the animal stumbled onto the ice. A third shot hit the bear in the head, releasing a spray of red that splattered the snowy surface red, and it thumped heavily to its side, motionless.

"Hide, quick." She lunged behind the closest tree. Big Kev followed suit.

She peeked around the trunk, watching as several shadowy figures emerged from the snow-filled landscape. A couple of the armed soldiers from the warehouse. She ducked back behind the tree, pressing her back to the rough surface and willing her breathing to quiet.

Realene looked at Kev, who'd assumed the same position she had. They had to be careful not to make a sound, only twenty feet or so separating them from the downed beast.

"Just a bear. Infected, I'd bet," one of the soldier's said.

"Haul it back," a tinny voice replied from the radio. *The colonel.* "Containment is priority one."

Then came a crinkling sounded like fabric, maybe a tarp of some kind.

The first man spoke again, saying, "Sir, we should send teams to sweep the perimeter and search the roads. It wasn't the bear that set off the alarm."

*Shit.* Realene hoped they'd be in the clear.

Grunting sounded, more crinkling. She waited, tried to ignore the cramp that clenched her tired leg. A slight rustle sounded beside her, the scrape of fabric on tree bark, and she angled a look at Big Kev. He had his eyes closed tight.

If the soldiers discovered them, they would be dead before she even had a chance to mention Harmon's name.

More grunting sounded, then more scraping. The noises faded, replaced by the bluster of the wind, the rustle of tree branches. Her fingers burned within her gloves, the cold seeping through the fabric, but she held herself in place, counting to five hundred before she turned, very slowly from her hiding spot behind the tree. No one there. Just an empty lake slowly being consumed by the storm.

"They're gone," she whispered, just loud enough for Big Kev to hear.

He slumped forward, bracing his hands on his knees. "Jesus, that was close."

"We're not safe yet. Come on." She trudged back toward the cabin, her muscles shaky. Icy pellets of snow stung her face, but she was glad for it, glad for the cover it provided them.

The soldiers would be searching the roads, meaning there was no way out. And holing up in the cabin wasn't an option. Any decent search around the lake's perimeter would include the place.

They hiked through the snow in silence, neither of them saying a word.

When they reached the cabin, she pulled Big Kev close. Only one option remained. "We have to split up."

"What? Why?"

"They're looking for whoever was at the warehouse, and we have to make them think it was just me. They can't know you were there." She didn't think the colonel would hurt Big Kev, but he'd gone to a lot of trouble to keep that meteor site a secret, even from the Canadian government, and she couldn't risk it.

Big Kev's brow furrowed, and Realene wondered if he was thinking about his dad, about what was done to him after he'd seen something unexplainable. "Yeah, okay. What's the plan?"

"They're covering the roads. I'm going to take the van and make sure they find me." She swallowed, her pulse clogging her throat.

"Are you crazy?" he asked.

"I already left a message for the colonel about Calvin. It wouldn't be that much of a stretch that I'd come up here looking for him."

The front door of the cabin opened, and the tip of a shotgun peeked through the gap. After a moment, Ana stepped out, lowering the weapon. "What the hell is going on? I heard gunshots."

Realene followed Big Kev onto the porch. "Is there any other way out of here?"

Ana threw her hands up in frustration but didn't ask any more questions, just said, "There's an old snowmobile trail just behind here that meets up with the main road farther east, I bet Uncle Cal's truck could make it."

"All right. Give me a head start, and we'll meet back at the hotel."

"As long as the colonel doesn't kill you," Big Kev said. "And none of us get, like, wormed."

"Wormed?" Ana asked, looking confused. Her confusion deepened after noticing the toy in Realene's grip. "Is that a Super Soaker?"

"Kev will fill you in," Realene said, figuring Ana needed to know the truth in case this plan all went to hell and they ended up back in the warehouse.

Realene marched toward the van and hopped inside, throwing the water gun into the back. She maneuvered the vehicle around and pressed the gas, barreling down the road as fast as the snowy gravel would allow, icy snow pelting the windshield. Her empty stomach clenched, anxiety taking hold. Nate had run away from the colonel. Or tried to, at least. Why the hell had Harmon taken him there?

Now she was going to throw herself at the colonel, confess to being places and seeing things she shouldn't.

She really wished Nate was here now. If she had actually come to Canada with him like he'd asked, they'd be facing this together. She hit a patch of ice and the tires slipped, sending her heart skipping a beat. Realene turned into the skid and straightened out, her practice and experience taking over.

Dad had still been alive when she learned to drive, would take her onto back roads and into empty parking lots in the worst weather. She still remembered him whipping donuts around the icy pavement until they were both laughing so hard they'd cried.

Realene reached the main road and was starting to turn right to drive around the lake and toward the warehouse when she had to slam on her brakes as another car sped past, barely avoiding clipping her bumper. After passing her, it slammed to a stop, brake lights glowing through the falling snow, and the doors opened.

The colonel stepped out, along with a couple of other guys.

Realene kept her hands on the steering wheel, watched as Harmon rounded the front of the van. He opened the passenger-side door and got in. The other guys circled the van, peering through the windows to make sure there was no one else in the car with her.

"I'm assuming that was you at the facility," he said.

"I tried calling you first."

"You spoke with the sergeant, who told you she would relay your message. Why didn't you wait for my call?"

"I was worried."

"Yes, and when I called you back you weren't there."

"You called me back?" She'd never checked her messages. Had meant to at the gas station, but then she saw Birdie.

"I did. If you'd been there to answer, I would have told you we tracked the meteor's path and discovered it broke into two pieces when it entered our atmosphere, but that we found the other half and secured it." He heaved a frustrated sigh. "We also found Calvin, injured but alive. He's in the hospital."

"Is he okay?" Tears welled up in her eyes. "What happened to him?"

The colonel turned toward her, pinning her in place with a stare. "Now you're here, when I specifically said not to come. In my message. Which you didn't listen to."

She pressed herself back against the door.

"You risked being infected. Or worse, shot. That's a heavily guarded site. Those soldiers have orders to keep the outbreak contained and to deal with trespassers with extreme prejudice."

"Does the Canadian government even know you're here?"

"They can't know. They're unequipped to handle this, would never accept our explanation of an alien infestation."

"So, you've, like, gone rogue or something?"

"I'm doing what needs to be done to prevent more loss of life, which includes keeping this operation secret from those who would only hinder the mission," he said, his words clipped.

"Then why'd you bring Nate?"

"Nate is not my responsibility, you are. I made a promise to your father I would keep you safe, to treat you like my own daughter." His jaw muscle twitched. "You're lucky he's not alive to see you behave like this."

Realene flinched, pain stinging her chest as if he'd punched her. "Nate could've been infected," she whispered.

"He was already here, and I thought he deserved to know. I was hoping to put his mind at ease, show him we had it under control. A decision I regret, since he clearly couldn't handle it." He shook his head. "And now I have to deal with you both when I should be focused on containing an extremely dangerous alien infestation."

Her cheeks burned. "I know. I… I'm sorry."

"You are to go back home immediately, understand?"

"But the storm—"

"You'll avoid the worst of it if you leave now."

Fluffy snowflakes covered her windshield, began to blot everything out. "Can I at least see Calvin? I want to make sure he knows I came."

"I'll tell him," he said. "Go home. I have enough to worry about without you around."

"Not until I talk to Nate." She raised her chin, didn't allow herself to look away. "I need to make sure he's okay."

"Nate deserves to enjoy his vacation with his girlfriend. It's no secret you hate that girl."

"I do not hate her," she said. But hadn't she treated her badly at every chance?

Harmon pinched the bridge of his nose. "What exactly are you trying to accomplish here? You're in over your head. Yes, you helped last time, but now we know what it takes to beat these things, and we don't need you getting in the way because you want to play the hero again."

She sucked in a breath. "I didn't say…I don't think I'm a hero."

"I know you mean well, but sometimes when you try and help, people just get hurt."

"You're talking about Ma."

He met her gaze, didn't look away.

Realene blinked rapidly, trying to hold back the tears. She knew it. He'd been lying to her this whole time, telling her she was a hero when he thought the opposite. The only thing she was good at was interfering, getting the people most important to her hurt.

A knock sounded on his window, and she jumped. One of the soldiers waited outside.

Harmon opened the door and stepped out, speaking to the man in hushed tones. After a moment, the colonel turned back to her and said, "Go home."

She didn't say anything, just sat gripping the steering wheel.

He closed the door, and he and his men got back into their vehicle. They backed up, allowing her to turn onto the road heading away from their facility. The tears she'd been holding back spilled down her cheeks.

# Twelve

**REALENE'S DRIVE BACK** to the Holiday Inn Holidome was forty-five minutes of pure stress. She prayed Big Kev and Ana made it back to the hotel, that they weren't stranded in the woods somewhere, or captured by the colonel's men.

A good inch of new snow blanketed the parking lot, but visibility wasn't too bad yet. The radio warned that the cold front was close, would result in high winds and over sixty centimeters of snow accumulation over the next twelve hours. She couldn't remember the conversion of centimeters to inches, but it seemed like a lot.

The weather was better farther south. Harmon was right that if she got on the road soon, she'd be able to avoid the worst of it. She just wanted to go home, never should have come in the first place.

Realene scanned the Holidome parking lot, saw Calvin's truck but not Nate's.

Her throat tightened.

Nate was going to be okay. The colonel would make sure of it.

She parked and ran to the entrance of the Holidome. People packed the pool area, music and drunk voices filling the atrium. She blocked out the annoying people crushing her in the elevator and rushed to reach the quiet of the room.

Big Kev lay on the far bed, his feet poking off the end. The TV was tuned to reruns of *Kids in the Hall*. She recognized the sketch he was watching—"Are Aliens Dull?"

She normally loved *KITH*, and Dave Foley in particular, but right now she wasn't in the mood.

Big Kev hit the mute button on the remote and sat up on his elbows. "Dude, you made it."

Ana's coat was tossed on the bed, and the bathroom door was closed.

Realene slumped onto the other bed. "I did. You guys okay?"

"Yeah. We slipped right out of there, no problem. How 'bout you? Did you talk to the colonel?" He sat up. "Have you been crying?"

"Yeah and yeah." She shrugged, not ready to share the details of her many failures. "I talked to Harmon. They found Calvin. He's okay. He's in the hospital."

"Why? What happened?"

She frowned. "I don't know." *She'd asked, hadn't she?* But the colonel didn't say.

"Can we see him?"

"No. The colonel was pretty pissed about the trespassing and everything. I'm actually gonna head home. I just wanted to make sure you were okay first. You're welcome to come with me."

"No fucking way. I don't trust Harmon, and I'm not going anywhere until I see Uncle Cal myself and get proof that it's all true, that my dad was right about everything."

"You can't tell anyone about this. It's too dangerous."

"No duh, it's dangerous. This is an alien invasion we're talking about. And who knows how many other sites are out there?"

"It's a crash landing, not an invasion, and this is the only other site," she said. "The meteor broke in half upon entry into our atmosphere."

He pointed at her. "Just because you went along with the cover up and lied to everyone about what happened doesn't mean I will too."

The bathroom door opened, and Ana stepped out. "I thought about just staying in there, but I can hear everything you're saying anyway, so..." She leaned back against the wall, hands in the pockets of her overalls.

"No way are we keeping quiet about this," Big Kev said.

Realene rubbed a hand over her tired eyes. "I just don't want you to get hurt."

"More like you don't want to make your buddy Harmon mad."

She stood and grabbed her duffel bag. "Whatever. Do what you want, I don't care."

"You're really leaving?"

Realene sighed. "Yeah, I never should have come here in the first place."

"Have you even talked to Nate?"

She stared at the ratty hotel carpet. "The colonel will take care of him."

"Jesus. You just don't question a thing he says, do you?"

A knock sounded on the door, and Ana answered it.

A Shakey's delivery guy in a parka stood in the hall. "Almost didn't make it," he said. "Bunch of animals out here."

"Sorry, man." Ana pulled out some cash to pay him. "Appreciate you braving the weather. And the idiots."

She took the two pizzas and a two-liter of Big 8 Cola from the guy and started to close the door, but Big Kev crossed the room and grabbed the door before it closed.

He took one of the pizzas. "I'm gonna take a walk and check my AOL account, see if there's any news from the Alien Alliance." He started to go, then turned back to Ana. "Oh, and in case you didn't hear, supposedly Uncle Cal is fine, because her military buddy said so, but we can't see him. So that checks out, eh?" He let the door slam closed behind him.

Ana sat on the far bed, placing the pizza box beside her. "Kev told me about those, uh, alien worm things. Pretty messed up."

"Messed up?" Realene gripped the handle of her bag, her nails digging into her palm. "Hundreds of people died, you know, the first time."

"No offense, but you seem on edge. Maybe you should eat something."

"I should go. Get on the road before the storm gets worse."

"Suit yourself." Ana opened the box and pulled out a slice for herself.

The smell of meat and cheese hit Realene's nose and made her stomach growl. She had to admit she was pretty hungry. "Fine." She dropped her bag and grabbed a piece. "Hawaiian?"

Ana finished chewing her bite. "What's not to love about salty and sweet? Invented in Canada too."

"Huh." Still standing, Realene took one bite, then another.

She had to admit, it was the best pizza she'd had in a long time. Before she knew it, she'd finished everything, including the crust, and Ana was grinning at her.

"Guess I was hungry," Realene said, her face heating.

Ana grabbed two glasses from the desk where they sat on their little cardboard coasters and turned them upright, then poured some Big 8 in each one. She handed a glass to Realene.

"Thanks. And sorry for disparaging your national pizza, it's pretty delicious."

"You're welcome." Ana sat back down. "Now that you're a bit more rational, are you still driving back home tonight without first seeing... What's his name again? Nate?

"I saw him at the site. He looked fine. I mean, physically fine. I think he kinda freaked out. Anyway, I'm guessing he wouldn't be too excited to see me. I was a jerk the last time we talked."

"Boyfriend trouble?"

"Ew, no. Nate and I are just friends."

"So what's the problem then? Just let him slug you or something and move on."

Realene chuckled, then helped herself to another piece of pizza. She took a bite and savored it.

"Sorry, but I just want to get this straight. Instead of staying inside, where you have a warm room, good pizza, and fantastic company, you're going to run away into a literal blizzard."

Realene leaned against the desk and narrowed her eyes. "I'm not running away."

Ana raised an eyebrow and took a sip of her drink. "Could've fooled me."

"I messed up coming here, okay? Getting you and Big Kev involved." Realene set her half-eaten slice back in the box, her appetite souring. "This isn't a joke, you know? My ma was murdered, and a lot of other people died."

"I remember her, but only a little. I think we were playing in your yard, and I fell, scraped my knee. She took me inside, patched me up, then gave me this weird flat, rolled-up bread. It was, like, sweet."

"Lefsa." Realene smiled, the memory of the flavor on her tongue. "Homemade. With butter and sugar."

"Yeah, lefsa." Ana wiped her hands on a napkin. "You know, I talked to Uncle Cal after everything happened, and he was cagey about it. Wouldn't say much. But he did talk about you, said you saved his life, that you looked out for him."

"Not this time," Realene said. "He needed me. Called me for help, and I missed it."

"Okay, but you're here now. And tomorrow we'll figure out where Uncle Cal is and go see him."

"Harmon made it pretty clear I'm not welcome."

Ana scoffed. "Screw that guy."

"You sound like your brother."

"Yeah, well, we've got good reasons for not trusting government types. They like to keep secrets, don't care who suffers for it."

"Kev told me a little about your dad, what happened."

Ana exhaled heavily. "I was only eleven, but I remember us being happy before, you know? It just…changed everything. My dad, he's never been the same."

"What did he see?"

"An aircraft of some kind, said he was totally transfixed by the thing. Couldn't move. It came closer and blasted this bright hot light that burned, then he blacked out. Woke up with a serious burn on his leg and found some weird pieces of metal."

Realene's instinct was to say the experience had nothing to do with aliens, but if they could hitch a ride on a meteor, wasn't it possible there were others with ships? "Do you think it was a UFO?"

"Maybe. My grandma used to say we're in the stars and what's in the stars is in us." Ana looked up at the ceiling as if she could see through it to the night sky. "What I know for sure is something happened that people in power wanted to cover up, and they made sure Dad was seen as crazy. We were a family before, not perfect but normal, happy. After, everything changed. I try to do what I can to help him, but I feel like it's never enough."

"I'm sorry." Realene didn't know exactly what Ana was going through, but she understood what it was like to watch your parent lose a part of themselves, to be responsible for them. Watching Ma slip away while Realene couldn't do a thing about it was torture.

"You lost your dad, too, yeah?" Ana asked.

"Three years ago. Cancer." Realene wiped her hands on her jeans. "I know you think Harmon's a dick, but he really helped after that, made sure me and Ma were okay."

"Noted," Ana said. "But that doesn't excuse him hiding things from you and getting mad for coming after your friends. You did what was right, even though you were scared."

Realene inhaled a deep breath, thinking of the last time she'd gone over to Nate's to hang out. They were young, eleven or twelve, and his dad, Dick, was drunk. He corned Nate, seemed about to hit him. Realene didn't think, just grabbed the closest thing she saw and threw it at Dick. A can of beer that bounced harmlessly off the man, then burst open and sprayed the foamy liquid everywhere.

Dick called her dad, who was also his boss, to pick her up, and she thought she was in big trouble. Instead, her dad said he was proud of her for sticking up for her friend, for doing what was right. He said she'd been brave. He also said she was never to set foot in Nate's house again.

Harmon accused her of wanting to be a hero, but that wasn't why she came. She had no interest in saving the day. Realene just wanted her friends to be okay, wanted to be there for them when they needed her. The guilt that had coiled in her chest eased at the realization she had nothing to feel bad about, that Harmon's demands for her to leave her friends behind were bullshit.

If her dad were still alive, he wouldn't be mad. He'd say she was brave.

"You're pretty smart," Realene said.

"Don't you mean pretty and smart?" Ana glanced over and her lip twitched. She tapped the corner of her mouth. "You have something."

"Oh." Realene pulled a napkin from the pile, cursing the ravenous appetite that made her eat like a slob, and swiped at her face.

"It's so much worse." Ana laughed. Standing, she swiped at the spot with her own napkin. "There. Got it."

"Thanks." Now so close, Realene picked up on a scent coming from Ana, something earthy and slightly sweet. Sandalwood maybe?

The room door opened and Realene backed into the desk, grimacing as the sharp corner jabbed into her hip. Ana stayed right where she was.

Big Kev looked between them. "Why is your face so red?" he asked Realene.

"Pizza sauce," Ana said, giving Realene a wink.

"Okaaay. Anyway, I checked in with Flint. Nothing new to report, and don't worry, I was careful about what I told him. I let them know about the warehouse, since they were already watching the area. They're gonna try and get someone to keep an eye from a distance, but it's gonna be tricky with the storm. You really set on driving home tonight?"

"Drive home tonight? What kind of crazy idea is that." Realene grinned.

Big Kev shook his head. "At least you came to your senses."

Ana closed the pizza box and set it on the desk beside the TV. "In that case, I challenge you to a game of snooker."

"I'm sorry, you what now?" Realene asked.

"It's a form of billiards," Big Kev said. "You know, pool."

"Ah, okay, yeah. I'm in." Realene wasn't usually one for athletic contests, but she and Nate had gone through a billiards phase together, and she still had a knack for the game. They'd played at the YMCA just about every day after school their senior year, back when Nate was spending as little time at home as possible, so as to avoid his dad's alcoholic rage.

Hanging out downstairs could serve a double purpose and help her catch a glimpse of Nate, make sure he was okay, without disturbing his time with Trish.

**THE HOTEL ATRIUM** was packed, but more so in and around the swimming pools, allowing Realene to claim one of the two pool tables with ease. They had billiards not snooker, which Ana called a tourist fueled national travesty, so they decided to play eight ball instead. The tables were located beside a small, shabby-looking towel hut with a fake thatched roof and dirty towels piled high inside a hamper that hadn't been emptied all day. There were also several buckets of cheap plastic sunglasses, the kind with neon-colored bows.

A guy in a Hawaiian shirt who was much too tipsy to be a hotel employee had cleared a spot on the counter to set up a makeshift bar. A handwritten sign detailed the prices for beer, mixed drinks, and shots. Realene wondered how long he'd stay in business before someone from the hotel shut him down.

Big Kev got them each a Molson Ice, then sat in a patio chair near the billiards table while Ana explained the difference between pool and snooker. Apparently, snooker used a square table and different balls, but Realene missed the details after that. She was too distracted by how cute Ana looked in her denim overalls.

Realene had changed out of her dad's gray flannel. It was a nice security blanket but admittedly stunk because she refused to wash it. To freshen up, she put on a red-and-black flannel of her own, wishing that she'd brought something cuter to wear.

"Care to make it interesting?" Ana inserted a loonie in the coin slot and the balls dropped into the channel at the bottom of one end of the table. She started racking the balls.

"Watch out, she's a shark," Big Kev said.

Realene decided to play along. "Sure, what's the wager?"

"If I win, you take me out on a date tomorrow night, and if you win, I take you out."

Realene suppressed a grin. Seemed like a win-win. She'd have to stay in town an extra night, but they already had the room booked, and maybe Nate was right. Maybe she did deserve a break. "You're on."

"FYI, she murdered her last girlfriend with a tire iron to the eye socket," Big Kev said to Ana.

Realene gaped at him. "I told you that was self-defense."

"No talking about exes on a first date," Ana said. She lined up her shot, her long, beaded earrings brushing the felt of the table, and knocked in a solid.

Realene chanted *be cool, be cool*, in her head, even though she wanted to squeal like some kind of schoolgirl. "This is a date?"

"I bought you dinner, didn't I?" Ana took another shot but missed.

"And it was delicious. Consider me converted." Realene sipped her beer, then took a shot at a stripe, which missed by a mile. Perplexed, she crouched until she was eye level with the table and saw that the surface was far from flat. "I think this is going to be more about luck than skill."

"Good thing I'm talented *and* lucky." Ana took another shot and made it.

A girl wandered near Big Kev, and he popped to his feet. "Something I can help you with, little lady?"

She giggled, pointing at his jersey. "Are you a hockey player?"

He puffed up his chest. "Not anymore. Used to play, though. Goalie."

Ana came up beside Realene and whispered, "That was in the third grade. He got cut from the team after he kept ducking every time the puck came close."

Big Kev flipped them off behind his back and led the girl toward the pool, where a dozen people lounged on pool floaties, even though the water was four feet deep at most.

Realene scanned the pool, looking for any sign of Nate and Trish, but didn't see them.

"You okay?

"Oh, uh, yeah." *Hockey. They were talking about Hockey.* "What about you? Ever play sports in school?"

"Not really," Ana said. "Did a lot of hunting with my dad before the incident. But as I got older, I focused more on my classes and stuff. Guess you could say I'm more of a nerd than an athlete."

"Same. Definitely the last one chosen for dodge ball."

Ana took a swig of her beer. "Kev said you're starting university in the fall."

"Yeah, I'm thinking of going into psychology. What about you? Any plans?"

"Just working and saving up. I'd like to get out of Winnipeg, go somewhere warm. But my dad, he needs support."

"Yeah." Realene understood the feeling of being trapped, but in hindsight, it was better than being alone. "I bet he appreciates you, though. And it's nice you still have him around. My ma, she, uh, suffered with dementia before, you know. I used to take care of her."

"I bet she appreciated you, too." Ana gave Realene's hand a quick squeeze. "So, were you guys really attacked by a bear today, or was that bullshit?"

"Not bullshit." It wasn't funny at the time, but she chuckled thinking about it now. "But that was nothing compared to the hordes of infected prairie dogs."

"Prairie dogs? What are they? Like, wild dogs or something?"

"No, they're little. Like gophers but smaller. I think you Canadians call them ground squirrels."

"What? Those aren't scary, they're adorable."

"Not when they're linked *Children of the Damned*-style in a synchronized attack of claws and teeth."

Ana snorted beer from her nose and swiped at her face with her sleeve. "Oh my God. Now I'm picturing them with little blond bobs."

Realene laughed so hard at the visual, she had to hunch over to catch her breath. "Seriously. It was scary."

"Closest I got to being featured on *When Animals Attack* was saving Kev from a cougar once."

"No way."

"Yes, way. We were up near the sand lakes looking for UFO remnants, and he got too close to her den. She just, like, appeared, and started growling at him." Ana raised her arms, fingers curled into claws. "I tried jumping, making myself look taller, all the things they say to do, and he was able to crawl away."

"Jesus," Realene said, enthralled.

"Then she came for me, like ran right at me and took a swipe." Ana unclipped one side of her overalls and pulled up the shirt beneath to show a Freddy Krueger-style set of claw marks across the side of her stomach. "I was able to fire my gun in the air before she did more damage. Scared her off."

"Amazing." Realene got closer to examine the scars, reached out to touch them but stopped herself just before her fingers made contact. She cleared her throat and stood.

Ana lowered her shirt before fastening her overalls back in place. "Guess I, uh, owed you anyway, since you showed so much skin earlier."

"Ugh, don't remind me. I cannot believe you saw me in those ridiculous boxers."

"Come on. You looked cute in them."

Realene took a long drink of her beer to hide her smile. She wanted to scream, *Ana thinks I look cute!* Instead, she said, "So, you help Kev with his UFO hunting?"

"Mostly to keep him and dad from getting into trouble." She leaned back against the pool table. "They'd both be in jail or in some secret government facility if I wasn't there to stop them from trespassing or stealing stuff that isn't theirs."

"Sounds like a big job."

"Someone had to look out for them after my mom left." Ana played with the thin, beaded choker at her throat, then seemed to catch herself, dropping her hand. "Besides, they've calmed down a bit. Dad mostly spends his time doing the conference circuit these days, tries to spread the word about his story that way."

"Conference circuit?"

"For UFO enthusiasts." She rolled her eyes. "They're a wacky bunch, but they love Dad. Treat him like a rock star. And they pay pretty good, so it helps keep a roof over our heads. We actually just came from one in Saskatoon." A frown pulled at her lips.

"You okay?" Realene asked.

"Oh, yeah. Just thinking I should probably go home soon and check in. He can get a little squirrelly after talking so much about the encounter."

"That's understandable." She didn't say it but figured he probably had PTSD.

The image of Nate freaking out beside the crater in that warehouse popped in her head. Hell, she didn't want to go anywhere near the lake knowing there was another meteor close by.

Yeah. There was plenty of PTSD to go around.

Ana lined up a shot and hit the eight ball solidly into the corner pocket. "Oops, looks like I lost the bet."

Realene didn't call her on the purposeful scratch, just smiled.

"Hey," Big Kev called out, appearing from the throng of bodies packing the pool area. "Look who I found."

Nate trailed behind him, clad in a Hawaiian shirt, swim trunks, and a pair of those ridiculous free sunglasses.

A relieved smile spread over Realene's face, then faltered. He might be pissed at her for crashing his trip.

His face broke into a grin, and he jogged over, wrapping her in a hug, then pulling away. "You made it."

"Yeah, I, uh, I'm sorry. I didn't want to spoil your party or anything. I'm really sorry for—"

"Trish," he called, looking back the way they'd come. "Look who's here."

Trish wore the same sunglasses, along with a pink-and-yellow polka dot bikini. Her steps faltered at the sight of Realene. "What are you doing here?"

"Hey, Trish, cute swimsuit." The compliment wasn't fake. Trish *did* look cute, in a Beach Barbie kind of way. "I came to check on Calvin. He left me this voicemail and, well, we thought he might be in trouble."

"Oh my gosh." She raised one hand to her mouth. "What happened? Is he okay?"

"Yeah, Harmon actually found him. Said he's in the hospital. We're gonna try and see him tomorrow."

"You talked to Harmon?" Nate leaned in closer, his breath reeking of alcohol. "So you know about the, uh, thing in the woods?"

She nodded.

Big Kev threw his arm over Nate's shoulders. "Heard there's some kind of spring break party next door at the Merry Moose. You guys want to go check it out?"

"Yeah, man, let's do it. I think I've earned a few more drinks after today." He laughed, but it sounded brittle. Forced.

Trish gave him a worried look but said, "Sounds good, baby. Whatever you wanna do."

"You coming?" he asked Realene.

"Oh, no. I don't want to interrupt your vacation. I was thinking I might just hang out around here." She gestured toward the pool table but knew she would end up returning to the room as soon as the rest of them left.

"No way in hell are you staying here. You're coming with us," Nate said.

Realene gave Trish an apologetic look. "Okay, yeah, sounds fun."

"You kids have fun," Ana said. "I'm gonna head home." She gently touched Realene's hand, sending a tingle over her skin. "See you tomorrow night?"

"It's a date." She barely contained the grin that wanted to split her face as she watched Ana walk away.

"Hold on… Date?" Nate said. "You picked up a girl? You stud."

"Dude, that's my sister," Big Kev said, knocking back the rest of his drink.

"Ana?" Nate asked. "Nice." He gave Realene a high five.

She noticed his hand was bandaged, remembered it had been bloody after the fight at the warehouse. "You okay?"

"Oh, yeah. You should see the other guy."

"If we're going to the bar, I need to change," Trish said. "Come on, baby." She took Nate's arm and pulled him in the direction of their room. They had to weave around two girls that were shoving each other and shouting.

"We'll see you guys over there," Big Kev called, then hooked his arm with Realene's and led her away from the increasingly rowdy coeds packing the pool area and toward the hallway with the elevators.

# Thirteen

**AFTER GRABBING THEIR** coats from the room, Realene and Big Kev made their way toward the lobby. She dreaded hanging out with a bunch of drunk idiots, but she didn't want to pass up the chance to talk to Nate. He hadn't seemed mad at her, but she owed him a real apology. Plus, she wanted to make sure he was holding up okay after seeing the other half of the meteor.

A group of drunk kids ran past, spraying each other with water guns. She barely dodged the spray, but Big Kev wasn't so lucky. He sniffed his coat sleeve. "Does Caribou Crossing stain?"

A whiff of the whiskey hit Realene, and she grimaced. "I'm not sure, but it definitely smells."

The lobby area between the atrium and the front doors had become the location for an impromptu dance off, and a crowd of people surrounded an open circle where two guys were facing off to "Intergalactic" by the Beastie Boys blasting over a boombox.

"Think I should get in there?" Big Kev asked, then proceeded to demonstrate his running man.

Realene cringed, at which point he started doing the sprinkler.

"Maybe save it for the bar." She started to turn away, when she noticed a Cruella de Vil-haired old lady barging into the center of the dance circle: Irene, followed closely by Birdie. She waved a bundle of brochures. Birdie grabbed her arm, tried to pull her away, but she shook off his grip. Border patrol hadn't stopped them after all.

"Repent, sinners, the end times are upon us," she yelled, her voice carrying over the music

Realene grabbed Big Kev's arm and pulled him to the side, out of Irene's sightline. "How the hell did they figure out where we're staying?"

Someone grabbed the brochures from her hand and flung them in the air, letting them rain down over the crowd. One floated over to land at Realene's feet, and she bent to pick it up. The trifold brochure said, "Judgment Day is Coming" and featured flames that looked like they'd been colored red and orange with magic marker.

Big Kev grabbed the brochure and folded it open to reveal three panels of ranting about Reverend Zebediah the martyr, and depictions of people burning in a lake of fire. "Yikes."

"You're the one who thought they might be onto something, remember?" she said.

"I mean, sometimes the enemy of your enemy is your friend."

"Wait," Realene said. "Who was the enemy? Me?"

He shrugged. "Well, yeah, maybe a little at first, but mainly the government, the colonel. You know, the ones who've got my uncle somewhere."

The front doors opened, and several uniformed Mounties walked through, bundled up in winter coats and hats—or *toques*, as they called them up here. The officers moved through the crowd, which parted like the Red Sea at the appearance of cops. Someone switched off the boom box, and the crowd quieted.

Chrissy came out from the behind the desk, looking frazzled. Her previously perky ponytail sat lopsided on top of her head. She pointed to Irene. "That's her, the one I called about. She's been harassing our guests and won't leave."

Irene stooped to pick up one of her discarded brochures. "Nonsense. We're doing God's work. Can't you see the end times are coming?"

Birdie backed away, giving Irene what Realene could only describe as a death stare. Not as loyal as her precious Lieutenant Braun, then. Or at least not willing to get arrested.

One Mountie looked at the other, a small smile ticking the corner of his mouth. "That may be, ma'am, but this is private property, and you've been asked to leave. Do you have somewhere you can go?"

"I wanted a room, but they wouldn't give me one."

"We're all booked, ma'am. I told you that," Chrissy said, chewing her gum aggressively.

A shout sounded from the area of the mini golf course, and she yelled toward the commotion, "Hey, break it up!" before rushing over to try and corral the crowd.

"Sorry, ma'am, it's time to go," the Mountie instructed. "If you don't have a place to stay, we'll take you in for your own safety." He took Irene's arm.

She waved the brochure in his face. "The end times are upon us. You'll see. False prophets, wars, and loose morals."

Big Kev laughed. "Loose morals."

"That's one of her favorites," Realene said.

Irene looked in their direction, and her eyes widened. "There are devils in our midst."

Realene couldn't resist. She raised her hands on either side of her head and gave herself little devil horns.

Irene freaked out, started screaming, "They're here among us, don't you see? Satan's minions!"

"Ma'am, I'm sorry, but if you don't come willingly, we will have to restrain you."

"He spoke of this day. Prophesied the time would come. Fire and ice from the sky. Devils among us!" She pointed at Realene, her face twisting into something completely unlike the woman who'd once been Ma's best friend. She used to be such a nice, normal person, but none of that remained. It had been stripped away by fear, brainwashing, and ignorance.

Realene frowned at the thought.

The Mounties got on either side of Irene and led her forcefully through the front doors.

"There is more going on here than you know. That demon Harmon is hiding something!" she screamed.

That much was true, and Realene was glad the Mounties would dismiss whatever was said as crazy rantings. The colonel was wrong for many reasons, but he was right to keep the meteor a secret from the Canadian authorities.

The crowd started chanting, "Nah nah nah nah, hey hey hey, goodbye."

Birdie slunk out the doors after the cops and Irene, maintaining a safe distance.

Big Kev sang along with the crowd, waving his arms in the air as they moved toward the door. Realene found herself walking to the beat. At least they wouldn't have to worry about Irene anymore, but Birdie and the Olsons could still be a problem.

She considered calling the colonel to tell him, but he'd only yell at her for not leaving. Besides, he'd made it very clear he had everything under control, and he didn't want or need her help. That was fine by her. She could focus on having some fun for a change.

**REALENE AND BIG** Kev followed the line of people from the hotel to the Merry Moose, wind slowing them as soon as they exited the front doors. Icy flakes filled the air and pelted their faces as they made the trek through the already accumulating snow to the bar that was only a few hundred feet away, but barely visible. She was surprised the bar had decided to stay open, even with the captive audience of spring breakers.

She cringed at the realization that she was wearing the same flannel as the moose on the bar's sign. Not that she had anyone specific to impress now that Ana was gone, but Realene also didn't relish feeling like a lumberjack among a bunch of hotties.

Inside the rustic, cabin-like building, a large bar sat in the center like an island circled by barstools. The lodge-theme continued with stuffed animal heads mounted along the walls, including a moose on the back wall that was equipped with sunglasses. One half of the room featured high-top tables and a TV mounted in each corner; the other half featured a dance floor and a fancy CD jukebox. Most of the patrons were wearing shorts, skimpy sundresses, or bathing suits under their winter coats. Many had donned plastic sunglasses with neon bows, and a few wore Canadian tuxedos—denim from head to toe—which made Realene think of Jeff Hozak, aka Reverend Zebediah, who'd fancied the look. May he burn in hell.

Realene scanned the packed room but couldn't find Nate and Trish in the crowd. "I think we beat them here," she said, suppressing her urge to flee the pressing-in of people from every direction.

"Let's grab a drink." Big Kev marched through the crowd with ease, his massive size acting as a sort of people-plow for Realene to follow.

They passed a pair of girls talking to a guy with a camcorder, who was offering them free *Ladies Gone Crazy* T-shirts in exchange for flashing their boobs. Realene guessed the *Girls Gone Wild* crew had chosen a more beachy location and didn't care if some cheap knockoff decided to stake its claim in Canada. The girls started to unzip their jackets, and she kept walking. She liked boobs as much as the next person, but not at the expense of some drunk girl's dignity.

Now at the bar, she waited behind Big Kev, who was trying desperately to get the bartender's attention. A bartender wearing a red-and-black flannel. *Great,* she was dressed like one of the employees.

"Tubthumping" by Chumbawamba played over the speakers, and she groaned at the terrible song choice.

Big Kev finally got the drinks and handed her yet another Molson Ice. Not Realene's favorite, but when in Canada, one honored the local customs.

"From the land where ice was born," he said, quoting the commercial, and they clinked bottles.

Realene swigged back half of hers, the cold stinging her throat. She could use a bit of liquid courage.

They made their way to the high-top tables, snagging one as another group moved to the dance floor. Both TVs played *MuchMusic*, the Canadian version of MTV. Instead of bikini clad girls dancing on a beach, there were ski bunnies dancing at Whistler resort.

All around her, girls wiggled and danced to the music, their coats hanging open to reveal their skimpy clothes beneath. Several of the guys wore swim trunks with snow boots and coats, displaying bare chests and puka shell necklaces.

She spotted Nate and Trish at the bar getting drinks. Under their coats, Trish wore a sundress with hot pink leggings, and Nate had switched to jeans with his Hawaiian shirt. Both of them still wore their complimentary sunglasses.

Big Kev raised his hand, yelling to get their attention. "Nate, Trish, over here."

Nate looked around. He saw them and half danced his way over.

Realene held back a grin. He must be tipsy already, and he wasn't the only one. She found herself bopping to the music.

He and Trish set down their drinks on the table, some kind of bright blue concoctions with umbrellas, and beamed intoxicated smiles. His cheeks were rosy, and he swayed a little on his feet. "This isn't so bad, is it?"

Realene figured she should get her apology out of the way before she chickened out. "Not really my scene, but I figured I owed you guys a drink."

"For what?" he asked.

"I'm a jerk. I should have come with you when you asked. And Trish, you seem really nice. Sorry I've been such bitch to you."

Nate laughed, and Trish gaped at her. "Oh, um, thank you, I guess. I appreciate that."

"I know we're crashing your vacation, and we're going to leave you alone after this. I promise. We'll just finish our drinks and head back to the hotel."

Big Kev eyed his already empty beer bottle. "What? We will?"

"Oh, great," Trish said. "I'm so glad you understand. Like, I would normally love to hang out, but this is supposed to be a couples thing, you know."

Nate smacked one hand on the table. "No way are you guys leaving. Let's have some fun. Get another round."

Trish angled a look toward the packed dance floor, her face hopeful. "But baby, I was thinking we'd dance."

Realene snickered. Nate did *not* dance in public, ever. He was the one who stood off to the side at every school function they'd ever been to, making fun of everyone else who dared to let loose.

"Yeah, let's do it," Big Kev said. "I do a mean Roger Rabbit." He started doing a miniature version of the move while edging backward.

"Oh, I, that's awesome…" Trish said. She looked back at Nate. "Are you coming?"

Nate gave her a kiss on the cheek. "I'll be there in a sec, muffin. I need to tell Realene about the *you know what* first."

She looked between him and Realene, gnawing at her lip. "Okay, baby, but don't take too long. I want to see your best moves." Trish and Big Kev left for the dance floor.

"You're really gonna dance? Like in front of all these people?" Realene asked.

"Sometimes you do stupid stuff for the people you love."

She choked on her sip of beer. "Love?"

"I mean, yeah." He fiddled with the umbrella in his drink.

She noticed his lips were tinted blue and stifled a laugh. Big Kev had been right about staying, about making up with Nate. "Hey, I really am sorry about how I acted."

"It's okay. I know the funeral was tough."

"The worst." She took another swig of her beer, tried not to think of Ma lying in that frozen ground. "But I should have just talked to you about it."

"Maybe, but I shouldn't have pushed you. You've got a right to grieve."

"Yeah, but I think you were right about trying to move on, too. All Ma ever wanted was to make people happy. She wouldn't want me to be depressed because of her." She looked at her mood ring. It was a bright green. Saying the words out loud, that Ma would want her to be happy, released some of the guilt inside her. Realene had to allow herself to move on, to stop blaming herself. For Ma.

"So, what's going on with Calvin?" he asked.

She told him about the call and about finding Calvin's things and the warehouse.

He leaned in closer. "So, you saw?"

She reached out and placed her hand on top of his. "I did. Are you okay?"

"I thought it was over." He hiccuped. "Thought I could just forget about all of it, move on."

"We can. We don't have to get involved this time. Harmon doesn't want our help anyway. Well, not mine at least." She told him about her conversation with the Colonel, about him ordering her to leave.

"That asshole." He bumped the table, and she managed to grab her beer before it tipped over. "You were just trying to look out for Calvin and me. And none of what happened in Demise was your fault."

Realene was actually starting to believe that. "That's what Ana said, too."

He gave a sly smile. "'Ana said,' huh? Do tell."

"Shut up." She shoved him gently.

"I heard you have a date tomorrow, so I guess you're staying for a few days at least."

Her cheeks flushed. "Yeah. I guess."

She glanced at the dance floor and at Trish, who was doing something that resembled the chicken. Realene suppressed her instinct to be judgmental, to see her from Nate's perspective, and by doing so, decided her dancing was kind of cute.

"About what you said earlier. Why are you so worried about crashing our vacation? We invited you, remember? Who said you'd ruin things?"

"No one, but I can tell that Trish wants privacy. She said it herself: This is a couples thing for you guys. Besides, you deserve some alone-time after the past couple months." She bit her lip, not wanting to spoil his mood, but knowing she had to tell him his mom was at the Revelation church and that Irene had managed to follow them into Canada. "Hey, I have to tell you something about your mom and the cult. I saw her—"

"Nope. No cult talk. Not tonight." He swished his umbrella around in his drink.

"Okay, fine." She'd tell him tomorrow. Irene was in jail for the night and wouldn't be causing any trouble until then. She couldn't stop thinking about the meteor, though. Hanging there above the crater, worms infecting all those screaming rats. It wasn't that far from town, and if they got loose in a big city like this, it would be so much worse than Demise.

"Hey," Nate said, and she met his eyes. "It's gonna be okay. There's nothing we can do anyway, right? What's that thing your dad used to say? 'Not my circus, not my elephants.'"

She giggled. "'Not my monkeys.'"

"That's right." Nate gulped down his drink, then grabbed her arm. "We can worry about alien monkeys tomorrow. Tonight, we party!"

She giggled and said, "Hell yeah."

"Wait." He pointed toward the ceiling. "You hear that?"

She strained her ears to catch the beginning of "Gin and Juice" by Snoop Dogg fading in on the speakers. "Oh, no…" Realene mumbled. "I don't think so."

"Oh, yes," Nate interrupted with a grin. "This is happening."

They'd gotten drunk on gin and Hi-C and danced to this song in her bedroom shortly before Ma was diagnosed, but that had been just the two of them. Surely, he didn't expect her to relive the moment in front of all these people.

He grabbed her hand and pulled her toward the dance floor. "You need to let loose. Have some fun."

"Dude, this is so embarrassing." Where was the Nate that hated to dance? She could really use him right now.

"Who cares?" They reached the dance floor and maneuvered to join Trish and Big Kev.

They all started to sing along, as did everyone else in the bar, and Realene got caught up in the excitement. The liquor might have helped, too. She raised her arms above her head and belted out the lyrics. She hip-checked Big Kev, thankful he'd talked her into staying.

As the song was coming to an end, a guy clad in only a Speedo and flip flops sidled up behind Trish and grabbed her hips, grinding against her.

"Hey, watch it," she said, clawing at his hands.

Speedo Guy only gripped her tighter, nuzzling his face in her hair.

Nate shoved the guy, who let go of Trish and whirled to face Nate.

"Whoa, guys, settle down," Realene said, extending her arms between them. She shot a look at Big Kev, hoping to take advantage of his size, but he was in a shouting match with a couple of Speedo Guy's friends, at least she thought they were, since they were also wearing only speedos.

Nate smacked her arm away and got in the guy's face. "That's my girlfriend, asshole."

Speedo Guy laughed. "No way you landed a sweet piece of ass like that."

Trish put her hand on Nate's arm. "It's okay, baby, I'm okay. Let's just go."

"Yeah, *baby*, why don't you just go. Little pussy." Speedo Guy high-fived a friend of his standing nearby.

Realene gritted her teeth, wanting someone to teach this asshole a lesson, but she knew they should just walk away.

Nate, however, had a different idea. And his fist was already cocked and ready.

"Stop!" Realene shouted, but it was too late.

Nate punched the guy hard right in the mouth, bloodying his bottom lip good. But Speedo Guy barely budged. He just smiled through bloodstained teeth and lunged at Nate, tackling him to the dance floor.

# Fourteen

**SPEEDO GUY LANDED** on Nate, tackling him to the ground and knocking the sunglasses from his face. The people closest stopped dancing and backed away, forming a circle around the fight. Speedo Guy hopped on top of Nate and nailed him with a couple hard punches before Realene and Big Kev grabbed the guy by the arms and lifted him off, hurling him into the surrounding crowd. He smacked into the people on the perimeter, who caught him and kept him from falling.

The *Ladies Gone Crazy* camera guy shoved his way into the fray and started filming.

Speedo Guy swiped his hand across his face to leave a red smear. He licked the blood from his lips, probably a mix of his and Nate's, and made a "come get me" gesture.

Realene sneered at the jerk, wanted to punch him herself.

Trish knelt by Nate. "Please. It's not worth it."

His Adam's apple bobbed in his throat, but he gave a sharp nod, then got up and stormed across the dance floor. Realene swiped Nate's sunglasses off the floor and gave one last glare at the jerk, who was now getting pats on the back from his friends as if he'd done something great.

Nate and Trish moved to the outside edge of the crowd, against the wall, and Realene and Big Kev caught up to them. Nate had a cut lip and a bloody nose but didn't look too badly hurt. Trish grabbed a couple drink-ring marred napkins from the closest table and used them to wipe away the blood from his face. She gasped and took a step back, her free hand coming up to cover her mouth.

"That bad?" Nate asked.

"Let me see," Realene said, stepping closer. She'd seen Nate get in plenty of fights, usually defending other people. He'd never been very good at delivering blows, but he had lots of practice taking a punch.

"No." Trish snatched the sunglasses from Realene's hand and placed them on Nate's face. "I just, I hate to see you hurt. It's okay. I'm okay. Everything's fine." She blanched at the sight of the bloody napkins in her hand, and Nate grabbed them from her.

"She's got a thing about blood," he said.

"We should go now. Get back to the hotel," Trish said.

He stuffed the napkins in his coat pocket. His face was mostly clean of blood, just a bit remaining on his bottom lip. "No. I'm not letting that dick ruin things. Let's get another round of drinks."

Realene tended to agree with Trish that leaving might be a better plan. "Are you sure?"

Big Kev smacked him on the back. "Yeah, man. I'm buying. Well, I mean, technically Calvin's buying, eh?"

Realene watched Nate scan the crowd, looking like the Terminator in his shades. His gaze landed on Speedo Guy, who was back on the dance floor, grinding with a girl who somehow did not seem repulsed by him.

Realene grabbed Nate's arm. "Let's see if we can get seats at the bar."

They had to wait a few minutes, but eventually a couple stools opened up. She and Trish took the seats, sitting with their backs to the bar, and the guys stood. Big Kev talked them into a round of kamikaze shots, and they raised the blue-green concoctions to clink their glasses, then downed them in one gulp.

They actually tasted better than Realene had expected, certainly more palatable than straight liquor. She was a lightweight, and though she'd only had three drinks, she felt pleasantly warm and actually giggled when Big Kev told a dumb joke about beavers. She found herself swaying to the music and realized she was having a good time. She noticed Trish was definitely not, her hands gripped tightly in her lap.

"Hey, you okay?" Realene asked. The music had become louder to combat the noise of the crowd, so she had to shout to be heard.

"Yes, yeah, of course. Just a little tired. I'd really like to go soon."

She was probably still shaken up from the fight, from seeing Nate get hit, not to mention getting accosted by that guy. "Me too," Realene said, feeling like a jerk that she hadn't supported the idea earlier. She'd been too caught up in her own fun to notice how miserable Trish looked. "I'll tell the guys."

"Okay, thanks. Sorry, I just, like, I think we should go." Trish hopped from her stool, zipping up her coat.

Nate and Big Kev were deep in conversation about the sale of the Winnipeg Jets to Arizona. "Do they even play hockey in Arizona? I mean, isn't it just a bunch of sand and cactuses?" Big Kev said.

Realene shouted in Nate's ear, "It's too loud in here. Let's go."

He squinted at her, then half-yelled something unintelligible, proving her point.

"Trish wants to go," she tried again.

He gave a thumbs up and they started toward the door, Trish leading the way.

A scream cut through the music.

Realene looked back toward the dance floor, figuring it was probably another fight. The people in the crowd began to jostle each other.

"Guys, come on," Trish said, her high-pitched voice barely audible.

Another scream sounded, this one more like a shriek, and the crowd quieted.

"Help! Help us!" someone cried, and Realene took an involuntary step toward the cry before a hand caught her elbow.

Trish.

"Please. No more fights," she said, her lips and chin trembling.

The crowd seemed to split open, as if forced apart, and a guy came stumbling out, catching himself on a high-top table just a few feet from them. "He fucking bit me," he said, one hand cupped over his throat. Blood dribbled through his fingers. He stumbled off toward the bathroom, a girl trailing after him.

"Someone call an ambulance," Realene yelled, and several heads turned toward her. She made eye contact with a bartender, who held up the phone, showing he was already on it.

The guy had been bitten. Not punched or kicked. *Bitten.*

Nate came up to stand next to her, and she said, "I think… What if…? Are they here?"

"No," he said. "No."

Another scream came from the dance floor. Speedo Guy stood at the center, blood drenching his face, neck, and chest. A guy sat on his knees nearby, clutching his face. Realene was pretty sure it was one of Speedo Guy's friends.

Trish dug her nails into Realene's wrist. "We have to go. Now."

Speedo Guy seemed to hear Trish's voice, though that shouldn't be possible, and he came strutting toward them. Realene snatched a beer from the hand of a girl standing beside her, grasping it by the neck and holding it high as she shoved Trish behind her.

Speedo Guy stopped inches from Realene's face, staring down at her, as he was at least a head taller than her, grinning.

Little black worms wiggled in the whites of his eyes.

Realene froze, her entire body going numb. Speedo Guy clocked the bottle in her hand, and his lips peeled back in a growl.

This was it. This was how she would finally get infected. Maybe die.

A blur at the edge of her vision barreled into the guy. His friend, who'd been on his knees a minute before, knocked Speedo Guy into one of the high-top tables, which crashed to the ground with the two of them in a heap.

The bottle slipped from her grip and shattered on the floor.

A bartender hopped up on the bar. "The cops are on their way. Please stay where you are."

That was the wrong thing to say.

Everyone started to yell and press toward the door in a crush of bodies.

All the lights flipped on extra bright, and the speakers began playing "Closing Time" by Semisonic, likely on some sort of autoplay.

Several flannel-clad employees blocked the door, yelling for everyone to stop, but the bar patrons had turned into a mob that would not be reasoned with. The employees were pushed out of the way, and one of the guys fell to the ground. He cried out as the crowd stomped over him. Realene reached for his hand to pull him up, but she was swept outside in the swell of the crowd before she could help him.

The blizzard had eased slightly, at least allowing her to see a few feet ahead of her, but the air was still frigid cold.

She stumbled toward a tall figure she thought was Big Kev, grasped his arm.

"Jesus. That was a hell of a bar fight," he said.

"The worms." She gulped in a breath, tried to slow her racing heart. "They're here."

"I know, the meteor—"

"No," she said. "They're here. That guy in there, attacking everyone, he was infected. I saw his eyes."

"What?" He yanked her toward the parking lot. "We've got to get the hell out of here."

"Not without Nate and Trish." She didn't say Nate might be infected too. He'd fought Speedo Guy, got his blood all over him, but she wanted to see him first before assuming the worst. "And we've got to call Harmon."

She ran toward the hotel entrance. Someone slammed into her as she was entering the sliding doors, and she stumbled and fell, dropping to her knees in the slush-slicked entry. She looked up, expecting someone to lunge at her, bite her, predator taking down prey. But the kids running past, many of them with coats hanging open and exposed skin red from the frigid temperature, were giggling. Just kids running from the bar.

Getting the outbreak under control was the first priority, but it was happening so much faster this time. In Demise, it had taken several hours to progress from confusion to aggression. And how the hell had Speedo Guy been infected to start with?

Big Kev helped her to her feet, and she saw a wall of Mounties surrounding the atrium area, where raised voices and screams drowned out any music.

Realene rushed to the front desk, where Chrissy was watching the people scamper around the lobby. A wad of pink gum was stuck in her hair, wild strands of which had escaped their scrunchie to crown her head in a ratty halo. "No running," she yelled.

"Hey, I need a phone," Realene demanded.

"This is for staff use only," Chrissy snapped. Her smeared black mascara made her look like a tired raccoon.

Big Kev reached over and snatched the phone from the handset, stretching the cord over the counter and handing it to Realene. "It's an emergency."

Chrissy huffed and threw up her hands. "Whatever. I'm not even supposed to be here. Fucking Dave." She edged from behind the desk to yell at the guests still streaming in through the front door. "I said no running!"

"Number?" Big Kev asked, and Realene recited the colonel's cell number so he could dial it on the keypad.

"Look for Nate and Trish," she said, angling her head toward the door, and Big Kev turned to scan the crowd.

After two rings, the colonel picked up. "Harmon."

"Colonel, there's an outbreak," she said.

"Realene?"

"At a bar in Winnipeg. Next to the Holidome. We were there with Nate and Trish, and a guy started attacking people. I saw them, the worms in his eyes. It's happening again."

"I thought I told you—"

"You need to get this under control," she said. "There're at least a couple people infected, probably more, and it's spreading fast. Where are you?'

"Close," he said. "Nate and Trish, they're with you?"

"No, but we'll find them."

"Get back to your room, now."

"Not without them."

"I'll find them. Get to your room."

"Hey, over here!" Big Kev yelled and took off toward the door, where Nate and Trish had just come in.

"They're here," she said into the handset. "Hold on."

"Realene, listen to me," Harmon said, but she lowered the phone, his voice fading.

"Are you guys okay?" She asked, scanning Nate and Trish for injuries.

"Other than almost getting trampled." Nate winced, pressing his fingers to his temple. His sunglasses sat crooked on his nose. "I'm really feeling that beating."

"What do you remember? Tell me," she said.

"What?" he asked.

"Describe to me what happened, from when you first arrived at the bar until now. Quick." *Please, please, don't be infected. Not again.*

"Uh, okay. We went to the bar, we ordered those blue drinks with the umbrellas, then you guys came and there was the jerk on the dance floor."

"Okay. You're okay." All the air gushed from her lungs. She pressed the phone back to her ear. "They're here, they're okay."

"You're with them? I told you—"

"We'll call you later, after we get somewhere safe."

"Stay there, I'm on my way—"

The line went dead, and Realene saw Chrissy standing behind the counter, her finger depressing the hook switch button. "If you need to talk more, do it from your room."

Realene gritted her teeth and chucked the handset at the woman, who caught it with a huff and slammed it back on the cradle.

Realene turned back toward her friends. "We've gotta go."

"The worms are here. That guy in the bar was infected," Big Kev whispered.

Trish looked at Nate, then back at the others. She swayed, as if she might pass out.

"Nate's okay," Realene said. "If he were infected, he wouldn't remember what had happened. But we've got to get out of here while we can." She turned to Nate. "You got your keys?"

"They're back?" he said.

"Harmon's close. We'll let him handle it." She would not allow them to get quarantined again, to be forced to fight for their survival. To risk being infected or killed. Not this time. She held out her hand. "Give me your keys. We'll need your plow in this weather."

"Okay, yeah." He dug through his pockets and extracted his keys, handing them to her.

"We should wait here for Harmon," Trish said, gripping Nate's elbow. "He'll know what to do. He's coming."

A shriek sounded from the pool area.

"Stay here," Realene said. She crept past the front desk, trying to see past the line of Mounties. Several of them grappled with partiers clad in bathing suits. She stepped up onto one of the AstroTurf berms and gripped the palm tree, craning to see over the heads of the officers.

The pool area had broken into a full-on riot. People wrestled on the ground and traded punches, knocking over patio chairs and tables. In the arcade, one guy lifted up another guy and launched him into an *Addam's Family* pinball machine, triggering the bells and lights. Someone had grabbed a pool cue and was charging through the space like a medieval jouster, knocking people left and right. Swimmers fought each other, too, clawing and shoving each other beneath the water, which now swirled with blood. The floats that held drunk idiots had been ripped to colorful plastic shreds.

Officers tried to break up the fights, pulling people apart and placing them in handcuffs, but they were outnumbered. Realene watched as one of the people who'd been handcuffed on the ninth green of the mini golf course turned to the person cuffed next to him and bit them. Hard.

Heart hammering in her chest, Realene hopped down from her vantage point.

A girl wearing a swan-shaped pool floaty around her waist raced past the officers, coming straight for Realene, teeth bared. Realene grabbed the swan's head and swung the girl in a circle, shot-put-style, sending her rolling into one of the pool tables. The girl knocked out the closest leg and the table collapsed on top of her. Her legs stuck out like those of the Wicked Witch, except still kicking. The pool balls rolled from the table and into the crowd.

Realene ran to the first tee of the mini golf course and grabbed four putters from the bucket. A guy in swim trunks and, for some reason, a white fur coat, stalked toward her, arms outstretched. She knelt down, gripping the bundle of putters by the handles, and swept the guy's feet out from under him. He screamed and went down hard.

Gasping for breath, she rushed back to the others and handed them each a putter. "Anyone comes at you, bash 'em. Got it?"

"Bash 'em?" Big Kev asked.

"Either that or get bit."

"Just hold on," Trish said. "Harmon's coming. We should wait for him. He'll know what to do."

"This whole place is about to go up." As if to prove her point, a couple broke past the police line, a girl chasing a guy. She leapt onto his back, tackling him to the ground just a few feet from the group, and chomped into his shoulder.

A pool ball flew from the atrium area, cracking into the window beside the entrance and leaving a perfect circle.

Realene rested her own club on her shoulder like a baseball player coming up to bat, and strode toward the exit, which slid open to let in a gust of snow and a chorus of screams. "Let's do this."

# Fifteen

**THEY STEPPED OUT** the doors and into the blowing snow of the blizzard. Past their area of visibility, shadowed figures moved. The main road that ran past the hotel and bar was totally obscured, only the streetlights glowing faintly through the white haze. A shiver shook Realene, and she took a moment to raise her hood and pull on her gloves. She was grateful for the storm, which would hopefully keep the outbreak contained until Harmon arrived.

The four of them walked side by side, scanning the area for threats. A police car was parked by the bar, whose neon beer signs blazed from the windows. The car sat empty, the lights flashing in a strobe of red and blue against the falling snow. The bar's front door sat open, light spilling into the night.

A shout sounded within, followed by a gun shot, and a figure appeared in the door. A mostly naked figure. Speedo Guy. He saw the four of them and charged, flip flops slipping in the snow as he ran.

Trish gave a battle cry and raced toward the guy.

"Stop!" Nate cried, going after her.

"Leave us alone, you dick," Trish screamed. She raised her pink putter and brought it around in a perfect arc to nail the guy in the jaw. His head whipped to the side, and he spun in a circle before slumping to the ground on all fours, moaning.

Nate grabbed Trish's arm and dragged her away. She panted, huffing plumes into the cold air.

"Nice hit," Realene said, then led them along the building, past the front doors.

A shout came from the direction of the bar, and a Mountie stumbled out. He weaved toward Speedo Guy, clearly injured.

Speedo Guy looked up, and though she couldn't hear it, Realene saw his mouth stretch and imagined him growling. He lunged, tackling the officer, and latched onto his neck. She flashed back to three months ago, to when she'd seen a child complete the same maneuver on what she assumed was its mother in the parking lot of the Cinema Twin.

"Come on," Realene said. They had to get out of sight before Speedo Guy finished with the officer.

"We can't leave him," Nate said.

"We have no choice." They had to focus on saving themselves now. And as long as the infected were only injured, not dead, the colonel could still cure them.

A girl in a long winter coat came racing toward them from the direction of the street, and Big Kev raised his putter, ready to strike. It was a good thing he didn't, because she broke into laughter as a snowball nailed her in the back and a guy came chasing after her, both of them running toward the hotel entrance. She hadn't been infected. Just drunk.

"Don't go in there," Realene called to the wasted coeds, but her voice was barely audible over the whip of the wind, and they disappeared into the white haze without hearing her warning.

The wind blasted into Realene, staggering her steps, as the four of them turned the corner of the hotel toward the lot where Nate had parked. The cars there were covered in snow, but a path still led behind and around the vehicles, only a foot or so of accumulation since the last pass of the plow.

They raced toward Nate's truck, snow pelting them in the face with icy needles. The truck was covered in white, so they quickly brushed off the windows and unplugged the power cord that extended to a nearby outlet.

Realene climbed inside the cab and started the truck. The engine struggled a little after sitting idle for so long but ultimately turned over. Realene wouldn't normally drive after drinking, but she was the most sober of the four, and at least the roads would be deserted due to the storm.

After cranking up the heat and defrost, she grabbed the long-handled brush-scraper from behind the driver's seat and handed it to Big Kev to clear the ice layer on the windows. "I've gotta grab something from the van."

Realene exited the truck and ran toward her van. She'd feel better having her super soaker and defibrillator, just in case. Almost there, an engine sounded behind her, and she turned to see a car careening toward her. At the last second, she threw herself to the side, landing in the piled snow between two cars as the out-of-control vehicle careened past. The back end of the vehicle fish-tailed back and forth as it barreled toward her parked minivan.

"No," she cried, climbing to her feet as the vehicle slammed into the van's trunk, the front end smashing fully into the rear bumper and crushing the trunk's hatch. No way she was getting her supplies out now. Barbara Eden might finally be beyond repair.

The doors of the crashed car opened, and two people tumbled out. She thought about warning them of the worms, but figured that nothing she'd say would convince a couple drunk assholes of their doom, and rushed back to the Nate's truck instead. She climbed into the truck's driver's seat, next to a grumbling Big Kev, who was sandwiched between her and Nate. Trish had to sit on Nate's lap.

"Where are we going?" Trish asked.

Realene had been too focused on just escaping. She hadn't thought that far ahead. Kev's house was close, but she was hesitant to involve Ana and their dad in this. Nate hadn't been infected, but any one of them may have been exposed and just not know it yet. "I… Somewhere without other people. We should self-quarantine, just to be safe."

"The cabin," Big Kev said.

She didn't love the idea of going somewhere so close to the meteor site, but they didn't have a choice. "There a phone there?" she asked, not recalling seeing one.

"Yeah. And food to last at least a few days."

She backed out, careful to watch for any more idiots, and pulled past the hotel entrance. Blood smeared the parking lot where Speedo Guy had attacked the Mountie. A shape hurled out of the darkness, smacking into her window. It was the employee who'd been trampled in the bar.

Everyone screamed as he clawed at the window, smearing bloody prints over the glass. "Stop!" he screamed.

"Go!" Kev shouted, shoving his foot down on the gas pedal.

Realene gripped the wheel as the vehicle surged forward, the guy falling away. They sped out onto the street.

"Get off." Realene kicked Kev's foot aside and replaced it with her own as she cranked the wheel to the side, careening between the lanes before righting herself. They blew through a red light, and she had to swerve again around an abandoned vehicle parked half on the shoulder and half in the lane.

It was large, about the size of a minibus.

The blowing snow made it impossible to tell if it was the Revelation bus. Irene had been arrested, but Birdie and the Olsons may be holed up inside the vehicle after being unable to get a room. She shook her head, couldn't worry about them now.

In the rear-view mirror, she saw several cars speed into the hotel parking lot, forming a line at the entrance as if to block anyone else from leaving. The colonel had arrived.

Realene exhaled a sigh of relief.

# Sixteen

**THE ROAD TO** the lake was packed with snow, so Realene kept the plow's blade lowered and crept along at no more than ten miles per hour, the blizzard outside disguising everything more than a few feet ahead of the vehicle. Long, orange rods stuck through the snow on either side of the road, marking the road's edges. She half expected a vehicle carrying Harmon's soldiers to emerge from the depths of the blowing snow, but none did, and judging by the condition of the road, no vehicle had traversed it in the last hour or more. At least that was her guess. The storm was dumping so much snow, it was hard to say.

Despite Trish sitting on his lap, Nate had fallen asleep, likely from all the alcohol he'd consumed. Head thrown back to rest against the seat, he snored softly. Trish looked out the windshield, her hands braced on the dashboard.

Realene wondered if Trish was thinking back to the night she lost her dad and sister.

Big Kev fiddled with the radio, flipping from station to station but finding only static. He finally landed on an A.M. station that predicted the storm wouldn't clear until early morning. Realene hoped the storm would keep the outbreak from spreading. The weather in Demise hadn't prevented it from infecting the whole town, but that blizzard hit too late. Winnipeg had more than half a million residents, and Lake Winnipeg was huge, connecting to multiple rivers and draining into the Hudson Bay. If the worms got into animals that used those waterways, the impact would be catastrophic.

No. She had to believe they'd alerted the colonel in time. The worms wouldn't spread, not this time.

“There,” Big Kev said, and Realene slowed. Though she had been to the cabin that afternoon, she would never have noticed the entrance through the trees, which was barely visible in the storm. She slowed and turned, the truck bumping and scraping along the path, struggling despite the plow. The lake and warehouse weren’t far, but she wasn’t going to think about that.

Movement flashed in her peripheral moments before a deer leapt in front of the truck. She slammed on the brakes and caught a quick flash of the animal washed in the headlights before it was gone. “Did you see that?” *Had the tawny coat of the animal been streaked red across its side?*

“Just drive slow,” Big Kev said. “There are lots of ’em in the area.”

“I meant the blood.” She scanned the woods on either side.

“What?”

“I think it was… Might’ve been infected.”

“Shit.” He looked outside, but the animal was gone.

She eased forward. No rods marked this path, so the only sign they were still on the road was the gap in the trees. Their headlights barely penetrated the darkness, and she felt like Wendy Torrance trying to navigate that snowcat down the mountainside in *The Shining*. Finally, a blocky shape emerged from the dark, and her lights splashed on the front of the cabin. She shifted into Park and slumped forward, heaving a deep breath.

“Nice job.” Big Kev smacked her on the back.

Trish opened her door, letting a bluster of wind into the cab, and hopped from Nate’s lap. He groaned and shook himself awake, yawning. “Where are we?”

Trish yanked on his arm. “Come on, I’m freezing. Let’s get inside.”

Big Kev slid across the seat, following them.

Realene got out, flexing her hands to release the tension in her fingers. The trees towered around her, closing them in. She looked up, but couldn’t see the sky, only the snow that filled the air. Several feet had already accumulated on the ground, and Realene plodded through it, breath huffing from the effort.

She reached the front porch and glanced back at the truck. Even from this close, it was barely visible amid the snow. Somewhere beyond it, the dense forest loomed, providing protection for the cabin. There were worse places to hunker down during an outbreak. She pushed through the front door and shut it behind her, the sound of the storm now muted. Big Kev and Nate had already shed their coats and hung them on hooks on the wall, and she did the same before shucking her boots and leaving them by the door.

Big Kev knelt before the stone fireplace. He'd already stacked some wood for a fire and was working to get it lit. Trish led Nate into the bedroom and closed the door. Hopefully they knew that now was not the time for any hanky panky. Trish was starting to grow on her, but Realene still had no interest in hearing any of their private business.

Luckily, Trish came back out quickly. "He's sleeping it off." She scanned the room, then strode over to the tan phone fixed to the wall at the end of the kitchen counter and picked it up. She scowled, pressing the button on the base several times. "It's not working."

"Weather probably knocked down the lines," Big Kev said. "Happens out here." He dusted his hands off on his pants as flames crackled in the fireplace, warmth beginning to spread throughout the room.

"But we need to talk to the colonel. Tell him where we are." She pressed the button several more times, then slammed the handset back onto the base.

"Hey, it's gonna be fine," Realene said. She put a hand on Trish's shoulder, but the girl shrugged it off and slumped onto the couch.

"That was faster, right?" Trish asked. "Like, spreading faster, I mean… We had more time in Demise, didn't we?"

"Yeah," Realene said. The faces of all the infected in Demise flashed through her mind. Lunging, attacking, biting. She often forgot that Trish had lived through all that, too. Had also experienced loss. "I'm sorry," she whispered, "about your family."

Trish rocked in place on the couch, looking swallowed up by the puffer jacket she still wore over her sundress and leggings. "My dad. He was bit first. By our neighbor. Always was an asshole, used to complain about me and Mindy being too loud. Mindy's my little sister, if you didn't know. Anyway, my dad was confused at first, but then he, like, started attacking. I had to… Well, you know."

Realene wanted to comfort Trish, but there wasn't anything that could help with those kinds of memories. "Yeah. I know."

"He got my sister before I could stop him. Before I knew what was happening. Normally, he'd never hurt us. I locked her up to keep her safe, then went to get help, but by the time I got back, Mindy was gone." Trish picked at her cuticles, and one started to bleed. "I always wondered what happed to her. I never knew."

It might be a blessing not to know, Realene thought, not to see those final moments.

Trish looked up, her expression stricken. "I'd give anything to get Mindy back. Anything."

Realene took a seat on the couch. "I get it. I feel the same way about my ma." She, too, would give anything for one more hour with her, one more chance to hug her tight, to tell her how much she loved her.

Big Kev grabbed the fireplace poker and probed the logs, sent a flurry of sparks into the flue.

Realene stared at the flames. One of the logs gave a pop, punctuating the silence. She pulled an afghan, not unlike her Oma's, from the back of the couch and draped it over her lap, like Ma used to do. She hoped Pumpkin was doing okay, that she would get home to him soon.

Big Kev took a seat on an ottoman. "You guys beat these worms once already. We can do it again."

Realene didn't feel like she'd beaten them the first time, more like they beat her. They took the things she cared about most and turned her into a killer. But she refused to let that happen again. She would get her and her friends out of this, without losing anyone or killing anyone. This time would be different.

"What are the odds that someone at that bar would be infected, eh?" Big Kev gave a short laugh.

"I was wondering the same thing," Realene said. "How did he get infected?"

"One of the animals probably escaped from the perimeter of the crash site."

"Maybe. It's not that far to the hotel." But she hadn't seen any animals running around, or any other people who looked infected. Only the bear, and Speedo Guy wouldn't have survived a bear attack.

"Whatever," Trish said. "It doesn't matter now. The colonel is taking care of it. He'll make sure everything is okay."

"I'm telling you, we can't trust that guy," Big Kev said. "All these government assholes are the same. They lie to protect their own interests and don't care who they hurt in the process."

"No. I don't believe that. Even if he is lying, I'm sure he has a good reason." Trish pulled her legs up, hugging them to her chest. "I'm sure."

The bedroom door opened, and Nate stepped out. He'd finally taken off those ridiculous sunglasses.

Trish jumped from the couch, took his arm as if to lead him back into the room. "What are you doing up? You need to sleep."

"I need Aspirin. And water." He shuffled past the couch into the kitchen, and Trish trailed behind him. "Something to eat. Soak up the alcohol."

Realene's stomach gave a little growl, and she realized she was starving too.

Big Kev took Trish's spot on the couch. "Should be some stuff in the cupboards."

Nate opened the far cupboard. "Pretty slim pickings." Grimacing, he pulled out a package of salmon jerky and set it on the counter.

Realene joined him, opening a cupboard above the sink that held a few dishes. She grabbed a coffee mug that said "Sorry" above an image of a maple leaf and filled it with tap water.

"Go back to bed," Trish said to Nate. "I'll find something for you. Bring it in."

"Jackpot." Nate held up his prize, a half bag of Lays ketchup chips.

"Nice." Realene didn't normally get the appeal of ketchup chips, but the alternative of tinned fish sounded worse. She held out the cup of water to him and froze. Something shifted in the whites of his eyes.

Little black worms.

Realene's breath whooshed from her lungs, and a buzzing filled her ears. The coffee mug slipped from her hand, cracking as it hit the wood floor.

# Seventeen

**REALENE STARED AT** the black specks in Nate's eyes, knowing he may turn aggressive and attack at any moment. The wind gusted, rattling the cabin's windows.

"Smooth move, butterfingers." He put down the chips and bent to pick up the chunks of glass from the broken mug.

"No! I got it." If he cut himself, he'd bleed. If he bled, the worms would spread.

He raised his hands and grabbed the bag of chips, fishing one out. "Jeez, calm down."

"That's Uncle Cal's favorite mug," Big Kev said from his spot on the couch. "You're in big trouble. I mean, assuming he's still alive."

"Shut up, Kev," Realene snapped. With trembling hands, she carefully gathered up the glass shards and discarded them in the trash can.

"What the hell, dude? *You* shut up," Big Kev said.

Trish grabbed the hand towel from the edge of the sink and bent to wipe up the spilled water.

Nate held out the open bag of chips to Realene. "Want some?"

"Yuck. No. You know I hate those things." She watched him put another chip in his mouth. She couldn't remember seeing anyone infected take a bite of food. Usually, they just bit other animals or people.

"What's wrong?" he asked, mouth full.

Trish threw the wet towel in the sink. "I'm tired. Really tired. Let's go to bed, okay? Come on."

Big Kev walked up to stand beside Nate. "Did anyone think *I* might be hungry? Or do you only care about yourselves?"

Realene grabbed a pack of salmon jerky and handed it to Big Kev.

"Oh, hell yeah. That's the stuff," he said.

Her pulse pounded in her throat. "Can you come here for a minute?" She grabbed Nate by the elbow, leading him from the kitchen.

"You were right, these *are* gross. And stale as hell." He made a show of swallowing them, then tossed the bag in the fire. It flared bright orange as it burned. A foul, chemical smell filled the cabin.

"Seriously, I'm exhausted. Can we go to bed now? Please?" Trish gripped Nate's other arm, pulling him toward the bedroom.

Realene stopped him. "Nate, listen to me. Something's wrong."

"What?"

"Go look in the mirror." She could tell him, but maybe something was wrong with her. Maybe she'd imagined the worms, maybe she'd imagined that deer too.

"You're freaking me out." But he did as she said, went into the small bathroom and flipped on the light.

Realene watched from the open doorway as he examined his face in the mirror. Trish came up beside her, saying nothing.

Just then, Nate slammed back into the wall, then leaned close again, tugging down his eyelid with one finger. "What the fuck?"

The fire crackled and popped as Big Kev stabbed it with the poker. "Hope we have enough wood to keep the fire going tonight. It's cold as balls out there."

Nate looked back to meet Realene's gaze. His chest rose and fell, his breath speeding up. The terror on his face propelled her forward. She placed her hands on his shoulders. "It's okay. Deep breath in, then out. We're pros at this, remember?"

His whole body trembled.

She sat him down on the toilet and scanned the room for a hair dryer or a shaver—anything to electrocute him with. To cure him.

"How did this…? I mean, I feel okay. Normal." He braced his hands on his knees. "It was that guy right. At the bar. The fight."

"Had to be."

"But I remember. I think." He looked up at her. "We left the bar, saw that cop get attacked in the parking lot. That car hit the van. Then we drove here. Right? Am I missing anything?"

"No, that's it." Realene chewed her thumbnail. He might be contagious, but he didn't seem dangerous. Not yet at least. And he wasn't forgetting things. When Calvin was bitten he'd immediately lost several hours and eventually lost years.

"You guys telling secrets in here or what?" Big Kev came up beside Trish, who was lingering just outside the bathroom door, looking about ready to vomit.

This is why she wanted him to stay in bed. She already knew and didn't want the others to find out.

Realene grabbed Trish's arm, dragged her close. "You knew."

"Hey, leave her alone," Nate said, standing.

Trish shook her head but didn't try to pull away.

Realene gritted her teeth, angled a look at the girl. "Nate. She knew you were infected."

"Whoa, infected?" Big Kev stumbled back into the corner of the couch and toppled over it to end up sprawled on the floor.

Trish's eyes filled with tears.

Realene let go of Trish's arm, moved away from her. The smoky air of the cabin scraped Realene's throat, made it hard to breathe.

Nate's brow furrowed. "When did you realize? Why didn't you tell me?"

Her behavior at the bar suddenly made sense. So did her reaction to Nate after the fight. *After* she'd taken off his sunglasses. It wasn't the blood that had freaked her out.

Big Kev got back up. "I thought people who were infected were dangerous. Like that guy at the bar." He pointed at Nate. "But he doesn't seem dangerous."

Nate's shoulders slumped. "I am, though. We just don't know it yet. You should tie me up, lock me up. Something. Anything. Before it's too late."

Realene knew what the progression was, had watched Brooke and Calvin and plenty of others. "No. This is different. You haven't lost your memory, and it's been hours since you were infected. Do you feel angry? Like you want to attack someone?"

"No." He rubbed his hands over his face, drawing attention to the bandage wrapping his knuckles.

Realene thought back to the fight he'd gotten into at the warehouse, when he'd punched the soldier and gotten pushed into the cages. "What if it wasn't Speedo Guy that infected you? What if it happened at the warehouse?" She pointed at his hand. "You had an open wound when you were shoved into those cages, didn't you?"

Nate's mouth dropped open. "Those animals were infected. Even a drop of saliva would've done it."

"Whoa," Big Kev said. "That means it was the other way around. You infected Speedo Guy."

"And the people in the pool," Realene whispered. He had that cut when they were swimming.

Nate swayed and sat back down on the toilet with a thunk. "Oh, God. All those people. Hurt. Maybe dead. Because of me." He dropped his head into his hands.

"It's not your fault," Realene said.

"Right. It's that asshole Harmon's fault," Big Kev said, now standing in the far corner near the kitchen table, as far away as he could get. "He's the one who took you to that warehouse."

She frowned, wanted to argue, but Big Kev was right. Even though Harmon hadn't intended to, he'd put Nate in harm's way.

"No," Nate said softly. "It's my fault. Harmon just wanted to warn us about the second site, but I couldn't handle it. If I hadn't freaked out, none of this would have happened."

"I'm so sorry," Trish whispered.

Realene whipped around to look at Trish and advanced on her. "Why didn't you say anything? You knew, but you let us stay at that stupid bar."

Trish backpedaled, smacking into an end table with her leg, then maneuvering past it. "I was scared. I didn't know what to do."

"You were scared?" Realene shoved Trish against the cabin's front door. There was nowhere else for her to go.

"I messed up, okay. I'm sorry. I just… I didn't want it to be true." Trish covered her face, started to cry. "I'm sorry. I'm so sorry."

Nate came up beside Realene, watched Trish for minute, then exhaled a long breath. "It's okay. When I saw the meteor, I mean, I flipped out. I get it."

Realene scoffed. How could he be so quick to forgive Trish? This wasn't some little mistake. Her actions had put all of them in danger, had risked the worms spreading even more.

Headlights lit up the darkness, flashing across the front window.

"Someone's here." Realene pulled back the gauzy curtain to peek outside, saw a vehicle parked behind Nate's truck, the headlights streaming over the truck bed. "You got other family that would come out here?" she asked Big Kev.

"Just Ana and my dad, but they wouldn't be out in this storm," Big Kev said. "Could be military. Your buddy the colonel?"

"Yeah. Maybe. We're close enough to the meteor site." Realene was unsure whether to be worried or relieved at their company. Harmon was their best hope to help Nate, make sure he was cured, but he'd also been the one to get him infected in the first place, even if it was by accident. "What are they doing out there?"

A knock sounded on the front door and Trish yelped.

"Should I answer it?" Big Kev came over, apparently forgetting about keeping his distance from Nate.

"I mean, they know someone's in here," Realene said.

"Wait." Trish grabbed the sunglasses from the coffee table and held them out to Nate. "Here. So no one sees."

He grabbed the sunglasses and put them on.

The knock sounded again, pounding louder this time.

Big Kev opened the door, and a gust of snow blew in and hit him in the face. He flinched, then said, "What are you doing here?"

Realene edged up behind him, peeking past the door to see who he was talking to. A man stepped forward, the light spilling out to illuminate his face. It was Birdie. And the vehicle in the driveway was the stupid cult bus.

Birdie pulled down his hood and craned his neck to look past them, as if trying to see who else was in the cabin. "I could ask you the same thing."

"I live here, dude," Big Kev shot back.

"No, but really," Realene said. "What the hell are you doing here?"

"Some kind of mess going on at the hotel. Just looking for some shelter. This was the first place I could find."

"Bullshit. I don't know how, but you followed us. I'm sure of it."

"Oh, uh, crap." Big Kev winced. "Listen, this is going to sound bad, but, uh, I might have planted tracking devices on Nate's truck and the van."

"What?" Realene yelled.

"Listen, we can talk about this," Birdie started.

"Shut up. I don't want to hear a word from you." Realene pinned Big Kev, the traitor, with a glare. "You're working with them?"

"I mean, not anymore. I just, I didn't trust you, thought you were in cahoots with the colonel." He raised his hands in surrender. "They said they'd keep track of you both, and so, yeah, I, well, I planted the devices back in Demise. In case you took off. That way I'd know where you were. But that was before. We're cool now. And I got rid of the one on the van. But, uh, I guess I forgot the truck. Sorry. Are we cool?"

"We're pretty fucking far from cool." She thought back to Big Kev messing with the van in the parking lot.

"It's freezing out here. Can I come in so we can talk?" Birdie asked.

Realene stepped outside to block the door. "I'm assuming your psycho bus has heat."

Something moved behind Birdie, and someone emerged from the blowing snow to thump up the porch stairs. The figure was short and bundled in a puffy mauve coat that looked familiar. A scarf wrapped their head and neck, but not their face.

"Irene," Realene said, her voice cutting through the howling wind. "Shouldn't you be in jail?"

The woman lunged at Realene, not to attack, but to wrap her in a hug. "Oh, thank God."

Realene tried to push the woman away, but she stayed latched on.

Big Kev met her eyes and shrugged.

"I thought told you to stay put?" Birdie said to Irene, as if talking to a child. "Come now, let's get you back to the bus."

Irene pulled away, sniffling, and her mouth fell open. "Realene. You look so…grown up. My goodness. You were just a girl when I saw you last. How long has it been?"

A tiny "Oh," escaped Realene's mouth.

This was the same reaction Calvin had after they'd cured him. He'd lost a good ten years of his memories, thought Realene was still a little girl.

"You said hello, now let's get you back," Birdie said. He tugged on the old woman's arm.

"Is Marion here?" she asked.

Realene's throat tightened. "No," she managed. "Ma's not here."

"What in the world are you wearing? You'll catch your death of cold." Irene unzipped her coat and slipped it from her arms.

Realene froze as the woman draped the coat over her shoulders.

"There. How's that? Better?"

"See," Birdie said. "We don't mean you any harm. Can we come in now?"

"You can leave, dude," Big Kev said.

Irene caught site of Nate. "Is that…Nathan? Oh my goodness, you're so grown-up, too."

The wind gusted, peppering Realene's face with icy shards. She ushered Irene inside, not ready to send her away, "Come on. Let's have a talk." They walked past Nate and Big Kev, and Realene said to them, "Do not let Birdie in. I don't trust this."

"Me neither," Nate said. He, Big Kev, and Trish bundled up and stepped outside with Birdie.

Realene led Irene into the bedroom and encouraged her to take a seat on the bed.

Irene reached out and grabbed Realene's hand, pulling her to sit down. "You're shaking." The woman put one arm around her, rubbing her back.

Realene's muscles tensed with the desire to lash out, to punch Irene in the face until she gushed blood.

Irene looked around the room and out the bedroom door. "Are you sure your mother's not here?" The cabin was too small to hide anyone, but she still called out, "Marion?"

A tear slipped down Realene's cheek. After Ma was diagnosed with dementia, Realene had so many conversations with her just like this, but about Dad. *Where's your father? Will he be home for lunch soon? I made his favorite.* Realene always said yes, even though he was dead and had been for years.

At the sight of Realene's tears, Irene pulled her in close. "Oh, sweetheart. Don't cry."

But Realene couldn't stop. Something about getting Irene—the *real* Irene—back, broke her wide open. The woman had been good and kind before she got mixed up with that reverend. This was the woman she remembered as Ma's best friend, not the one who'd betrayed them.

"Shh, shh. It's okay."

Realene sniffled and pulled away. "Sorry."

"It's all right, dear. We all need a good cry sometimes."

Realene saw the flicker of black worms across the whites of Irene's eyes and grimaced.

"What is it, dear?" She patted her frizzy hair self-consciously. "I don't recall the last time I had my hair done. I must look a sight."

"You look fine," Realene managed.

Irene had not, like Calvin, been infected and cured. She was still infected. Only, like Nate, she wasn't aggressive.

None of it made any sense.

"What is this place?" Irene clasped her hands between her legs, looking incredibly small. "What are we doing here?"

Instead of answering, Realene said, "Never mind that for now. How did you get here? Do you remember?"

"No. That young man in the other room said I hit my head, but I don't know." She gave a slight shake of her head.

"Which young man? Birdie?"

"Oh, is that his name?" Her brow furrowed. "I don't like this. It's all wrong. I want to go home. Can you take me home?"

The words cut through Realene's chest like a hot knife. They were the same words Ma had spoken when they'd tried to flee Demise to escape the infection. But she failed to get Ma out, and only hours later she'd died in Realene's arms, died protecting her from the psychotic cult leader who Irene had led right to them.

"You're such a beautiful young lady." Irene reached out and brushed a lock of hair from Realene's forehead. "You look just like your ma when she was your age. How old are you again? I don't… I can't remember."

"It doesn't matter." Realene wiped her tears with her sleeve. "I'm gonna help you, okay? Get you home. Does that sound good?"

Irene gave a forced smile. "That sounds lovely, dear. Thank you." Her face became troubled again. "Where's your mother? Is she okay?" She called out again: "Marion?"

Realene helped the woman put her coat back on. "She's back home with Pumpkin. Probably watching *I Dream of Jeannie*."

Irene giggled. "Don't tell your father, but I think she's got a bit of a crush on Larry Hagman."

Pain spiked through Realene's chest. In Irene's mind, Dad and Ma were both still alive. "Come on," Realene said, helping Irene stand.

Now to see what Birdie was up to.

# Eighteen

**NATE PULLED THE** cabin's door closed behind him, stood on the front porch with Big Kev and Trish. She looked at him, then averted her gaze. "It's gonna be okay," he said, not putting his arm around her, though he wanted to. None of this was her fault. She was just trying to deal with it like the rest of them.

"Listen, we don't want any trouble," Birdie said. The cult bus idled behind him, the headlights illuminating the cabin.

Nate wondered who else was inside, how many cronies Irene had brought with her. "So, what *do* you want?"

"I told you already. Shelter from the storm." Birdie gave a smile that quickly faded. "Okay, you're obviously not a Dylan fan."

Big Kev crossed his arms over his chest. "This is private property, and you're not welcome."

"Don't want to work with us anymore, huh?"

He winced. "That was a mistake."

Birdie took a step forward. Behind him an older couple Nate recognized, the Olsons, stepped off the bus. "Well, we're not done with you. And all we're asking for is a little help."

Nate had started to really like Big Kev, couldn't believe he'd been stupid enough to team up with the Revelation psychos.

Another figure—petite, with long brown hair—came down the bus steps, stopping on the last one and peeking out the door.

"Mom?" The sight of her stole the oxygen from Nate's lungs as if he'd taken a hard punch in the stomach. She couldn't be here. He took several steps toward her.

Birdie's expression changed from friendly to serious as he pulled a gun from his waistband and aimed it at Nate. "I have to ask you to stop right there."

Nate stared at the gun, a tremor shaking through him. "You let her go. Now."

"I'm fine, Nathan," his mom said. She stepped down from the bus, and he noticed she was wearing his dad's old coat. "I asked to come."

Birdie gestured at Nate with the gun. "Turn around and put your hands behind your head."

Trish rushed up to stand beside Nate. "Leave him alone."

Rage bubbled in Nate's gut at the sight of his mom standing beside Birdie, being manipulated by a man who didn't give a shit about her. Just like with his father, just like with the reverend, she'd fallen for the same kind of abuse again. "You joined up with them? After everything they did? Can't you see they're manipulating you?"

Nate's mom stepped forward, but Mr. Olson grabbed her arm, keeping her from getting too close to her son. "I knew the colonel was up to something, and I've come here to prove it. If you ask me, you're the one being manipulated."

"I told you," Big Kev said. "You can't trust that guy."

"You should talk, traitor," Nate snapped.

"Quiet, all of you," Birdie yelled, the gun still aimed squarely at Nate. "Just turn around already, would you?"

Nate's mom shook off Mr. Olson's hold on her sleeve and marched toward Birdie. "Put that gun away."

Birdie glared at her. "You're not in charge here. Get back on that bus. Now."

"Don't talk to her like that," Nate said.

The door to the cabin opened behind them, and he glanced back to see Realene emerge, one arm wrapped around Irene's shoulders.

He took a few steps back to get closer to them but kept an eye on Birdie.

Realene left Irene near the door, spoke to Nate in a quiet voice. "She's infected. It's like when Calvin first woke up, yeah? She remembers me but younger, keeps asking about Ma. It's like everything in Demise never happened."

"So, she was infected and cured?" Nate asked.

"Not cured." She tapped one finger beside her eye. "But it's not like Speedo Guy, or everybody at the hotel. She doesn't have the aggression, just the memory loss."

"What's happening?" Irene asked. "Is something wrong with me?"

Realene angled her chin toward Birdie. "He told Irene she hit her head."

"She's a lunatic," Birdie interrupted. "You should be thanking me for what I did." He threw up his hands, still holding the gun. "Now, Irene, would you please get back on the goddamn bus?"

And suddenly it all made sense. "You infected her on purpose," Realene reasoned out loud. Something rustled in the woods, and Nate peered into the darkness but saw only trees through the blowing snow.

"I don't like him," Irene said of Birdie and nestled further under Realene's arm. "Don't make me go."

"It's okay, we won't," she said, her tone soft, like the one she used to use with Ma.

"These people are dangerous," Nate said to his mom. "Even Irene knows it. Stay with us. Please."

His mom looked at Birdie, as if trying to decide between this new leader and her own son. "I'll get my things." She turned back toward the bus, putting one foot on the steps.

"No one move." Birdie raised his gun, again pointing it at Nate.

Nate froze, but not without effort. Anger roiled in his stomach, urging him to attack the asshole, but he couldn't risk someone getting hurt.

"You put that weapon down and get off my property," Big Kev bellowed, giving it a good try, but a loud voice was no match for a gun.

"I'm just trying to do my job, but you all keep making it so damn difficult." Birdie took several steps forward, his weapon trained on Nate. He fished a zip tie from his pocket with his free hand. "Hands behind your back. Now."

Nate's mom grabbed Birdie's elbow, which caused his aim to veer left, and seeing his opening, Nate lunged and tackled

Birdie to the snowy ground, sending the gun flying into a nearby snowbank. His mom fell, too, giving a soft cry.

Birdie headbutted Nate in the face, splitting the bridge of his nose and knocking off his cheap sunglasses. Nate hissed at the sharp pain he recognized as a broken nose. Not his first. Blood trickled from both nostrils.

"No!" Birdie swiped handfuls of snow over his face to wipe away any trace amount of blood that may have gotten on him. "Did you infect me? Did you?"

"You know I'm infected," Nate said.

"Infected?" his mom said. "Infected with what?" She looked between Nate and Birdie. Like most of Demise, she didn't know about the alien worms, had been told everything that happened in town was the result of poisoning by Reverend Zebediah. She didn't believe that story, but she had no idea how insane the truth actually was.

"Everybody inside. Now." Birdie yanked Nate's mom to her feet, then pushed her toward the door. He grabbed his gun from the snow pile and used it to intimidate the rest of them into complying.

Nate waited for everyone else to go, waited until it was just him and Birdie. He stared at the young man's face until he saw it: a hint of black flitting across the white of his right eye. The countdown on Birdie's sanity had begun.

# Nineteen

**REALENE WATCHED AS** Nate strode across the dining area into the kitchen, pulling off his coat and shirt and piling them on the floor. The rest of them ended up standing against the far wall, with Trish by herself in the corner, the Olsons and Sophia closest to the bedroom door, and the rest of them clustered against the wall nearest the kitchen.

That asshole Birdie beelined for the phone and tried unsuccessfully to dial it while also aiming his gun at whoever was currently giving him the wrong kind of look. No one told him the phone didn't work.

Nate cleaned himself up at the sink, scrubbing harder than was necessary.

"Is Nathan sick?" Irene asked, clutching Realene's arm.

"He's fine," Realene said. She still wasn't sure why, though. While Irene's side effects seemed different from what they'd seen before, his were non-existent. "Stay here, okay?"

Realene joined him at the kitchen sink, watched the blood-tinged water run down the drain. "I should have told you, but I saw Irene and Birdie at the hotel. I didn't know your mom was with them, but I did see her at the church before I left."

He pressed his lips into a tight line, nodded.

Birdie hung up the phone, picked it back up, pressed it to his ear.

Realene gestured discreetly in Birdie's direction. "You think they're trying to start another apocalypse. Pick up where Hozak left off."

Nate shrugged. "Probably. Doesn't seem to be going so well, though. Idiot got himself infected." He grabbed his clothes from the floor.

"He's infected? How do you know?"

Nate pointed to his eye. "Saw the buggers myself."

"Shit."

"Dammit." Birdie slammed the phone back onto the cradle, dislodging the whole unit from the wall and sending it to the floor with a crack.

"You're paying for that," Big Kev said, exiting the bedroom holding a flannel that must have been Calvin's.

Nate crossed the living room, and the Olsons pressed their backs to the wall. He threw the clothes and towel into the fire, sending a black plume of smoke into the room, and took the shirt from Big Kev, putting it on.

Sophia walked over to him, arms crossed. "What is this about an infection? What's that Harmon gotten you into?"

"Stay away from him." Birdie leapt over the couch, almost falling as he stepped from the cushions to the floor. He aimed his gun at Nate, who was still standing by the fireplace. "He's dangerous."

Realene edged closer, knowing Nate wasn't the one they had to worry about. Birdie was already an aggressive asshole. Once the worms took hold, he would turn into a raging lunatic, just like that guy in the bar.

Nate moved to block his mom. "What are you planning?"

The Olsons took defensive positions on either side of Birdie. "We're trying to protect people, to save them from that demon Harmon and his minions," Mrs. Olson said.

Irene left her spot against the wall to huddle beside Realene. "Who is that man? Why is he threatening Nathan?"

Realene felt a familiar irritation bubble up inside her, the irritation she'd felt with Ma day after day as she became more and more confused. She wished she had all those days back. "Just stay quiet. It'll be okay," she said, patting Irene's hand.

"Protect people? By infecting them?" Nate asked. "Lying is a sin, you know."

"Nate," Realene said, but he wouldn't look at her. They needed to keep Birdie calm, not rile him up.

"I didn't infect you. You infected me. Yeah, I know I'm infected. I can feel 'em in there." He knocked the gun against his head. "I'm not stupid." He then jabbed the gun at Nate. "If you'd just stayed at the hotel, this wouldn't have happened."

Realene flinched at every movement of the gun, afraid it would fire. "Birdie, hey, look at me. You understand what can happen with this infection, right? People get out of control, do things they normally wouldn't do. So, why don't you give me that gun? Just to be safe."

He looked at the weapon in his hand. "How do I know you won't kill me with it? I've heard the stories. I know what you did to the infected in Demise."

Realene flinched. Unfortunately, he had a point. "Just dump out the bullets then. I'll keep the bullets, you keep the gun."

Birdie seemed to be considering her suggestion when Mr. Olson made a grab for the gun. "Do not be fooled by these conniving devils," he said.

Birdie wrenched the weapon away just in time, keeping hold of it for himself. "Get away from me. Back up. All of you."

Nate's hands flexed into fists at his side, as if he was considering jumping Birdie again. Behind him, Sophia saw the action and flinched. Realene wondered if she was seeing Nate in that moment or remembering her dead husband, who had often used his fists on her.

Irene swayed back and forth, agitated. "Make him stop that. He shouldn't do that."

"Shh, shh," Realene said, then raised her arms and put herself between Nate and Birdie. "Hey, let's everyone calm down, okay?"

Birdie pointed the gun at her. "I said I'm in charge here, not you."

"Stop it!" Irene screamed. "Don't do that!"

"It's okay. I'm okay," Realene said, trying to convince herself more than anybody. She stared into the black void of the gun's barrel, willing her shaky limbs to be still. Behind Birdie, she watched Big Kev inch toward the side wall, where a shotgun was mounted beneath a stuffed deer head. "I get it. You're the boss. We're all good." She raised her hands above her head.

"Shut up. Just let me think," Birdie said, jabbing the gun at her.

Irene shoved in front of Realene, grabbing his wrist and pulling it toward the floor. "Leave her alone."

"Stop!" Realene yelled. She reached for the woman, gripped the back of her jacket.

"Irene, let go." Birdie grunted. He wrestled his wrist from her grip and a loud crack split the air.

A gunshot.

And a scream.

Irene fell back into Realene, clutching her stomach.

"*No.*" The word came out in a desperate gust of breath as Realene went down to the floor under Irene's weight, ending up cradling the woman in her lap.

Blood bloomed across the chest of Irene's purple coat. She'd taken a bullet meant for Realene. Just like Ma.

"No, no, no. Not again. Please, no."

Voices sounded around her, shouting.

Irene looked up at Realene, face going pale. "You're such a beautiful girl, just like your mother. And brave, too."

Someone grabbed Realene's arm, yanking her to her feet. Birdie.

"This is your fault," he yelled, spittle flying from his mouth. "No one was supposed to get hurt."

"You shot her, you fucking psycho!" Realene screamed.

His expression turned pained. "That wasn't… I didn't. She grabbed my gun."

Big Kev stepped up, cocking the shotgun and jabbing it into Birdie's back. "Drop it."

Nostrils flaring, Birdie followed orders, letting the gun clatter to the floor. The fact he was able to stop meant the worms hadn't taken over yet. He'd shot Irene dead all on his own.

Trish grabbed the dropped weapon and pointed it at Birdie, the gun shaking in her unsteady hands.

Big Kev directed Birdie toward the door with the shotgun barrel. "Get in the bedroom. Go."

Birdie let go of Realene's arm and backed through the bedroom door, his posture hunched. Defeated.

Mrs. Olson gave a shriek and lunged at Trish, who moved surprisingly fast, not firing the gun but smacking the old lady in the forehead with it. Mrs. Olson cried out in pain and quickly slunk away,

"Both of you get in there too," Nate said, looking at the Olsons. They did as they were told, clutching one another as they walked.

Realene wondered if they'd been at the church the night the reverend ordered his lieutenant to kill that reporter. How many people did they have to watch suffer before realizing that they were the devils they warned about?

Big Kev closed the bedroom door, and Trish ran up with a dining room chair, wedging it beneath the doorknob.

Realene looked back at Irene, and her blood turned to ice in her veins as the old woman's head lolled to one side.

"Irene," Realene whispered. She reached for her, but Nate grabbed her arm and stopped her.

"Careful. The blood," he said.

She sunk to her knees and backed away from the pool of red that puddled beneath Irene's midsection. Realene had wished so many times for this exact thing to happen to Irene since she'd ambushed them in that movie theater, gotten Ma killed, betrayed her best friend.

But this wasn't that same Irene. This was the woman who'd cooked three hot meals a day for her and Ma the month after Dad died. This was the woman who had loved them. Loved Realene. Loved her enough to die for her.

Realene's head fell to her chest, and she sobbed.

# Twenty

**NATE PLACED A** hand on Realene's shoulder, watched as she sat huddled on the floor beside Irene, sobs racking her body. He didn't say anything, couldn't. Anger clogged his throat, and any words that came out wouldn't help.

A scream sounded from behind the bedroom door.

"Let us out," Mrs. Olson begged, followed by her husband shouting, "He's going to kill us!"

Nate's mom made a move for the door, but he caught her elbow, holding her back. More screams came from the room, cries from Mr. Olson of, "Get off me!"

"We can't just leave them in there," she said, yanking her arm away.

Nate felt nothing for the Olsons but anger, couldn't find even a spec of sympathy for them. He hoped they got what they deserved.

"She's right." Trish moved to grab the chair she herself had put beneath the doorknob.

"Don't touch that," Nate said. "Kev, little help?"

With a sigh, Big Kev stepped in front of the door, blocking it.

"It's too late, anyway," Nate said. Birdie had already attacked the couple. In another ten minutes, they could turn aggressive too. "Let them out, and you're putting the rest of us at risk."

"What is this infection? Harmon's behind this, isn't he?" Sophia asked.

Nate heaved a breath. "You know the story about the poisoning in Demise was a cover up, right? Well, it was actually a sort of infection, one that's contagious. It can make people confused and affect their memory, like Irene, and it can make people extremely aggressive, like *him*." He gestured toward the closed bedroom door, which rattled on its hinges. "If you let them out, you risk everyone here."

"It's not right to leave them in there. They might die."

"You suddenly care about what's right?" Nate gritted his teeth. "You watched them kill that reporter and did nothing to stop it. How could you go back—"

"Stop it," Realene said. She climbed to her feet, her body threatening to collapse with exhaustion. "We need to get ahold of the colonel, tell him we have these guys locked up."

"No way," Big Kev said.

"You don't get an opinion," she said. "Your tracking device is the reason they found us. This whole thing is your fault."

He opened his mouth, closed it. Gave a sharp nod.

"Harmon's the only one who has the resources to contain this," Nate said. "We need him."

Trish pointed to the phone where it trailed from the handset to the floor. "Okay, but how do we call him when we don't have a phone?"

"I brought a phone. The satellite kind," Nate's mom said, staring at the bedroom door. Nate's dad had bought her one years ago as part of his doomsday prep.

Something slammed into the door, causing the wood to split down the center.

"We should go." Realene took a last look at Irene's body, then grabbed her coat and put on her gloves.

Nate took a random coat from a hook by the door. It reeked of tobacco, and he wondered if it was Calvin's. Nate went out the door first, followed closely by his mom, and stood looking at his truck, which was blocked in by the bus.

"The truck's blocked in," Big Kev said, coming to stand beside him.

"No shit." And now that his mom was there, it would be an even tighter fit.

"Guess we're stealing the doomsday bus." Realene marched through the snow to the side door of the hulking vehicle.

A light snow fell, but the blizzard had passed, meaning their visibility should be okay. It had been several hours since they'd plowed their way to the cabin. Hopefully the way was still clear enough for the bus to make it back.

Trish and Big Kev were the last out, and he stopped to lock the front door.

Nate didn't think it would hold long if Birdie broke out of the bedroom but didn't say that. He grimaced at the thought of the three infected getting loose, spreading the worms. He made his way to the bus and ascended the stairs. Ahead of him, Big Kev plopped into the driver's seat and started perusing the controls.

"Can you actually drive this thing?" Realene asked, standing directly behind him. The first few rows of seats had been removed, leaving an open space.

"Oh, sure. Piece of cake compared to a big rig." He glanced between her and Nate. "I'll get us out of here. Least I can do after…you know."

Nate continued past them down the bus's aisle. He passed Trish, who plopped down in the first available seat. His mom sat in the back row of seats at the outer edge, and he spotted a shape beside her. Trout raised his head and gave a short bark, his tail thumping.

"Hey, buddy," he said, scratching the dog as irritation prickled inside him. "You had to bring him on this wild goose chase, too?"

"I couldn't very well leave him alone. And it's just me at home. I don't have anyone else to watch him, do I?" she said.

He eased out a breath, told himself to calm down, to be reasonable while he still could. The worms hadn't gotten to him so far, but they still might.

She handed him the phone from her bag, one she apparently hadn't told Birdie about. Nate took it up to Realene, then returned to the back of the bus to talk to his mom. "Why did you join up with them again?"

"Someone has to stop that Harmon. I knew he was using you for some kind of evil." She gripped her hands in her lap. "This infection. It's him. I know it."

"Mom, no, he's trying to contain it. To stop it."

She scowled. "No. That Harmon is the one who brought you here. This is his fault."

Nate didn't say she might be right, that the colonel bringing him to the meteor site could have been the source, but feeding into her paranoia wouldn't help matters, and he couldn't tell her the whole truth about the meteor and the worms anyway. She'd never believe him.

The bus's engine roared to life.

"And Trish is such a nice girl, now she's all wrapped up in this too," his mom said.

"I know." He was supposed to protect her, but all he seemed to be able to do was put himself and everyone around him in danger.

The bus began to back up. He stood and walked to the front, where Realene was putting the satellite phone down on the dashboard.

"The colonel is sending reinforcements," she said. "Asked for us to meet him at the warehouse."

Going back to that base, putting themselves even closer to the source of the worms, made Nate want to puke. "Guess we have no choice," he said.

Big Kev struggled with the shifter, the gears grinding. "It's cool," he said, sounding more than a bit unsure. "Just shaking off the cobwebs."

"I don't think we'll be there long," she said. "He said he's gonna get us somewhere safe."

"Did he say if the quarantine worked? If the infection spreads here..." Nate didn't have to finish his sentence. They all knew that hundreds of thousands of people would be hurt or killed if it wasn't stopped.

"Didn't say. You still doing okay?" she asked, touching his arm. Not being careful not to touch him, not trying to keep her distance.

He wanted to give her a hug for that but didn't. "I feel fine. Hey, um, I'm sorry about Irene."

"Yeah, me too." She gave a wry laugh. "Never thought I'd say that after how many times I wished she'd drop dead."

"She was different. Like before."

Realene frowned. "I don't get why, though. She wasn't confused like everyone in Demise was when they were still infected. This was different."

"Like me, too," Nate said. "I mean, I'm glad I haven't lost my memory and turned rabid, but I don't know why."

Realene bit her thumb nail, chewing it to the quick.

The bus lurched backward, and Big Kev flipped on the brights, washing the cabin and the trees on either side in light. Just then, the cabin door burst open, and Birdie and Mrs. Olson ran toward them, or tried. They struggled through the knee-deep snow, half crawling.

"They're out," Big Kev yelled, extremely unhelpfully.

Nate's mom came up the aisle. "What do we do?"

"Don't worry, we'll be safe in here," he said.

Outside, Mrs. Olson shrieked at them, her face blotchy and red. She was definitely infected. There was no sign of her husband, and Nate tried not to think about the possibility the guy might already be dead.

Birdie and Mrs. Olson struggled their way free of the snowbank and past Nate's truck, making it onto the plowed road. They charged the bus.

"I can't see a damn thing back there." Big Kev continued backward, squinting at the rearview mirror. The path behind them was barely lit by the reverse lights.

Birdie reached the hood and smacked it with both hands, then leapt up to grab the massive grill that covered the hood and began to climb.

Mrs. Olson rounded the bus, pounding at the door and screaming. "Filthy demons!" She jumped up to balance on the lowest step that extended past the doors, clutching the top lip of the armor that still encased the outside of the bus. "When God releases his fiery wrath, it will incinerate your souls!"

Realene stayed on the interior steps, gripping the lever that held the door closed.

Birdie reached the windshield and sat back, balancing on his knees as he raised his fist and punched the glass. He howled and clutched his hand, which was probably broken. A red smear marred the glass where he'd hit it.

Big Kev increased speed, driving backward along the road. He'd changed tactics, now looking over his shoulder as he attempted to navigate them down the dark, tree-lined route.

"You will be judged!" Mrs. Olson screamed, her spittle freezing in droplets on the door. She bore no resemblance to the sweet old woman who'd sold him chocolate-covered potato chips at their candy store. "God will cleanse the world of filth like you!"

The bus thumped over something, and Mrs. Olson slipped off the step, disappearing.

A scream sounded and Big Kev swerved, smacking the back end of the bus into a tree. Nate was thrown backward, ended up splayed on the floor next to his mom. Birdie smacked face first into the windshield, then rolled off the hood.

Trish rushed over, kneeling beside Nate. "Are you okay?"

"I'm fine." Nate looked at his mom, who winced and rubbed her shoulder. "Mom?

"I'm okay," she said.

"What the hell, dude?" he shouted at Big Kev.

"You try driving backward in the dark," he snapped, glancing back at the tree they'd hit.

Nate got to his feet and helped his mom up, peering outside. "Where are they?"

The only sound was the chug of the engine. He looked out the windows, trying to pick up any sign of movement in the dark. His mom came to stand beside him.

"What are you waiting for?" said Trish. "Let's go."

"What if they're under the bus?" Big Kev asked. "I don't want to run 'em over."

Nate didn't like Birdie or this new Mrs. Olson very much, but he also didn't want to see them squashed beneath the massive tires, their blood and guts bursting onto the snow.

"There," Big Kev said, pointing outside toward the cabin.

Birdie wobbled and clutched his head with his good hand. He looked up, his lips pulling back from his teeth in a snarl.

A blurry shape erupted from the open door of the cabin and tackled him to the ground.

For a moment, Nate wondered if it was an animal of some kind, but it was only Mr. Olson. He sat atop Birdie, lunging at his face and neck with teeth bared, but Birdie managed to throw him off and stand, stumbling once more toward the bus. Mr. Olson ran after him, latching onto his back, and to counter, Birdie spun in a circle, grabbing at the man's arms where they encircled his neck.

"Let's go, hurry," Realene said, and Big Kev shifted into drive, then pressed the gas. They lurched forward, back onto the narrow road as the headlights bounced over the scene before them.

Mr. Olson latched onto Birdie's ear now, taking a bite. Birdie shrieked and bent forward, flipping the man off his back to land hard in the packed snow.

Nate's mom pressed her hand to her mouth, watching the fight with horror. He wondered if she was remembering his dad, remembering what she'd seen Nate do to him.

None of them said anything else as Big Kev shifted into reverse and started back down the darkened road. Soon the headlights revealed Mrs. Olson, her dead body crushed into the snow.

Birdie again stumbled down the road after the bus, stopping to clutch the truck bed for support as he passed it. After a moment, Mr. Olson sat up, looking like Michael Meyers popping back up after you were sure he was dead.

Nate tore his gaze from the scene, acid singeing his gut.

"Jesus that was fast," Realene whispered.

They'd seen the same thing at the bar, but this just proved that wasn't a fluke. Whatever this strain was, it escalated in minutes instead of hours. And in Demise, the infected attacked those who weren't infected, not each other.

Nate's mom slumped against one of the seats, bracing herself.

Trish, who'd been watching the whole scene in silence, turned to Nate, tears streaming down her face. "I'm so sorry."

"This isn't your fault," he said.

"I should have told you," she whispered.

Nate's mom turned to stare at him. Her gaze was frightened and unsettling.

"Mom, are you okay?"

"You. Just stay away from me," she said, edging past him down the aisle. "Stay away." The look in her eyes was that same one from the day he killed his father.

"Mom." He reached for her, but she shrunk away from him. Trout whined and took a few steps toward Nate as if to comfort him.

"Trout," she said. "Come here, boy." The dog gave a forlorn look at Nate, then obeyed, jumping up on the seat beside her.

Nate slumped into the seat two rows ahead of his mom, resting his head against the window. The frosty glass stung his skin, but he didn't move, just closed his eyes and prayed the chill would spread and turn him numb.

# Twenty-One

**REALENE CLUTCHED THE** bar at the top of the stairs and peered into the darkness behind them, watching for anything she may have to warn Big Kev about. After a tense few minutes, they reached a clearing that widened the road, and he was able to turn the bus around so they were facing forward again. He cracked his neck, then started forward.

"Impressive driving." It couldn't be easy navigating these things backward, Realene figured. Especially not in a life-or-death situation. "We wouldn't have gotten this far without you."

"What can I say? I'm a pretty big deal."

"I haven't forgotten about those trackers, you dick."

"I'm sorry, okay? I messed up." He heaved a deep breath. "Do you want to punch me? That's how I settle up with Ana. One punch to the face, as hard as you can hit."

"That won't really work with you driving. But I'll take a rain check." She wasn't even close to forgiving him and definitely didn't trust him. But her priority now was getting Nate help. She looked back to see him resting his head against the window, eyes closed. Trish sat by herself a few rows ahead of him and just stared absentmindedly at the floor.

Speaking of people Realene didn't trust…

She made her way over and sat down beside Trish in the spot closest to the window. The girl tensed, as if expecting Realene to yell or hit her.

Realene kept her voice soft so Nate wouldn't hear if he awoke. "He loves you, you know."

Trish dropped her chin to her chest.

"I don't know how much he's told you about everything that happened, but I wouldn't be alive without him," Realene continued. "None of us would. He was always the one that said we had to try, no matter the odds, that we couldn't wait for someone else to save us." She paused, then said, "Before the worms, what it was like for him at home, with his dad. He ever tell you about that?"

"Yeah, some."

"He's always been the one to protect everyone else. He deserves someone who will do the same for him."

The bus rocked to a stop as they reached the spot where the side road ended. Big Kev turned onto the main road, which seemed clearer, as if vehicles had been driving through the newly accumulated snow. Probably Harmon's military vehicles.

Trish swallowed, then whispered, "I love him, too."

A bare hint of morning light broke on the horizon, illuminating the frozen lake coming up on their right. Trees lined the road on the other side. "That's a start. But would you die for him? Kill for him? Because I would, and I did." She rubbed the scar on her palm from their blood pact as kids. Best friends forever. "You understand me?"

Trish clasped her hands in her lap, knuckles turning white. "I do."

"Then you need to tell me the truth. You know how this happened, don't you?"

Trish glanced behind her, back to where Nate was sleeping, his breath still ragged. She nodded.

"Tell me everything."

Trish exhaled, raised her head to look at Realene. "It wasn't the cult—" But before she could finish, her eyes widened, and she screamed, "Look out!"

Realene turned in time to see something smash into the side of the bus, rocking the vehicle and causing the back end to swerve. Trish slid sideways, pressing into Realene, whose skull smacked the window hard. She shook her head and saw a giant shape stumble back from the bus and shake its own massive head. It was a goddamn bison.

Startled cries erupted from everyone on the bus as it slid slowly to a stop until it was sitting askew horizontally across both lanes of the road. Big Kev released a tirade of curse words.

"What happened? Is everyone okay?" Nate asked, standing from his seat.

Head pounding, Realene half stood to see how they'd fared. No one seemed seriously hurt. "I think so."

The bison was still outside, but seemed dazed, was slumped onto its front legs and huffing. She'd seen an infected bison up close in Demise, and it wasn't something she wanted to repeat. This beast had managed to shove them several feet, would attack again if they didn't get away.

"Drive!" she yelled at Big Kev.

They lurched forward, and she gripped the back of the seat, glancing outside. The bison wasn't alone. Another of the huge beasts erupted from the trees and barreled toward the bus.

"Everybody hold on," she yelled, watching as their new attacker passed its dazed cohort to slam into the bus, shoving the vehicle fully off the road this time. Screams erupted again as they began to slide down the snowy escarpment that led to the lake. The engine roared in defiance as Big Kev tried to right their course, but his efforts were futile. The wheels just spun until the entire rig became stuck.

A rumbling growl sounded from outside and two more hits came, smacking into the bus one after another, rocking them sideways until the bus teetered on two wheels. Trout yelped and slid across the floor.

Realene dropped to her knees and grabbed the dog's collar, yanking him close to her and wrapping her arms around his body. She looped her leg around a support of the bench seat.

Like a slowly falling tree, the bus continued to tip until finally it thumped fully over, landing in the snow with a dull thud that knocked the air from her lungs when her back hit the windows. Trout trembled in her embrace, and she nuzzled his head. "It's okay, buddy. We're okay."

She sat up, grimacing. Luckily, the bus was decked out with metal plates and bars on the outside, so none of the windows had broken when the side of the bus became the floor.

"Trout? Where's Trout?" Sophia called, and he wiggled from Realene's embrace to pad across the windows toward her. On his way, he stopped next to Trish, who lay crumpled on her side. He whined and sniffed her hand.

Realene crawled over, saw blood in Trish's blonde hair, and pressed two fingers to the girl's neck until she felt the steady beat of a pulse.

Trish came to, giving a soft moan.

Nate stumbled over, using the seats to hold himself up. Realene scanned him for any sign of injury, didn't see any. He dropped to his knees beside his girlfriend, reached for her then stopped, maybe thinking about spreading the infection. She started to sit up.

"Careful," Nate said, backing away from her to give her space.

She touched her forehead, wincing.

A curse sounded from the front of the bus, and Big Kev appeared, climbing over the driver's seat.

"Kev, you okay?" Realene asked.

He took a few wobbly steps toward them. "Were we just attacked by a goddamned bison?"

"Two, actually." She scanned the bus for a first aid kit but didn't see one.

"They're peaceful, though."

"Yeah, but the worms aren't. Those bison are for sure infected."

Sophia sat huddled between two seats, now holding Trout close. "God, please protect us from this evil, keep us safe from harm. You are our refuge and fortress, dear God."

A deep, growling bellow sounded from outside, and something shoved into the bus's undercarriage, sent them sliding once more down the remainder of the escarpment, all the way to the edge of the frozen lake at the bottom.

"God, what have I done to deserve this?" Sophia wailed. "Why is this happening again?"

"There are aliens among us, lady. Keep up," Big Kev said, yanking on the lever that would open the front door, which was now hung from the "ceiling" of the bus.

"Shut up, Kev." Realene made a mental note to punch him in the face as soon as she had the chance.

"Lying lips are an abomination to the Lord," Sophia said. "You're liars, all of you."

"You really want the truth?" Nate bent over his mom, his posture tense. "This infection, the one that the colonel is actually trying to contain, it's alien worms. Look for yourself." He opened his eye wide with forefinger and thumb.

Sophia shrieked, and Realene grabbed Nate's arm, pulling him away. "You're not helping."

Nate yanked his arm from her grip, glanced back at his mom. She'd continued her prayers, now muted because she had her face buried in Trout's fur.

Another bellow sounded from outside, and the bus was hit again, sending them sliding onto the lake's frozen surface.

Realene held on to the back of the seat, now positioned over her head. Another hit followed the first, propelling them farther from the shore.

"We gotta get outta here," Kev said, when they came to another stop.

"No way," Nate said. "At least inside we're protected by the bus."

A sharp smell wafted through the air, stung Realene's nose. "Gasoline."

Big Kevin took his own whiff of the air. "Shit, she's right. They must've hit the tank."

Nate grabbed the emergency latch on the bus's backdoor, grunting and straining. "It's jammed."

Realene climbed the seats and stretched to reach one of the windows above them, flipping open the latch. It would be a tight fit, especially for Big Kev, but they'd have to make it work. Then she remembered the bars crisscrossing the windows on the outside. "We're trapped."

"The roof hatch." Nate moved to the square emergency exit that sat in the center of the roof, now the bus's side. A metal ladder was folded across the square opening, and he pulled it out, then bent to remove the metal pin and pushed open the hatch. A gust of cold wind whipped through the enclosed space.

"Go, hurry." Realene nudged Big Kev toward the opening, and he jumped through.

She approached Sophia, who got up, Trout clutched in her arms.

"Out of my way," Sophia demanded and shoved past Realene, putting the dog through the hatch first then climbing out after him.

Trish went next.

The smell of the gasoline strengthened, making Realene dizzy. She stepped to the opening and saw they'd been pushed about a hundred feet from shore. She jumped, landing hard on the snow and ice. Nate landed beside her a few seconds later, and Big Kev helped them both to their feet. Ahead of them, Trish stood beside Sophia, who held Trout by his leash.

They were on the opposite side of the lake from the military installation, which was just beyond the tree-lined shore across the water. The storm had eased up just enough for her to see the first of the pines there.

An aggressive snort sounded from the other side of the overturned bus.

"Run!" Realene shouted and bolted away from the bus, pushing Big Kev forward. Nate grabbed Trish's and Sophia's arms, with Trout in tow, and dragged them along, high-stepping at speed through the heavy snow that covered the ice.

The crash of a bison slamming into the undercarriage of the bus sounded behind them. The vehicle slid across the ice, the roof clipping Realene's heel as she threw herself forward, diving across the ice on her belly like a demented penguin.

When nothing crushed her, she looked up to see the rest of them were still alive and running. She turned over and sat up. Beyond the front end of the bus, she caught sight of one of the bison. It seemed to notice her, to lock on with its bottomless black eyes. Breath puffed from its nostrils, and it emitted a terrible, keening cry that was totally unnatural.

She wondered if bison had sharp enough teeth to bite, if it would try and infect her or just stomp her to death beneath its massive hooves. Maybe her death would give the others enough time to get away.

"Rea!" Nate cried, running up to her, pulling her to her feet. He'd come back for her. Of course he had.

A loud crack sounded, one she felt reverberate up through her feet, and she and Nate froze. Several more cracks sounded, multiplying, spreading from the weight of the bus. Wasting no more time, Nate helped Realene to her feet and sprinted with her after the others. They didn't look back as the cracks nipped at their ankles, threatening to swallow them into the depths.

# Twenty-Two

**THE GROUP OF** them half ran, half slid across the ice, angling toward the lake's far shore and the military base beyond. They closed the gap to twenty feet, then ten. Trout made it first, climbing over the crusted snowy berm, followed by Trish, Sophia, and Big Kev. Realene and Nate were last, leaping forward and crashing into the snowy shore as the loudest crack of them all split the ice like the Red Sea and swallowed the bus and both bison whole. Realene watched from her back as the three titans sank like rocks into the water's black and frigid depths.

"You're bleeding," Sophia said to Nate. Trout nuzzled her leg.

Nate scrambled to his feet, pressing a gloved hand to his bleeding nose. "Stay back."

"Listen to him," Sophia said, frantic. "He's got the disease."

"Not a disease." Big Kev stood and brushed the snow from his coat. "Alien worms. Real life E.T.s. We told you this already."

Realene didn't have the energy to tell him to shut up this time.

Sophia sneered at Big Kev. "Blasphemy. His creation is Heaven and Earth. This alien talk is just more lies."

"It's not a lie," Big Kev shouted. His outburst caused all of them to jump. It was the first time any of them had heard Big Kev raise his voice in anger. "There are hundreds of sightings of unidentified flying objects every year. Not to mention reputable firsthand accounts of alien encounters. Just ask my dad if you don't believe me. He'll tell you."

Sensing now what was going on, Realene placed a hand on his back to calm him. "Hey."

He whipped around, looking ready to fight, but something in her face must have changed his mind, because his shoulders slumped and he relaxed. "Sorry."

"Save your energy, okay. She's not worth it."

"It's not aliens," Sophia said, her voice now colder than ice. "He did this. Colonel Harmon. This is *his* doing."

"C'mon," Realene said to the rest of them. "Harmon's just on the other side of those trees. Let's get this over with."

Big Kev and Nate followed slowly after Realene, but Trish stayed back with Sophia and Trout.

"Wait," Trish said, the look on her face troubled. Following a deep breath, she closed her eyes and blurted, "She's right. Sophia's right. About Harmon. Or at least I think she is."

Realene froze in her tracks. "What are you saying?"

"Harmon." Nate stared at Trish; pain etched into his face. "He did this to me?"

"That's not possible." It couldn't be true. He would never do something like that. The colonel had saved them. Saved her. Realene stalked toward Trish. "You're lying."

Trish looked to Nate with tears in her eyes. "It was supposed to be a quick test," she explained. "Infect you, study how you reacted, and cure you before any complications arose. He said it wouldn't hurt and he'd make sure you didn't remember."

Nate laughed—a harsh, grating sound. "This whole thing was a setup then. Inviting us here. Harmon needed a guinea pig, someone to infect on purpose, and I was the one he chose."

"Dude," Kev mumbled. "That's really messed up."

Realene caught the sob that wanted to escape her mouth. This was more than messed up. It was a complete betrayal. She'd trusted Harmon, and he'd infected the person who mattered to her most in the whole world.

"How do you know all this?" Nate said. "You were what? In on it?"

"No. It's not like that," Trish said. "I didn't know about the plan, not until after we got up here. I thought it was just a fun trip. But then Harmon told me I had to help get you to the warehouse. Once we got there, you freaked out and that alarm started going off. The experiment never happened, and we left. After that, I thought everything was okay, that I'd never have to tell you the real reason we were there, but I was wrong."

"If the experiment never happened, then how did Nate get infected?" Realene asked.

Nate rubbed his hand where the cut was, where he'd been shoved into the infected animals. "The cages. I was infected when I touched them."

Realene strode toward Trish. "That's why you were being so secretive. Why you only wanted to talk to Harmon. You were just trying to protect yourself. You wanted to make sure that Nate never found out."

Nate looked more broken than Realene had ever seen. Worse than the time she'd visited him in jail. Worse than the day his parents had kicked him out. Worse than when they almost died at the hands of the reverend.

Filled with an anger she could no longer contain, Realene shoved Trish as hard as she could, which caused the girl to stumble backward but not fall. "Why'd you do it, huh? Why'd you help Harmon? What's in it for you? Say something, or I swear—"

"I had to." Trish sobbed. "I had no other choice, okay?"

Sophia jabbed a finger in Trish's face. "Deceiver! You helped that devil corrupt my son. You'll pay for this. You'll burn."

Trout gave a sharp bark at the nearby trees and growled, drawing the group's attention to whatever it was that had raised the dog's alarm.

"Please no more bison," Big Kev said.

But the shape that moved just behind the trees was too small for that, barely a slinking shadow. Realene squinted, watched as the animal stepped from the trees to reveal silver fur and a sharp-toothed snout. A wolf.

"Uh-oh," Realene said.

"At least there's only one," Trish said.

"Uh, wolves travel in packs." Big Kev pointed at the trees, where more shapes began to emerge, a half-dozen in total.

"What do we do?" Nate asked.

"Stay calm." Big Kev walked backwards in the direction of the military's warehouse, which was still a good hundred yards away.

"Calm." Realene choked on the word, could barely talk with her pulse pounding in her throat.

They all followed Kev's lead. Trout kept growling and barking, but Sophia yanked his leash, pulling him along.

The wolves stayed where they were, watching from the tree line. They looked too skinny, bony, but not bloody or injured. Maybe they weren't infected.

That first wolf, the alpha, raised its head and howled. The rest howled, too, forming a chorus. They stopped, and a growl rippled through the pack.

"Kev?" Realene said.

The wolves lunged as a group, running through the snow.

"Run!" he screamed.

Realene tore her gaze from the animals and ran as fast as her short legs would allow. The trees loomed ahead, getting closer. She pushed herself harder, focused on the warehouse now visible between the many firs and pine. The road there was also coming into focus. Her legs ached and her lungs burned.

The growls behind them gained ground, still sounding faint, but getting closer.

Realene pulled her pocketknife out and flipped open the blade, watching the backs of her friends as they raced through the snow. They were coming up on the warehouse, passing the edge of the trees that hid the building. A snarling bark sounded right behind her, and she stumbled, then fell. She flipped to her back, ready to stab out with the knife. But before she could, a blur of fur barreled past her, colliding with the wolf midair and sending the animal sprawling in the snow.

Trout stood tall beside Realene, legs wide and back hunched, growling and baring his teeth.

The wolf jumped up and stalked toward Trout. The only thing injured, it seemed, was its pride. The rest of the pack advanced, coming up behind their alpha.

Realene struggled to her feet, then stumbled forward ahead of Trout.

The wolf lunged.

**A LOUD CRACK** split the air.

A gunshot.

The bullet missed its target but grazed the wolf's side enough to cause the animal to yelp, then turn and run. The rest of the pack followed the alpha in retreat.

Trout whined and Realene turned, closing the knife and shoving it back in her pocket. "It's okay, buddy." She crouched to let him lick her face. "You're such a good boy."

"Trout," Sophia said, and the dog went to her. She fished some treats from her pocket, her hand visibly shaking.

Nate and Kev rushed up to Realene while Trish hung back behind the group.

"Thought you were a goner for sure," Big Kev said.

Nate bumped his shoulder into Realene's and grinned. "You brought a knife to a wolf fight."

"Where did that shot come from?" Realene asked.

Nate turned back and pointed to a sniper on the roof of the warehouse. "My guess is him."

"Not much of a shot," Big Kev said.

"Maybe he meant to miss," Nate replied.

The garage door beneath the sniper opened, and a cargo van pulled out, followed by a sedan.

Realene and crew trudged through the snow to meet the vehicles at the road.

The sedan pulled up first, and Harmon got out. He still wore his civilian clothes, but a gun was now visible inside a shoulder holster beneath his unzipped parka.

"Everyone okay?" he asked.

None of them said anything.

He frowned. "All right, well, let's get you inside."

The driver's-side door of the van opened and a man, one of Harmon's soldiers stepped out. He was huge, dwarfed even Big Kev. He opened the rear doors of the van. An empty cargo bed waited. Did he want them to get inside? Because that didn't make any sense. They were only a hundred yards from the warehouse. Close enough to walk.

"What's happening?" Realene asked. "What's the van for?"

Harmon gave an exasperated sigh. "I'm done playing games with you, Realene. This is for your own good. Now get inside the van so we can get you somewhere safe. Wolves are the least of our worries."

"Yeah, okay. Sorry," she said. She couldn't confront the colonel yet, not until she had more proof to back up Trish's claims. In the meantime, she had no choice but to play along.

Harmon smiled at Sophia and reached out to take her hand. "Mrs. Haugen, I assume. My name is Colonel Harmon. I'm sorry we didn't meet under better circumstances."

Sophia scowled, refusing his hand. "Matthew 7:15," she recited. "'Beware of false prophets who come to you in sheep's clothing but inwardly are ravenous wolves.'"

"Mom," Nate said, his tone short.

Harmon's mouth pressed into a thin line.

"Please, Sophia," Realene said, trying to catch the woman's eyes. "I know you think he lied about the Reverend, but he's here to help us. He's gonna get us home."

"Yeah right," Big Kev mumbled, starting toward the van. Trish followed, saying nothing. Realene joined the two of them, but no one climbed inside.

A branch snapped somewhere in the trees, and she flinched, tension thick in the frigid air.

Sophia glared at the colonel, broadcasting her contempt. "I believed a false prophet once already. I will not fall prey again."

Shouts sounded from the area behind the warehouse, then the walkie clipped to the belt of the massive soldier squawked, issuing a loud beep. A voice on the other end said, "Fox 1, this is Fox 2. Sergeant Birdie has been apprehended. Repeat, Sergeant Birdie has been apprehended. He was attempting to gain access to the facility. Over."

Harmon grabbed the walkie from the soldier, pressed the call button, and said, "Roger. Detain and cure him. Over and out."

Realene sucked in a breath.

*Sergeant* Birdie.

It all made sense. He'd referred to the whole thing as a job, and he'd been the one to infect Irene, probably as part of Harmon's tests. Birdie was a spy.

The colonel clipped the walkie back to his own belt, then placed one hand on his holstered gun, the movement precise and calculated.

"Judas. Betrayer," Sophia said, apparently reaching the same realization about Birdie.

"Your ilk tried to poison the people of Demise," Harmon said. "We couldn't very well leave you unsupervised. We needed a man on the inside."

Sophia's eyes nearly popped from their sockets at Harmon's confession. She pointed at him, then at Nate, then at the rest of them. "Try and fool me, but before you do, know this: I am a vessel for God's righteousness, and He *will* reveal the truth to me, and the truth will set us free." And with that, she wheeled around and made a dash toward the warehouse, her dark hair whipping wildly in the wind.

"Mom, don't!" Nate yelled, running after her.

"Davis," Harmon barked, and the soldier that had been standing near the van sprinted after Nate, tackling him to the ground. Nate cried out, face twisting in pain.

Trout lunged, but Harmon snatched the dog's collar and raised him up off the ground with one hand. Trout growled and bared his sharp teeth in defiance.

At the sight of his abuses, Trish and Realene rushed into action.

"I'll get Nate," Realene said.

Trish nodded and ran over to Harmon, rescuing the dog from the colonel's grip. With Trout now safely in her arms, she dropped to her knees and comforted him. "Shh. It's okay, bud," she whispered.

Caring nothing for the dog, Harmon pulled his gun and instead aimed it at Realene. "No one move," he commanded. His expression was deadly serious.

Realene halted and raised her hands in surrender.

Sophia ignored what was happening behind her and kept going, half skating, half running on the icy road ahead. She was almost to the open warehouse.

Realene knew what she would see once inside: the crater, the suspended rats, and above that, the box holding the worm queen.

Sophia skidded to a stop and stared into the warehouse. Her hand rose, pointing, and she shrieked long and loud, shattering the surrounding quiet.

Atop the warehouse, the sniper adjusted his aim.

Realene had wanted to scream, warn Sophia of the danger, but it was too late. A deafening shot rang out and dropped Sophia where she stood. Her body crumpled lifelessly onto the road.

# Twenty-Three

**"STAND DOWN, I** repeat, stand down," Colonel Harmon yelled into the walkie, his gun now holstered again.

"Mom!" Nate screamed, the sound splitting Realene's heart in two.

He wrenched himself from beneath Davis to crawl toward Sophia. Davis got up and strode after Nate, towering over him. For one horrible second Realene thought the man would shoot Nate, too, but instead of a gun, Davis pulled a riot baton from his belt and clocked Nate hard on the back of the head with it.

Nate dropped to the ground, moaning.

"You bastard." Realene lunged at Harmon, but before she could land a blow, he grabbed her wrist and wrenched her arm behind her back. Subdued now, he turned her around so she was facing away from him and shoved her. She stumbled forward and landed hard on her knees.

Wincing, Nate sat up. He pressed a hand to his head, which was dripping blood.

She got to her feet, turned to face Harmon. "I hate you," Realene said, her voice cracking.

"That woman attacked a secure government facility, my men responded appropriately."

"That woman has a name. Sophia. And your sergeant, your little spy, he murdered Irene. The Olsons are probably dead too. And who knows how many people at the hotel. Because of you." She stalked toward him. "I can't believe I ever trusted you."

The muscle in his jaw twitched. "You were never supposed to be here. None of this would have happened if you hadn't shown up."

"No." She would not let him manipulate her, blame her, again. "This is your fault. You planned to infect my best friend for some stupid little experiment, and you fucked it up. You let it get completely out of control."

Harmon looked down at Trish and reached for his gun, removing it from the holster. "Now how would you know about that?"

Trish stood, backed up until she bumped into Big Kev. "They figured it out on their own. Please. I'm telling you the truth."

"You gonna murder her now too?" Nate asked, managing to stand and take a wobbly step toward the colonel. "Just use her to get what you want then kill her? You spineless snake."

Big Kev eyed the colonel's gun. "You won't get away with this, people know where we are, they'll come looking for us."

But Harmon would just get rid of those people too. Big Kev's dad. Ana. His Alien Alliance friends. None of them were safe.

Harmon raised his gun, pointing it at Big Kev and Trish.

"Please, Colonel," Realene said. "No one else has to die."

"I agree with you," Harmon said. He turned to Davis and nodded a silent command.

Acting under orders, Davis pulled his gun, aimed it at Nate, and pulled the trigger, firing a tranquilizer dart into Nate's neck.

Nate collapsed into a medicated sleep.

"Restrain the rest," Harmon said.

Davis started with Big Kev, fastening his hands behind his back and loading him back into the van. Next came Trish, then an unconscious Nate. Trout jumped in after Nate, nudging him with his nose and whining.

When Davis came for her, Realene didn't resist. She let him fasten her hands behind her back, let him force her into the van.

He slammed the door in her face.

The driver's seat was visible, no barrier between it and the cargo area, and a moment later, Davis climbed in, his large frame crammed into the small cab. He turned on the car, and "Know Your Enemy," by Rage Against the Machine blasted from the speakers.

Realene swallowed a laugh. Good advice she wished she'd paid attention to sooner. So many people tried to warn her about the colonel, but she wouldn't listen. Now, Sophia was dead. Maybe Calvin, too.

Davis turned down the volume and shifted into drive. Big Kev and Trish sat in silence.

Realene watched from the rear window of the van as the colonel got into his car. She prayed for another bison to come and crush him to a pulp inside his vehicle or shove the car into the lake so she could watch him drown, but her petition went unanswered.

The radio inside the van squawked. "Fox one, this is fox five. Alert. RCMP approaching. Over."

Royal Canadian Mounted Police.

Davis slammed on the brakes, and Realene slid into the sleeping Nate.

Big Kev whispered, "Hell yeah. It's the calvary."

Realene craned her neck to see out the back window. At the far edge of the lake, half a dozen people in dark coats and wide-brimmed hats rode horses straight toward them. She turned back to Davis, watched him grab the radio from the van's center console and say, "Roger. What are they doing here? Over."

"Going to arrest your asses for detaining Canadian citizens," Big Kev said.

The voice on the radio said, "According to their radio chatter, they received several reports of gunfire and came to check it out. Over."

"They still ride horses? Over." Davis asked, voicing Realene's exact thought.

"They were on snowmobiles but couldn't get past the downed tree we used to block the road. Guess they commandeered the horses from a rancher. Over."

"Roger. Over and out." Davis swore and hung up the radio, then hopped from the van, closing the door behind him.

Shoulders threatening to tear from their sockets, Realene looped her bound wrists beneath her butt and under her legs.

Pain tore through her muscles, but she managed to work her wrists past her feet, ending up with her bound hands in front of her.

"How the hell did you do that?" Big Kev asked, wiggling as if trying to emulate the feat.

Trish, on the other hand, copied the move successfully, and got her hands in front of her with ease.

Outside the window, Davis met up with Harmon, who had exited his sedan.

"What do you think they're talking about?" Big Kev asked.

"I'm not sure I wanna know," said Trish.

"What's that supposed to mean?" Realene asked.

"It means you don't know what he's capable of. What he's *really* capable of."

"Jesus, would you quit with all this cryptic bullshit. Just tell us," Realene demanded.

"Look," Big Kev said, nodding at the scene outside the window. A look of uncertainty had come over his face, like something bad was about to happen.

In the distance, the Mounties had paused their approach, and two of them dismounted their horses in favor of investigating the giant hole in the ice that the cult bus and the two bison had disappeared into earlier. They watched with amusement as a beaver rose from the frigid water and climbed atop a floating sheet of ice, where it stood on hind legs and beat its flat tale against the bobbing perch.

Even from this distance, Realene could see the damage to the animal's side. Gruesome injuries that exposed both muscle and bone. Injuries no normal animal could survive.

"Oh, crap," she mumbled.

Before anyone could react, the creature launched itself at the closest Mountie and latched onto his face with sharp claws. The man screamed and spun in a circle, but the animal didn't let go, its tail flying out straight behind it and smacking the gun out of the other Mountie's hand. Desperate now, the man ran wildly up the embankment toward the other four men in his crew.

Harmon and Davis jogged down the road toward the men.

The four Mounties who'd remained on the road quickly dismounted and surrounded their wounded colleague. One of them was able to bat the beaver free with the end of his saber and another was able to grab it and fling it through the air. The little monster, however, executed a perfect front flip and landed neatly on the mount of one of the horses. The horse bucked, but the beaver held on to the mare's neck with bared teeth and claws, drawing blood. It even rode the horse for a few seconds before ultimately being ejected and stomped to death beneath its hooves. All that remained was a bloody, furry mess. Blood dripped down the injured Mountie's face, which he cupped with a gloved hand, while two of his fellow Mounties helped him sit. The other three men worked to calm the six horses, especially the one that had been bitten.

Harmon and Davis closed in on the Mounties, and Harmon said something, gesturing with his hands, seeming to offer his help. But as he got closer, he pulled a weapon from his belt, and Davis did the same.

Realene screamed and grabbed at the door handle, thinking she'd try to jam her knife into the mechanism, but the door swung open.

That asshole Davis had left it unlocked.

She tumbled out onto the icy road and watched as Harmon and Davis opened fire on the six Mounties, dropping them one by one. Tranquilizer darts protruded from the fallen officers' necks.

When the colonel looked back to the van, he saw Realene had escaped and shouted for Davis to respond.

Realene looked around her, thought of making a sprint for the trees, but the memory of the wolves stopped her.

The van.

It was still running.

She would take it and drive, get them all out of there. Big Kev knew all the back roads, even those not on a map. This was their chance.

She turned to charge for the driver's seat, but immediately froze, gasped at what she saw. Big Kev was slumped over in the back of the van, a smear of blood on his forehead. Trish stood in the road, a gun pointed at Realene.

"Where'd you get that?" she asked.

The weapon was steady in Trish's bound hands. "It was Birdie's."

"Please, you don't want to do this."

"You're right." Her gaze locked on something behind Realene.

A shot sounded, and pain pierced Realene's shoulder blade. She felt dizzy, and her vision started to blur. "No," she managed before everything went dark.

# Twenty-Four

**REALENE WOKE IN** bed, gasping for breath. The memory of the world tilting, her friends knocked out in the back of the van as she fell to the icy ground, was still fresh in her mind. Where was she? A thin strip of light pierced the darkness of the room she found herself in, coming from beneath a door. Her eyes adjusted. Wood-paneled walls… Nirvana posters… Anatomy diagrams and high school honors…

She was back her in bedroom.

In Demise, North Dakota.

She shoved off her comforter, the one her Oma had knitted, and whipped open the insulated curtains that covered the bay window. Daylight streamed inside, and she squinted at the bright blanket of sparkling snow that covered the field behind her house and the meteor crater. She threw open her bedroom door.

The clang of a pan being pulled from the cupboard and placed on the stove sounded above the din of conversation and canned laughter from the TV. Sounds she hadn't heard combined since before Ma got bad, when she still cooked.

She sucked in a pained breath, made herself move down the hall and into the kitchen, stopping just past the edge of the tile.

Colonel Harmon faced the stove. He wore her dad's apron over his uniform, which said, "Best Flippin' Dad Ever" above an illustration of a spatula.

"Take that off," she said.

He gestured toward the dining chair closest to her. "Sit. You must be hungry."

"Where are they? What did you do to them?" She balled her hands into fists.

"We'll get to that," he said, his face expressionless. "Sit. Down."

She wanted to scream at him, punch him, tear his eyes out or at least try, but then something brushed her ankle.

Pumpkin.

The urge to cry rose up so fast she could hardly swallow it down. "Punky." She scooped him up and slung him over her shoulder, pressing her face into his soft fur, inhaling the scent of him. He purred and bumped his face in her hair.

"Took the liberty of picking him up for you." The colonel slid something from the pan onto a plate and turned off the stove before removing her dad's apron and hanging it back on the doorknob of the little pantry beside the stove where it had been for the last three years. She'd gifted it to him for Father's Day one year, and it still smelled of him, of his signature kraut burgers.

She gave Pumpkin one more squeeze before lowering him to the floor. He rushed past the colonel, giving a short hiss as he passed.

"Doesn't like me much."

"He's a good judge of character." She sat in the chair, back rigid.

The colonel set a plate on the table. The smell of the grilled peanut butter and grape jelly sandwich caused her stomach to grumble, and she tried to remember when she last ate.

"What day is it?"

"Tuesday." He sat down in the chair beside her. "Eat. I know you're hungry."

Starving would be more accurate, but she couldn't trust anything from him. Might be drugged.

"There's nothing in the food. Besides, I could've given you anything I wanted while you were out."

She looked for silverware, but of course a sandwich didn't require any. Smart. She definitely would have tried to stab him.

His lips twitched in a smile, as if he knew what she was thinking.

She considered smashing the plate over his head, but she had to play this out, had to find out where the others were, if they were okay. He couldn't tell her anything if she beat him to death, as satisfying as that might be.

Realene took a bite, chewed, swallowed. Didn't allow herself to think about whether it was good or bad. Her body needed food, and she needed Harmon to talk.

"Are you familiar with bees?" he asked.

"Uh, yeah, I know what bees are." She took another bite, forced the gooey peanut butter concoction down.

"When one queen dies, another takes her place. Remarkable creatures."

Another bite. Chew, swallow. Try not to gag. Definitely don't spit it in his face.

"After that day, the Meteor Murders, I guess we're calling it now, we managed to save a few prairie dogs, extracted specimens, but we couldn't get the creatures to replicate, couldn't get them to breed."

She forced herself to swallow down a bite of her sandwich, gagged a little. "Breed?"

"At first, we thought they used their hosts to reproduce, but that's only to spread, to increase in number. They reproduce through their queen, which you killed."

"You're welcome." She tore another bite from her sandwich.

"Only a temporary problem. Like bees, a new queen was chosen among the remaining specimens, but there's a limit to how many spawn she can produce, and we needed more. Then we discovered there was another piece of the meteor," Harmon said. "Having been separated from their queen upon entry into Earth's atmosphere, the worms north of the border went into hibernation. Apparently, their telepathic connection has geographic limitations. After introducing the queen to the hibernating worms, something incredible happened. The Winnipeg worms woke up. Thousands of them."

"Why is that a good thing? Why do you want more?"

"Why do you think?" he asked.

"If movie villains have taught me anything, you want to use them, control them. Make them a weapon." Her stomach turned and she gulped down a drink of water from the glass beside her plate. All that time she thought he was helping the town, helping her, but he'd been creating his own little monsters.

"Not just any weapon. A weapon to end all weapons. A weapon to end all wars. Imagine defeating an enemy without firing a single shot. Wars can't be fought if the soldiers don't remember why or who they're fighting. Hell, with enough testing, perhaps one day we can engineer a worm that will make an enemy combatant forget how to fire his gun. We're not there yet, but with controlled aggression, we can create our own super soldiers tomorrow." He leaned forward in his chair. "The worms changed everything, advanced our research by decades."

"And what happens when the soldiers you infect just start killing each other instead?"

Harmon shrugged. "There'll be casualties along the way, there always are, but it's the price we pay for progress."

Was he just telling her all his secrets to brag before killing her? She put the uneaten portion of the sandwich back on the plate, shoving down the urge to vomit. "You know you're evil, right?"

His brow furrowed, as if her words had actually affected him. "I never meant for you to get involved in any of this."

"You infected Nate." She pushed the plate away.

"For good reason." He squeezed the bridge of his nose. "After Calvin was bitten, it appeared those who'd been infected before were immune to any side effects. But I had to test it to be sure."

"Calvin came up there to see what you were doing, to prove you were a liar." Now he was probably dead or detained as a lab rat in some kind of secret facility where no one would ever find him.

Harmon gave a smug smile. "And ended up helping me instead. Between him and Nathan, we now know that infecting subjects twice is the key to eliminating side effects, yielding us carriers that can spread the strain but not be affected themselves."

"But why Nate? Why not one of your soldiers?"

"They would know what we were attempting. We needed a subject who would give us a genuine, objective result. And Nathan was a convenient choice."

She pressed her fingers to her eyes until she saw spots.

"He was supposed to be infected and cured in a controlled environment," Harmon continued. "We'd already extracted enough alien DNA to develop Omega and Beta strains for testing."

"Omega and Beta?" Seriously, he sounded like a super villain from some ridiculous movie. But this was real life. "Strains of worms?"

"Engineered from the original to accentuate certain characteristics. Omega for aggression, Beta for memory loss."

"Irene."

He took her plate and put it in the sink. "Sergeant Birdie infected her. We hadn't planned on her being involved at all, but we needed to test the Beta strain, and it seemed fitting. Better than she deserved, really."

There was a time Realene would have agreed but seeing Irene like that was brutal. She'd been so overwhelmed and scared, so much like Ma was the last year of her life. No one deserved that. And Realene had to watch her die, watch her give her life just like Ma had, which really fucking sucked.

She stared daggers at Harmon. He really thought that what he was doing was okay, justified even. "What have you done with Nate and Kev? Are they even alive? And where's Calvin?"

"They're fine."

"Just like Irene and Sophia are fine, right? How can I trust you?"

"I suppose you can't."

"So, what now, are you going to kill me too?"

"No. I promised your father I would protect you, and I intend to keep that promise. I don't want any more casualties in your family. Not after what happened to your dad, your mom…"

"What do you mean, casualties? Dad died of lung cancer and Ma was shot by the Reverend."

The colonel frowned. “Right.”

Had he said more than he intended?

Experiments. Specimens. Secret military facilities.

“You...you’ve done this before.” Realene remembered her dad talking about exposure, about the things that contributed to his cancer. She thought he’d been talking about Agent Orange. “You experimented on my dad?”

The colonel squared his shoulders. “They volunteered. They understood the risks.”

She choked out a laugh. “Risks.” She still remembered those final months, how much pain he was in. How he struggled to even breathe. She remained convinced the whole ordeal was what pushed Ma over the line, sent her dementia into warp speed. “Wait, you say *they* volunteered? Who’s they?”

Harmon looked at the floor. He was confident in his convictions about everything else, but not this.

“Ma?” she asked.

The dementia. It came on so fast. And there was no family history.

He said they’d been trying and failing to develop technology to wipe someone’s memory for years.

The colonel looked up, his own gaze steely. “They volunteered.”

They volunteered.

Not to lose their memories. Not to die. Not to leave her all alone. She couldn’t believe that. He’d tricked them, manipulated them. She had no doubt.

“It was after they found out she was pregnant...with you. Needed the extra income, stability for their new little family,” he said. “They wanted the best for you.”

Realene lashed out, punching him in the face. She felt the satisfying crack of his nose, of bone snapping. Pain throbbed through her hand, but she wanted it, savored it. She pulled back to punch him again, but he grabbed her by both wrists, holding her at bay as blood leaked down his face. “Calm down.”

“Where’s Nate? What have you done to them?” she yelled, straining against his hold, but he had her in a vice grip. No matter how much she twisted and struggled, he just held her there. It was the same tactic her dad used when she'd throw a temper tantrum as a kid. He'd hold her while she cried and kicked and tired herself out.

Her body trembled with exhaustion, threatening to collapse, and Harmon was not her dad. His embrace wasn't loving; it was repulsive. "Let go of me."

After a moment, he did, shoving her away from him. Realene hit the dining table at an angle, one hip screaming from the impact. She breathed through the pain, and it faded to a throbbing ache.

"Where are they?" She was done playing along with his grand confession, letting him distract her from what was really important.

He grabbed a dish towel, white and dotted with little carrots and tomatoes, and wiped the blood from his face before discarding the towel on the counter. "Trish, come in here," he said.

A shuffle sounded from the entry room, and Trish appeared in the living room, hands in her coat pockets.

Realene gaped at her. She'd been there that whole time. Listening. "You bitch." Anger burned in her gut. She was tired, but not so tired she couldn't get one good punch in on the girl.

Not that it would do any good.

The colonel grabbed Trish's arm, yanking her into the kitchen. "Give her the solution."

Trish pulled a clear plastic vial from her pocket and uncapped it. Her blonde hair had been pulled back in a tight bun, and her face was gaunt. Her sundress and leggings had been exchanged for too-big fatigues.

"What's in there? Which one is it?" Realene asked, staring at the vial, at the liquid that sloshed inside.

"Beta."

After all that, he was just going to wipe her memory. "Why the hell did you tell me all that? Just wanted to brag or something?"

"I thought you might understand that this is all part of something bigger, something important."

"Jesus. You know you're not the hero, right?" she said, twisting his words about her against him.

His face flushed. "I recall you saying you were jealous of those who'd lost their memories, wished you were able to forget what happened," he said. "Killing Brooke. Getting your mom killed. Now Irene and Sophia, too."

Her throat closed tight. She tried to swallow but couldn't.

"Now's your chance. We'll give it a day, then cure you."

She managed to suck in a shaky breath. "Right. You're doing me a favor, yeah?"

"It's a win-win." He pulled his weapon and cocked it, aiming it at her head, the alternative painfully clear. "You'll forget all of this, too."

"Drink it," Trish said, holding out the vial. The liquid was black, no sign of this new strain of worms, but Realene knew they were in there, would soon be coating her tongue and throat, filling in the whites of her eyes. Eating away, bit by bit, at her memories.

"Why are you doing this, working with him?" She shivered from a combination of cold and fear.

"I have no choice." Trish nudged Realene's chin up and tipped the vial into her mouth.

Realene gagged as the tasteless liquid hit her throat, thought of spitting it out but then what? A bullet to the head? Her blood splattered across Ma's funeral program?

Pumpkin gave a meow and twined around her ankles, as if reminding her he was still there, still needed her. She forced herself to swallow as tears leaked down her cheeks.

# Twenty-Five

**REALENE HELD THE** infectious liquid in her mouth, hoping for a chance to spit it out when they weren't looking. Trish reached out and plugged Realene's nose, forcing her to swallow.

"Used to use that trick on Mindy with cough medicine." Trish capped the vial and stuck it back in her pocket, refusing to meet Realene's eyes as if ashamed. She should be, traitorous bitch.

The substance moved down Realene's esophagus, and she wondered how long it would take to begin eating away at her memories. In her lowest moments, she had wished for this. Wished for the bad memories to magically disappear. But now the good ones would go with them, and so would her ability to help her friends. Her knowledge of what a monster Harmon was.

She'd go back to thinking of him as some sort of surrogate father, would be even more reliant on him with her memories gone.

"Let's go," Harmon said.

Trish walked through the living room and into the entry way.

Harmon rested his hand on Realene's shoulder, his touch burning her through her shirt. "This is all for the best."

"Where are they?" Realene asked, smacking his hand away. "What are doing with them? Are they even alive?"

He ignored her question, grabbing his coat from the back of one of the kitchen chairs and putting it on.

Bile stung her throat. "I hate you."

"For now."

Trish came back into the living room holding Realene's coat. "Put this on. It's cold in here." She moved behind Realene and finagled the coat onto her arms and over her shoulders.

Trish and Harmon them left, a frigid gust of wind whipping in through the front door as it opened, then slammed closed.

Realene went to the small entry room window that looked out on the driveway and pulled back the curtain. A sedan with a man she didn't recognize in the driver's seat was parked across the street. He gave a slight salute, like, "Yes, I see you, better stay put." She closed the curtain, catching a glimpse of the mood ring on her finger. Black as that liquid in the vial.

Pumpkin meowed from the doorway to the living room.

She picked him up, cradling him in her arms in a way he'd only ever tolerated from Ma. Today, he didn't struggle. She carried him to the recliner and set him down on Ma's afghan. He tenderized the blanket, then turned in a circle and laid down, settling his face on his outstretched paws. She smiled at the memory of him facing off against Murray the tiger at Lake Sauer, confronting a giant monster to protect her and Nate. The bravest of all of them that day. It was another memory she'd soon forget.

Ma and Dad beamed from their wedding photo on the wall, her so young and beautiful in her simple white dress and him so distinguished in his uniform. Starting their new life together.

About a year before her dad died, she woke in the middle of the night to the sound of someone crying and found him in the kitchen. She thought he was drinking again, but there was no sign of alcohol. He held her and sobbed and said he was sorry again and again.

Realene didn't know it then, but he'd just been diagnosed with cancer, and seeing him like that broke something inside her, shifted how she saw the world.

She'd assumed he was apologizing for getting sick, for leaving her and Ma.

Maybe he was sorry for saying yes to whatever the colonel did to him.

Dad's cancer. Ma's dementia. It was all Harmon's fault. He'd used them without hesitation. Probably thought he was being merciful toward Realene by wiping her memories, when really he was just sacrificing her as part of his grand experiments, like he had her parents.

Beside the photo hung an ugly macrame owl she made at camp one summer, which Ma declared beautiful and insisted on displaying prominently. Nate made a frog, which was even uglier. She wondered if Sophia ever displayed it, ever told him it was beautiful.

Realene snatched the owl from its hook and tore at the strands of yarn, unraveling them until it was just a bundle of string and a few sticks. Nate had saved her so many times, and she'd completely failed him. She agreed they should go to Harmon for help, was convinced he'd protect them, even after finding out about the secret warehouse. Kev tried to warn her. Told her of Calvin's suspicions, but she wouldn't hear it, wouldn't believe it. Now Harmon had them. And Sophia, who followed Realene to expose the Colonel, was dead.

Calvin might be dead already. And what about Ana and her dad? They'd notice Big Kev was missing. The colonel would have to take care of them, too, if he hadn't already. Big Kev had just been trying to prove his dad wasn't crazy, and because of Realene, both he and his dad might end up dead.

She paced the living room.

Maybe there was still time before she lost her memory to go after Harmon, storm the base, do something to try and save them. No. With that guard outside, she wouldn't get past the end of her own driveway. Realene wished she could go back to the moment Trish had tipped that vial into her mouth and spit it back into that bitch's face, make Harmon shoot her instead. At least then this would be over.

No. Her dad never gave up. He fought until the very end

And Ma died so Realene could live. She wouldn't just give up. She had to fight.

She grabbed the small memo pad and pencil by the phone, the one Ma used to write herself little reminders, and sat down at the table to capture her own thoughts before they were gone. She wrote about Harmon and what he'd done, who he was. Her scrawl was half cursive, half print, barely legible. She hoped future-Realene would still be able to understand the notes she left herself, and that Harmon wouldn't find and destroy them.

When she finished writing, she took down the wedding photo from the wall, hid the notebook inside the back of the frame, and rehung the photo in the same spot.

Wind rattled the trailer's corrugated steel exterior, the cold seeping into Realene's bones. Was it just the weather, or was that part of the infection taking hold, taking each little memory, freezing it solid and then smashing it to bits that melted and drained away forever?

"Remember the notebook," she chanted to herself. "Remember. Remember."

She shoved her hands in the pockets of the coat Trish had put on her and felt a piece of paper in the right one, tucked beside her glove. She pulled it out and unfolded it. A child's drawing, one from the box of mementos Ma saved. Little Realene had drawn a crude picture of her, Ma, and Dad standing beneath a circular orange sun. Nate was there, too, and so was Pumpkin. Just a kitten then.

Writing, done in purple crayon, covered the back, visible through the white page as she turned it over.

*Switched the vial you're not infected*
*Nate's at Steele AFB okay for now please help him*
*Tell him I'm sorry I love him*
*Before the warehouse Harmon said he has my sister*
*She's alive*
*I had no choice I can't lose her again*

*Trish*

*Not infected.* A relieved laugh escaped Realene's mouth, and Pumpkin raised his head to glare at her.

Trish had saved her.

Realene moved to the stove and turned on the burner, lit the corner of the paper on fire. It caught and spread, eating Trish's words, eating the childhood drawing of her family when they were happy. She dropped the burning message in the sink, watching it burn and turn to ash, then rinsing what was left down the drain.

She grabbed the counter, gripping it hard. That bastard Harmon had been outsmarted. Trish gave Realene another chance to save everyone she failed. To make it all right. Her vague reflection above the sink showed a feral grin, one with teeth.

Her smile wilted. She didn't actually know if everyone else was okay. Trish only mentioned Nate, and he was being held at the Air Force Base, which had armed soldiers. There was no way she could get past them. Even if she did, how would she know where they were keeping Nate or the others?

"Dammit." She slammed her hand on the counter.

A loud crash sounded outside, and she rushed into the living room to peek out the curtains. The sedan parked across the street had been hit, rammed head on. Colonel Harmon's henchman got out and started yelling at the other driver, who still sat in their vehicle.

"Serves you right, asshole," Realene mumbled.

A light tapping noise sounded down the hall to her bedroom, and she whipped her head toward the sound.

It came again.

She crept through the kitchen and down the hallway.

Another *tap, tap, tap*.

Someone knocking.

There was no window that offered a view, but whoever it was had avoided the front door for a reason. It had to be Trish. She must have gotten away, come back to help.

Realene pulled the door open, but it wasn't Trish on the other side, it was Ana, who spilled inside, then closed the door behind her. She wore a black stocking cap pulled low, and her coat was zipped up to cover half her face.

"Shit," she said. "I hope they didn't see me."

"You're not dead," Realene said, grinning. "Wait, what are you doing here?"

"It's my job to get my dumbass brother out of jams, remember?" Ana unzipped her coat, revealing a walkie talkie clipped to her waistband. She walked through the kitchen and living room, plopping down on the couch. "How'd you like my distraction?"

"You did that?" Realene asked, sitting down beside Ana.

She batted her eyelashes. "Sure did."

The relief at not being alone, at having someone to help so she didn't have to figure this out all alone swelled inside her like a giant soap bubble, getting bigger and bigger until it burst with a pop. Realene leaned forward and threw her arms around Ana, then pulled away quickly. "Sorry."

The other girl raised her eyebrows. "Guess you're happy to see me."

"Very." So much had happened, Realene didn't know what to say first, where to start. "How did you know to come?"

"A dude showed up at the house a few hours after I left you guys at the hotel, said he was with the RCMP." Ana snorted a laugh. "Yeah, right. Asked if we'd seen Kev, barged in and searched our place and everything."

"Were you hurt?"

"Nah. They took off quick when dad said he'd call the real RCMP, and we bailed as soon as they left, hid out at a friend's until the storm passed. Then I saw the hotel was all cordoned off. Official story was that a fight broke out at the bar, and the hotel had some kind of gas leak."

"There was another outbreak," Realene said. She explained how Nate unknowingly spread the worms, how they'd escaped to the cabin and been followed by the cult. Her voice broke as she first described Irene dying, and she full on cried when she recounted what happened to Sophia.

"We checked the cabin after the storm passed and they got the roads cleared, figured that's where Kev would go if he needed a place to hide out," Ana said. "Never seen the place so clean, they must've sent somebody in to cover up the mess."

Realene stared at her hands, which were clasped in her lap. "I'm sorry for all this, Ana. It was my idea to call the colonel. Kev tried to stop me, but I wouldn't listen."

"Hey, I make it point never listen to Kev, so…"

Realene appreciated the attempt at a joke but couldn't bring herself to laugh. "Now he has Nate at the base, and probably Kev, too. I don't know if they're okay. They might be dead, and it's all my fault." She squeezed her eyes closed against the tears and explained how she'd woken up to find the colonel and Trish, what she learned about her parents, and about the note Trish had left.

"That asshole." Ana shook her head. "And poor Trish. I mean, it sounds like she did some really messed up stuff, but I kind of get why."

"Yeah." Realene wouldn't excuse what Trish had done, but she understood. Given the same choice, the chance to have her ma back, she wondered if she would've been strong enough to resist. And Trish risked a lot to switch the vial. "So, what do we do now? I can't just waltz onto an Air Force base."

"We might have some help with that." Ana peeked through the gap in the curtains, then unclipped the walkie talkie from her waistband. "Come in Flint, this is Ana."

Realene raised an eyebrow. *Flint, as in cowboy UFO guy?*

"Go ahead Ana."

"We're a go. Meet us at Calvin's."

"Ten four."

"You're working with the Alien Alliance?" Realene looked outside, saw that two tow trucks had already hooked cables to the cars from the accident and were towing them away.

"They've been keeping an eye on things here since Kev left." Ana walked toward the entry room.

Realene was still wearing her coat and quickly put on her boots. "Keeping an eye, how? I thought they were just a bunch of nuts."

"Oh, they're nuttier than a Snickers bar, but they come in handy sometimes. They've been watching your place and Calvin's since Kev left, plus watching the base." Ana zipped her coat up, covering her face. "And we've got a secret weapon. Come on."

# Twenty-Six

**"WHAT DO YOU** mean secret weapon?" Following Ana, Realene closed the door behind her and rushed down the porch steps and across the yard toward the driveway. She surveyed the road but didn't see any sign of Harmon's goons. "And what did they see at the base?"

Ana strode around the front of Calvin's trailer, stopping beside the empty driveway. "They're posted up in the woods surrounding the base. Saw the colonel and a caravan of unmarked vehicles arrive yesterday, including a cargo van. Two people were dragged out of the van, and based on their descriptions, it was Kev and Nate. Oh, and a dog."

Realene wanted to sob in relief. "They're okay."

"As of yesterday." Ana's forehead creased with concern.

"The colonel said Calvin was accidentally infected, I bet they have him there, too."

A car turned in at the trailer park entrance to drive toward them, and Ana waved.

The car pulled into the driveway. Flint was in the driver's seat, and a beefy guy was in the passenger seat. Kev and Ana's dad. He got out and walked over to Realene with a pronounced limp. He gripped her by the shoulders and looked her straight in the eye. She cringed, readying herself for him to berate her for putting Kev in danger. Instead, he said, "We won't let those bastards get away with this," and pulled her into a bone-crushing hug.

"Come on, Dad, let her breathe," Ana said.

"Sorry." He pulled away and offered his hand, which swallowed Realene's whole. "You were just a little thing last time I saw you. It's Mac."

Realene smiled. "As in Big Mac?"

"How did you know?" He let go of her hand and pulled his daughter into an equally bearish hug. "How you holding up, Ana banana?"

His use of an adorable but embarrassing nickname made Realene's heart ache for her dad.

"I'll feel better once Kev's home." Ana extracted herself.

Flint got out of the driver's seat and walked around the back of the car, tipping his cowboy hat to Realene in greeting.

"You ready for the secret weapon?" Ana asked. She angled her head toward the car, where Flint had popped the trunk.

Birdie sat up, sporting a black eye, a mangled ear from Mrs. Olson's bite, and a bandaged hand from punching the bus window.

"What the hell is he doing here?" Realene reached in her pocket for her knife, ready to stab the guy if he tried to attack, but it was gone. Harmon must've taken it.

Flint helped Birdie from the trunk and shoved him toward Calvin's front door. "Don't worry, little lady. I took a few fast corners to give him an extra roughing-up."

The men started up the walk to Calvin's trailer.

"You know he's a spy for Harmon, right?" Realene said.

"He *was* a spy for Harmon." Ana held open the door, ushering Realene inside and locking the door behind them. "Now he's a spy for us. A double agent."

"Why would he do that?" She blinked rapidly, her eyes adjusting from the bright afternoon sun to the dim light of the trailer.

At the center of Calvin's trailer was a folding table, blueprints spread out across it.

Ana stripped off her coat, throwing it on the couch. "Tweety, tell her why you came to us."

"It's Birdie," he said, giving her a glare, then turning to Realene. "I never wanted that shit assignment, being forced to spend day and night with those goddamn crazies. But I never meant to kill anyone. Irene—she wasn't supposed to die. My dad was in the service, granddad too. Two Purple Hearts and a Silver Star between them. Lost my dad last year." He cleared his throat. "All I ever wanted was to follow in their footsteps, make them proud."

"Harmon said the worm venom would make us stronger, better than our enemies. But soldiers are supposed to be calm, controlled." His hands trembled and he curled them into fists. "I went completely berserk. Couldn't control myself, just wanted to rip apart whoever got in my way. He turned me into a monster. I can't let him to do that to my brothers in arms."

"How altruistic." She studied his face. "That's it? Really?"

"He knew I was out there. Infected. Made no attempt to save me. That's against the creed; you don't leave a fallen soldier behind." He fixed her with a cold stare that didn't suit his baby face. "I want to watch him die."

Realene narrowed her eyes, still not trusting him. "You and I have that in common, then."

"My turn. Why should I trust you?"

She scoffed. "He tried to wipe my memory and kidnapped my friends."

"But not you. He let you go." He studied her. "When you caught me on the phone at that gas station, I was talking to Harmon. You know what he said? That you were to be protected at all costs. So, what's so special about you?"

Realene didn't like the way he was looking at her, like a bug under a microscope. "He killed my dad and gave my mom dementia as part of his experiments."

"So? I'm guessing he's done that to a lot of people. Plenty with kids."

"Dude, I don't know, and we have more important things to do right now than trying to understand the motivations of a psychopath. He has my friends, and I will not let them die. Are you gonna tell me how you're planning to get us in there, or what? Because I'm going either way."

Birdie considered this, then said, "Come on." He led her to the table where Mac and Flint stood.

"This is a blueprint of the base. We saw the prisoners unloaded here," Flint said, pointing at the rear of the facility.

"How did you get this?" she asked.

Flint winked. “We have our ways.”

“That’s a decommissioned missile silo,” Birdie said. “It’s where Harmon’s been running his recent experiments.”

“Experiments?” Flint asked.

Birdie didn’t answer, just looked her way, leaving it up to Realene how much to reveal. She didn’t want to tell them more than she had to about the worms, but they needed help, and Flint was here for one very specific reason. She needed to give him what he wanted. “Using a recovered alien craft.” That was technically true. The meteor was a craft of sorts.

“Recovered alien craft.” Mac looked at Ana. “We’re going to get ’em this time, banana, expose ’em.”

She gave a tight-lipped smile. “The most important thing is getting Kev and Uncle Cal home.”

“They won’t be able to cover this up, won’t be able to do to them what they did to me.” He sat down at one of Big Kev’s computers.

Ana gnawed on her bottom lip, watching her dad.

Realene cleared her throat. “So, how are we going to get in?” she asked Flint.

“We’ve got a two-pronged approach.” Flint smacked Birdie on the back, hard. “First, infiltration. Tweety is going to get you in.”

“It’s Birdie,” he said. “There’s a one-room building above ground that’s unmanned. It houses the elevator for the silo.”

“And I called on some friends to help, cause a bit of a ruckus,” Flint said.

Mac looked up from the computer. “They just checked in, ETA two hours. We’re going today, this afternoon.”

A shiver raced up Realene’s spine. She was going to get her chance to save her friends, and she wouldn’t fail this time. If the colonel had kept them alive so far, it was to use them, and he wouldn’t hesitate to kill them if he thought he’d be stopped or exposed.

She remembered him standing proudly behind Senator Schmidt at the state capital as he talked about the importance of Steele Air Force Base. How would the senator feel if he knew the colonel was running a secret experiment on the base, was planning to turn U.S. soldiers into rabid guinea pigs?

Realene took a seat beside Mac at the other computer and pulled up Netscape. She searched for the site that had the list of their elected officials and contact information.

"What are you doing?" Ana asked, coming to stand behind her.

"Getting us a little insurance policy." She logged into her Hotmail and started typing an email to Senator Schmidt. The guy seemed like an asshole politician who'd leveraged the tragedy in Demise for his own gain, but politicians were extremely wary of scandal. He campaigned on his support of the armed forces, and she'd bet he wouldn't want to be implicated in secret experiments on the troops, especially if he was actually in on it. Might even see exposing such a thing as good for his re-election campaign.

She attached Kev's photos of the Canadian landing site, as well as the articles about the riot and gas leak at the Holidome. Schmidt would probably think she was a crackpot, but if Birdie betrayed them or things went badly at the base and the colonel won, she wanted someone to know the truth. She scheduled the email to send in two hours.

**SITTING IN THE** back seat of Flint's car, Realene couldn't keep still, kept checking her pockets. Stun Gun. Pepper spray. Flashlight. Surgical mask. No gun, though one had been offered. She'd never handled one, was afraid she'd end up shooting herself. The stun gun would have to be enough. Plus, it served double duty as a worm killer.

Beside her, Ana seemed equally nervous, her knee bouncing. They both wore blue scrubs beneath their winter coats and had their hair braided and tucked beneath surgical caps. It was decided they'd be more believable as medical personnel than military, since a few doctors and nurses worked in the facility where their friends were being held.

The one outlier in her outfit was her combat boots. More accurately, her dad's combat boots. They were a bit big but fit well enough over double socks. She hoped they'd give her a little of his bravery and courage, help her remember that she was doing all this not just for her friends, but for him and Ma too. For everyone Harmon had used and discarded.

Plus, steel toes wouldn't hurt if—or more likely *when*—things went downhill. Realene was pragmatic, and she knew that this would not be easy, that people would get hurt and maybe killed today.

"I wish you'd let me do this alone," she said to Ana.

"No way."

"Here we are." Flint turned into the Aspen Vista RV Park, which sat a mile west of the Air Force base. The place would've normally been empty this time of year, as it wasn't yet warm enough for the types that summered by traveling across the country in their motorhomes.

Tonight, there were at least a dozen RVs of varying sizes parked in the snowy lot. They could've passed for your average road warriors, except every one of them boasted roofs covered with antenna and satellite dishes and bumpers plastered with stickers that said things like "My Other Car is a UFO" and "Unmask Area 51."

They parked, and the doors of the vehicles opened, people spilling out to meet Flint. There were little old couples, young guys, middle-aged folks who looked like they belonged at a PTA meeting, and even one family with young kids.

Flint got out to greet them, and they chattered excitedly, as if this was some kind of fun adventure.

"This isn't some kind of party. People might get hurt," Realene said, doubting the crowd's usefulness on such a dangerous mission.

Mac turned around in the passenger seat, pointed at the group. "Did you know Flint lost his wife when a bright light descended behind their home? That was twenty years ago now. Martha was her name. Disappeared without a trace."

"That's awful." She thought of him as such an easy-going guy, kind of kooky. She never imagined that sort of tragedy was what got him involved in the search for alien life.

"Sleep paralysis, missing time, hallucinations. Being cut off from your friends and family, laughed at, called crazy. These folks deal with some perilous stuff. We're not going to let anything stop us from exposing the truth."

"Okay, Mac," she said, thinking of everything he'd been through just for saying he saw a UFO.

He got out and joined the others, several of whom ran up to him like he was some kind of celebrity.

She and Ana followed, standing a bit away from Mac and his friends.

"Seems like he's in his element, huh?" Realene said, remembering what Ana said about them being more like fans.

"I just hope they don't do anything stupid while they're trying to expose the truth or whatever." Ana pulled a candy bar out of her pocket. "I, uh, brought you something for luck. Canadian Kit Kat. Way better than the American ones."

"Thanks." Realene held back the grin that wanted to split her face, tried to be chill. She stuck the candy in her pocket but kept hold of it. No one besides her parents had ever given her candy, except Nate.

Another car pulled into the RV park, a nondescript gray sedan. Birdie. He got out, and the gathered group quieted, watching him. They'd been told the plan, that he'd be coming, but clearly they had reservations about working with anyone from the military. Realene shared their concerns.

Flint gave a two-fingered whistle. "Time to saddle up, folks."

Ana went over and gave her dad a long hug, probably worrying they may not see each other again. Realene had tried to talk them into letting just her and Birdie infiltrate the facility, but Ana refused. Her brother and maybe her uncle were down there, too, and neither she nor Realene totally trusted Birdie.

Flint flagged them over to one of the RVs. "Come on, time to get your IDs. You come too, Tweety," he called.

They climbed up the set of fold-out steps, ended up standing squashed together in the walkway that bisected the vehicle, a kitchenette on one side and a narrow banquette on the other. A guy appeared from the rear of the RV, pushing aside the black curtain that blocked off the space. He wore safety goggles perched on the top of his head and a lab coat. A stereo played "Who's the Man" by House of Pain.

"This is Augie," Flint said. "The best in the Midwest."

"Come on now, best in the country," Augie said in a voice that sounded young. If the guy was a day past eighteen, Realene would be shocked. He pulled out two laminated Steele Air Force Base access badges with metal clips attached, giving one to Realene and one to Ana. Each had their actual photos on them but fake names. Realene recognized her picture as the same one from her driver's license, meaning he'd probably hacked the DMV.

Birdie pulled out his own badge and compared it. "Damn good match. You're sure the names will work?"

"The names are honest-to-God civilian government employees, according to their system." Augie winked at Realene, clearly thinking himself quite the criminal genius.

She had to admit, the Alien Alliance was more well-equipped than she'd anticipated.

"Always a pleasure working with you." Flint handed the kid a wad of bills. "You comin' out to see the action?"

"I prefer to remain in the background. Ladies," Augie said, inclining his head toward them, then pulling the safety goggles back down over his face and disappearing behind the curtain.

The group of them exited the RV and found the parking lot empty, expect for Flint and Birdie's cars. They shook hands with Flint and wished each other good luck all around. Adrenaline thrummed through Realene's veins, making her a bit shaky.

This was it. They were really going to infiltrate a heavily guarded Air Force Base.

Ana slid into the backseat of Birdie's car, but Realene stood at the open door, just inches from him. "You're risking your career, maybe your life, doing this."

"You're welcome," he said, giving her a very self-satisfied look.

"In case this is a set up and you're really working with Harmon, or you have some last-minute change of heart, you should know we've taken precautions."

"What are you talking about?"

"You ever see the movie *Hackers*?"

"That's the one with Angelina Jolie, right?"

"Uh-huh." Realene pointed at Augie's RV. "These guys may seem a little crazy, but they include some of the most talented computer programmers you'll ever meet. The kinds of people that could wipe out bank accounts, credit records, and lots of stuff even more secure than that. And they know everything about you, your family, and your friends."

His lips pressed into a line. "Are you threatening me?"

"Oh yeah. I thought that was clear. So, now's your last chance. Are we doing this?"

"I'm not backing out, and the only one I'm betraying is Harmon."

"Okay then." She climbed in the back seat beside Ana and closed the door.

Ana chuckled. "*Hackers*?"

"Seemed appropriate. It's a worm that eats up all the pennies in that one."

"Nice."

Birdie got in the driver's seat and made a U-turn in the gravel paved lot, then pulled onto the highway. Realene looked out the window, not really registering her surroundings. She repeated the very simple plan in her mind.

Get in, find Nate, Kevin, Calvin, and Trout, and smuggle them out in what would be a very cramped trunk as quickly as possible. Without getting caught, shot, or infected.

*Easy peasy,* as Ma would say.

Birdie pulled over onto the shoulder about half a mile before the entrance, and Realene raised the binoculars hanging from her neck. On the horizon, barren trees stretched across the snow-covered landscape, and a large, rectangular, stone monument sign announced the entrance to Steele Air Force Base. The caravan of RVs turned in one after another, then pulled in side by side so each row was three vehicles wide and blocking the road so no one else would be able to enter or leave.

A squat, brick guard booth sat before a tall, metal fence topped with barbed wire, and behind the fence were two three-story towers on either side of the entrance that led to the barracks and other on-base housing. She knew from visiting with her dad that both the booth and the towers held armed soldiers whose edict was to protect the base. She really hoped none of the people from the Alien Alliance got hurt, especially Mac, who was particularly enthusiastic.

The camouflage-clad soldier manning the booth came out, waving his hands over his head and standing before the front row of RVs. The RV doors opened, and their owners poured out, now looking much less normal than they had.

Many wore tinfoil hats or Halloween-style alien masks, and most carried poster-board signs with slogans like "We Have a Right to Know" and "Stop the Cover Up of Alien Life" and "UFOs are Real." The outfits were sort of an inside joke, not something they'd normally wear, but they'd have an immediate impact.

A guy with a portable video camera balanced on his shoulder strode up to the soldier. He'd be telling the man that footage of this was being broadcast live over the internet for everyone to see. A petite woman wearing a springy alien-eye headband raised a bullhorn, calling out to the crowd of a few dozen people, who started chanting. Flint was nowhere in sight, since he was leading the team looping around the rear of the base to surveil the missile silo facility.

"They're in place," Realene said, struggling to keep her voice steady.

Birdie pulled off the shoulder, driving back down the highway. Either he was giving her the silent treatment after her threat, or he was as nervous as she was.

"You okay?" Ana reached out, grabbed her hand.

Realene focused on the warmth of Ana's skin pressed against her own, but that just increased her nerves. "Not really. A little freaked out."

Birdie turned, heading down the side road that led to the other entrance to the base, the one used by most base personnel.

"Why? Just because we're about to infiltrate a military base filled with highly trained soldiers?" Ana asked.

"That, yes." A nervous giggle escaped her throat.

"This is it," Birdie said, turning into the side entrance, which was similar to the front, with a guard booth and metal fence topped with barbed wire.

Realene let go of Ana and straightened, trying to look calm and professional. Nurse-like.

They pulled up to the booth and Birdie rolled down his window.

The guard stepped from the booth and approached the car. "Identification please."

She and Ana handed their badges up to Birdie, who gave them to the guard, along with his own ID.

This was it. Birdie might just give them away, say they were holding him hostage or something. Or he could blow it by acting suspicious.

"Wait here," the guard said, taking their ID's back to the guard booth.

This entrance had a single gun tower, but that was enough to end their plan and possibly their lives. Birdie could have easily slipped a note in with their badges, revealing their true identities to the guards. Or the fake names might be flagged because Augie wasn't quite as good as he claimed to be.

The sniper could fire at the car, killing them all before they even knew what happened.

Ana shifted beside her, knee bouncing double-time.

How had Realene ever thought this plan would work? Birdie said he was back in the colonel's good graces, but Harmon was a suspicious man. He could have flagged Birdie as dangerous or restricted his access. But they couldn't back out now.

A voice came through over the radio from the guard booth, but she wasn't able to hear what was said.

The guard came back toward the car, seeming to move in slow motion. Her pulse pounded in her ears, roaring like crashing waves.

"Go ahead," he said, handing the badges back to Birdie.

He rolled up the window and handed the girls' IDs back to them.

The gate rattled open, and they pulled forward, entering the base.

"Jesus," Ana muttered.

They weren't in the clear. Birdie still had to drive them through the center of the base and back toward the rear edge, which held no barracks or other buildings, just the missile silo and connected buildings.

They passed other cars on the road, and a plane flew low as it headed toward the airstrip. The base wasn't that big, was crossable in less than five minutes, but every second seemed to take an eternity.

Sweat coated her back, probably giving Ana a healthy whiff of BO.

They finally approached the rear of the base, marked by the surrounding fence, and a small, squat white building that looked like one of those nondescript offices at a construction site. Except this one disguised an elevator that led to Harmon's secret testing facility.

No sirens sounded. No vehicles zoomed down the road after them.

They'd made it. Realene exhaled a long breath.

Birdie pulled up to the building and cut the engine. "Now comes the hard part."

# Twenty-Seven

**REALENE GOT OUT** of the car, stretching to release some of the tension gripping her muscles. Beyond the chain link fence that circled the base, an open expanse of grass dusted by snow stretched out for a good half mile. Beyond that were several clusters of trees, then sugar beet and potato farms. Flint would be out there somewhere, but she didn't see any sign of him.

A few hundred feet away from the building that housed the elevator was a blocky cement structure that was the top of the silo. It wasn't like one of the huge cylindrical grain silos that dotted the prairie. Missile silos were built into the earth, and this top structure would have opened to allow the loading or launch of a missile.

Realene checked her pocket, making sure she had her surgical mask. Once inside the facility, they'd cover their faces. A thumping sounded from the back of the car, and Birdie frowned, moving toward the trunk. The thumping sounded again, and a muffled voice said, "It's me. Let me out."

"You have got to be kidding me." Ana stomped around the car, grabbing the keys from Birdie's hand to unlock the trunk.

Mac crawled out, rolling his neck. "Damn. It's cramped in there."

Realene resisted the urge to scream in frustration.

"What the hell are you doing?" Birdie asked.

"I can help. You might need back-up."

"We were planning to sneak everyone out in that trunk," Ana said. "How are we going to fit you all now?"

Realene eyed the back fence. Could they climb it and run? No. A square sign with a lightning bolt symbol signaled it was electrified.

"Jesus Christ. Get inside before someone sees you." Birdie led them past two other cars, including one Realene recognized as Colonel Harmon's.

Her heartbeat thumped in her chest. She'd expected he'd be there, wouldn't trust this operation and its prisoners to anyone else, but part of her had held out hope they'd miss him. At least other personnel were unlikely to recognize her. Harmon would know her regardless of any disguise, would realize his memory wiping plan hadn't worked after all.

Birdie unlocked the building's front door and ushered them in.

She glimpsed a vehicle approaching on the road toward them, the gravel path's only destination. "What do we do now? About Mac?"

"We've got to hide him," Birdie said.

The building was just one room with an unoccupied desk at one end, a couple of chairs against the back wall, and a ficus plant in the corner. The end opposite the desk was dominated by a set of elevator doors.

"The desk… Go." Ana pushed her dad.

He barely fit behind the thing, and Realene glimpsed his feet through the gap between the bottom of the desk and the floor, but they had no other option.

Outside, the approaching vehicle slowed and parked.

Realene and Ana stood side by side, trying to block the view of the desk while Birdie leaned out the partially open door to greet the driver. "Lieutenant," he said.

Realene wanted to rush toward the elevator, to escape, but they'd be more likely to be followed that way. Instead, she waited, tried to stop her hands from trembling.

"Sergeant Birdie," the driver said. "Heard you were up north for Operation Arctic Fox."

"Was. Just got back."

The lieutenant peeked through the open door. "Who are these lovely ladies?"

Realene gave a sharp nod she hoped was a respectful greeting. Beside her, Ana clasped her hands behind her back, posture rigid.

"Med staff. Just escorting them below." Birdie gestured toward the elevator. "We should probably—"

"I was heading that way, too." The lieutenant stepped past Birdie and through the doorway, surveying both girls as he went.

Realene prayed he didn't look too closely and notice Mac hidden behind the desk, or they'd end up in military jail or worse.

An alert sounded and he pulled a cellular phone from his pocket. "Lieutenant Johnson."

He scowled as the other person spoke, then said, "How many?"

More muted talking, drowned out further by the roar of a plane taking off above them.

"I'll be right there."

The lieutenant went back the way he came, saying, "Some kind of crackpot protesters at the front gate. Come lend a hand once you're done here."

"Yes, sir." Birdie closed the building's door and locked it, waited a moment until they heard the lieutenant pull away. "Jesus, that was close."

Mac climbed out from behind the desk, and the three of them turned to glare at him. He stood taller. "I've been working to prove the existence of alien life for almost ten years. I won't give up now."

Realene turned to Ana, giving her a meaningful look. "He doesn't understand what he's dealing with." They couldn't let him down there. He didn't even know about the alien worms, would storm around looking for some kind of spaceship.

Ana faced Mac, her posture saying she would not be argued with. "You have to stay here, Dad."

He took her hands in his. "This is my chance. Maybe my only one."

"Dad, this isn't about you getting proof. It's about saving Kev and Uncle Cal and Realene's friend. Can't you see you've already put them all at risk with this stunt?"

"I didn't mean…" Mac dropped her hands. His brow knitted. "They're going to be okay."

"You're staying here, even if I have to shoot out your kneecaps," Birdie said. "We just have to hope no one finds you."

Mac's eyes strayed to the elevator doors. Realene did not trust him to go along with their plan, not after everything he'd done to get there.

She pulled Ana away from her dad. "You have to stay with him."

"What? No. I told you I'm going."

"We can't be sure he won't do something risky," she whispered. "You've got to keep an eye on him, keep him up here and out of our way."

"Shit." Ana glanced over her shoulder at her dad. "What do I do if someone comes?"

Birdie heard the question and said, "Act like he's your prisoner."

Mac slumped into one of the plastic chairs sitting against the wall.

Ana said, "I'm supposed to be a nurse."

"Just zip tie his wrists and say I asked you to watch him." Birdie pulled a zip tie from his pocket, handed it to her. "Say he's one of those protesters, and he made it into the base somehow."

"That might work," Realene said, thinking a protester was a good cover. "And hopefully no one will come, anyway. If we hurry."

"Let's go then. Now." Birdie strode toward the elevator door.

Ana pulled Realene into a tight hug. "Be careful."

"I will. You too." She went with Birdie. He inserted a key at the top of a silver panel on the wall. A single button lit up, and he pushed it before withdrawing his key. At least Mac wouldn't be able to follow.

She stepped into the elevator, turned to see Ana sitting beside Mac. Her wish to go alone had been granted. A wish she was really regretting, because it was just her and Birdie now.

Inside the elevator there were only two buttons: Up and Down. Birdie pushed the Down button, and Realene raised one hand in a wave as the silver doors slid closed.

**THE FREIGHT ELEVATOR** descended several stories below ground as Realene stood beside Birdie, very aware she was now stuck with him. No back-up. This place that once threatened the ultimate violence of nuclear war had been silenced, but violence never quiets for long. Harmon had decided it was the perfect location for his efforts to develop a different but equally evil weapon, one that very few in the military even knew existed.

Pressure and heat seemed to build inside the car, and she wasn't sure if it was claustrophobia at being trapped in a box beneath the earth or panic at the plan they were about to enact. A plan that offered only one means of escape. She thought almost fondly of their battle at Lake Sauer. Being surrounded by a horde of infected animals and people while being pursued by armed cult members seemed far less dangerous than this, probably because she'd had Nate by her side. With her best friend, anything seemed possible.

Her vision grayed, heart beating so fast she worried she might pass out. This was for him, to get him, Big Kev, and Calvin back. She had to keep it together.

She counted to five as she inhaled a deep breath and counted again as she blew it out. The doors slid open to reveal a deserted, dimly lit hallway. The air felt stale and heavy, and the awareness of the tons of earth above them was impossible to ignore. The corridor held two doors on either side and a blast proof door at the end of the tunnel, directly ahead.

When Birdie mapped-out the space, he'd explained that the blast proof door, which resembled the kind you'd see in a bank vault, was the lab and would be the hardest area to get into. He'd accompanied Harmon inside only once. It had originally been the launch control center for when the missile silo was active but was later converted to a workspace for the program's most sensitive experiments and concoctions. Birdie saw caged animals inside, but not human subjects. They were kept somewhere else.

Realene put on her surgical mask. Nothing to see here, just a nurse.

Birdie led them down the corridor, his steps slow and precise so as not to make a sound. They stopped at the door on the left, and Realene pressed her ear to it.

"I will not tolerate your disrespect," Harmon said, voice raised.

"I'm not in the habit of respectin' a donkey's backside," another man replied. It was Calvin. He was alive.

Realene locked eyes with Birdie, who gave a quick nod.

Footsteps approached the door from the other side. Harmon. He would soon open the door and see them.

Birdie shoved Realene toward the door on the opposite side of the hall. "Go."

Thankfully, the knob turned in her hand, and she entered, closing the door just as the colonel must have exited the other room and seen Birdie. "Sergeant Birdie."

"Colonel Harmon, sir."

Realene pressed her back to the inside of the door and scanned the dark space. The dim light on what looked like a microwave was visible at one end of the room atop a kitchen counter. And the large blocky shape nearer to her must have been an island.

"What are you doing here, Sergeant?" Harmon asked.

"I've been experiencing some lingering side effects, sir. I thought it important to report it right away, see if you want me to talk to the doc."

A soft sound came from the shadows at the other end of the room. Someone crying. A young girl.

"What side effects?" Harmon asked.

"Flashbacks. Of the things I did while infected, sir."

"We designed the Omega strain not to eliminate memory," Harmon said. "You should be proud of your actions in service to your country, even when there's brutality involved."

Realene crept away from the door, toward the sound of the crying person. The room started to come into focus. A small couch had been pushed against the back wall and piled with an end table, a lamp, and another ficus. Someone was a big fan of those.

Huddled shapes pressed against the wall to her right, bars enclosing them. In front of the bars, a person lay on the floor, curled up on their side.

Harmon and Birdie still spoke in the hallway, though their exact words were no longer audible farther from the door. Almost everything appeared grayed-out in the dark, but Realene could still distinguish that the person on the floor had bright blonde hair pulled back into a tight bun.

"Trish?" she whispered, pulling down her mask to reveal her face.

Trish sat up, giving a hiccuping sob. "What are you doing? Get out of here."

Something shifted behind the bars, gave a low grumble, a sort of growl.

Realene pulled a flashlight from her pocket and flipped it on, illuminating the figures.

"No." Trish lunged for the light, forcing the beam to focus on the ground.

But in that split second, Realene saw the people huddled against the wall behind the bars of one big cage. People showing muscle and bone where the skin of their faces had been raked or torn. Their growls worsened in reaction to the light, but they made no move to attack, maintaining their huddled poses. She recognized them at once as the infected, like the deer and prairie dogs she'd battled. Walking corpses.

One was a little girl. Just a child.

Birdie spoke from the hall, his voice carrying. A warning maybe.

Trish shoved Realene across the room, toward the kitchen island.

"Hide," she said, looking toward the door.

Realene dove behind the island, pressing her lips closed to silence the sound of her breathing.

The door opened, the overhead lights blazed on, and Harmon said, "What's going on in here?"

"I'm talking to my sister," Trish snapped.

The little girl was her sister. Mindy. The one Harmon told her was alive.

Realene pressed her eyes closed against the threat of tears.

"She can't understand you," Harmon said. "You know that."

"What is this?" Birdie asked.

"A test of the long-term effects of infection," Harmon said. "How long the original Alpha strain of worms will continue to ambulate a body."

Footsteps sounded, moving away from Realene's hiding place, and a high-pitched growl sounded. Human but not.

"How long have you kept them like this?" Birdie asked.

"Three months," Harmon said. "But I suspect the effects will last for years."

Realene wanted to puke. He was keeping these people chained up to watch them rot away like zombies.

Trish's voice broke. "He's had her like this since that night, caged-up like an animal. Worms eating away at every part of her."

A scuffle sounded. Realene held still, though she wanted to leave her hiding place and help Trish give Harmon a well-deserved beating.

"Calm down," Harmon said. "I understand you're upset, but there was nothing to be done for her. She was too injured to cure, would've died immediately. This way, she can offer something of scientific value."

*Scientific value.* Like Realene's parents. Like Nate. He didn't care who he had to hurt to get what he wanted.

"You don't know that," Trish said through sobs.

A soft click sounded. A gun cocking.

"What do you think you're doing, Sergeant?" Harmon asked.

"Detaining you, sir," Birdie said.

*Yes!* Realene wanted to cheer. Birdie really was on their side after all.

"Put down your weapon."

"You don't care who you have to sacrifice, do you?" he asked.

*Shoot him,* Realene silently chanted. *Shoot him. Now. Do it.*

"You do not want to do this, Sergeant."

"All that talk about making us stronger. Better soldiers. That's bullshit. You want to turn us into monsters," Birdie said.

A shout sounded, a grunt, and the gun went off.

Realene tensed, forced herself to remain still, to look straight ahead at the cheap wood cupboard.

Trish cried out, and there was a thump of something landing on the floor. Then came more sounds of struggle, the rustle of clothing, grunting that could have been Harmon or Birdie.

Another gunshot.

Realene covered her mouth, holding in the scream that wanted to break free. Her breath wheezed in and out through her nose. Too loud.

Trish's choked sobs filled the room.

She was alive. What about Birdie?

A deep huff sounded, a grunt as if someone were struggling to stand. "Clean this trash up," Harmon said, sounding winded.

"No," Trish said.

"Do it, or I'll make things more painful for your boyfriend."

The door opened, then slammed shut.

Realene crept around the far end of the island, peeked past the edge. Trish stood with her back against the wall beside the door, sobbing as she stared down at Birdie, who lay discarded on the floor.

# Twenty-Eight

**REALENE RAN OVER** to Birdie and knelt beside him. The entry hole of the bullet beneath his chin was small and neat, leaking the barest hint of blood. The exit hole, if it could even be called a hole, had torn through a chunk of his forehead and one eye, revealing a grotesque cavern of bone, brain, and muscle. Bloody goop leaked from the wound, staining the industrial carpet.

"I'm so sorry," she whispered. He'd done terrible things, but in the end, he had a moral line he wouldn't cross and gave his life to stand up to Harmon. Birdie turned out to be someone she could trust, and now he was gone. Leaving her by herself.

No… not by herself. Nate was here. Harmon had said so. But he'd threatened to make things more painful for him. More painful than what? What had her best friend been enduring?

No. She wouldn't think about that. She just had to find him.

With bile rising in her throat at the sight of Birdie's demolished face, she stuck her hand in his pocket and pulled out his keys. She put them in her pocket.

Trish remained against the wall, paralyzed.

Realene placed a hand on Trish's arm. "Come on, let's go." She'd send the girl up in the elevator, get her out before Harmon decided he no longer needed her.

"I'm not leaving Mindy. Not again."

Growling came from the cage, uninfected blood seeming to turn the infected restless. Realene has a clear view of Mindy now. She was beyond saving, the skin and muscle missing along one side of her jaw and showing skeletal teeth.

"Trish, listen to me. That's not Mindy, not anymore."

"Leave me alone." Trish's gaze focused on her sister.

"At least help me get everyone out. That's what you want, right? Why you left me that note?"

"They're across the hall."

"And Harmon?"

"He was shot in the foot. He'll be with the doctor in the lab." She shuffled toward the cages, arms wrapped around her middle.

Realene promised herself to come back for Trish, to drag her out if she had to. She opened the door a crack and checked the hallway. Empty. A trail of blood led to the closed blast door. Realene ran across and into the room where she'd heard Calvin.

The room inside was brightly lit and lined with five gurney beds on wheels, two of which held Calvin and Nate, their wrists and ankles tied down with buckled straps.

Realene slumped against the wall, relief washing away the fear that she would be too late, that she would fail them. They were alive. Still held captive, still in danger. But alive.

"Hot damn," Calvin said, smiling to display his pearly white dentures.

"Rea to the rescue," Nate said. He still wore the flannel he'd changed into after the fight at the cabin.

She couldn't speak past the tightness in her throat. "Hey," she managed. Clearing her throat, she did a quick survey of the rest of the room. Trout had been muzzled and tied to the base of one of three tall, silver cylinders with windows near the top that sat against the other wall. He whined and thumped his tail.

"Just a minute, buddy, I'm coming," she said.

Calvin was closest, and she unfastened the restraints at his feet, then moved to undo his hands, one of which was wrapped in a bandage that wound through a gap between his pointer and ring fingers.

"Are you missing a finger?"

"Goddamn beaver bit it clean off!"

"Shhh, they'll hear." She wondered if that was the same infected beaver that attacked the Mounties near the lake.

After she finished letting him loose, he sat up, swinging his skinny legs over the side of the gurney. Realene hugged him, his body bony in her embrace. "Sorry it took me so long to get here." He'd been held prisoner for two whole weeks.

She released him, and he ducked his head. "Ah. I knew you'd come eventually."

Realene moved to Nate, gripped his hand in hers. "You okay?" The question was loaded with all the unspoken things that had transpired within the past few days that would most definitely make him not okay.

"Had a kinda shitty spring break. Should've gone to Florida."

"Nah, they've got gators." She studied his eyes before starting on the buckle at his wrist. No sign of worms. "They cured you."

"Tried to bite one of 'em. Guess they decided they didn't want to risk me spreading anything. Are you…?"

"Worm-free." She finished with one wrist and started on the other.

"We heard gunshots," he said.

"Harmon killed Birdie. He's actually the one that got us in, turned double agent." She finished that restraint and Nate sat up, helping her with his ankles.

"Us?"

"Oh, Mac and Ana are here," she said to Calvin. "They're upstairs waiting for us."

"How'd you get away?" Nate asked. "Don't suppose Harmon is dead, too."

"Unfortunately not. In fact, he doesn't know I'm here."

Nate stood, rubbing at the scar on his hand that matched her own. "When I woke up and you weren't here… I thought he killed you, too."

"I told him 'No way,'" Calvin said. "Knew you wouldn't go out like that."

"Only because Harmon tried to wipe my memory instead, but Trish switched out the dose," she said. "She saved me, made it so I had a chance to get to you."

He nodded once, his face expressionless. "She okay?"

"She's not dead, but I wouldn't say she's okay." Even after everything Trish had done, Nate still cared about her, at least a little. "Harmon told her he had Mindy captive, and that she was alive. That's why she helped him."

"Mindy's alive?"

"No, no. Not really. She's infected. Has been this whole time. Harmon's trying to see how long they can last like that." Realene cringed at the image of that poor girl, her face showing glimpses of muscle and bone. He'd basically become Dr. Logan from *Day of the Dead*, complete with the zombie test subjects kept captive in an underground bunker.

"She was just a little kid," Nate said. He went over to Trout, who did an excited little doggie hop, and unfastened the muzzle, then untied the knot in the leash.

"Goddamn mad scientist." Calvin gestured toward the silver tubes. "Tryin' to raise the dead, too."

Realene moved to look through the window in the center cylinder, which was cold to the touch. Inside, she saw Brooke's face, one eye socket empty courtesy of a tire iron.

"Fuck," Realene blurted, stumbling away. That empty socket had somehow stared at her.

"He's keeping them frozen, wants to see if he can use the worms to reanimate people." Nate's forehead creased. "Guess it would be handy if soldiers kept fighting even after they're dead."

"Jesus." Brooke's mother was still holding out hope her daughter might be alive somewhere, but in no way could she have imagined something so terrible as this. Realene squeezed behind the cylinders and yanked the plugs from the wall socket. She couldn't save Brooke or the other innocent people in those tubes, but she could ensure they wouldn't be used for more experiments.

"Where's Big Kev? Is he okay?" she asked.

Calvin came over to stand beside her. "They took him to that lab. Don't know what they're doing to him in there."

"Shit." Realene had hoped they would escape before the colonel noticed, but she wouldn't leave without Big Kev. "We've got to find a way to get him."

"I'll run in there, distract them. Wack them with something." Nate yanked on the metal handrail of the gurney as if it would be easy to dislodge, but it stayed firmly attached. "You guys can follow me, grab Kev."

That sounded like the worst plan Realene had ever heard, basically wasn't a plan at all. "Harmon's got a gun. You want to get yourself killed?"

"We've got to try something," he said. "This is my fault. If I hadn't run from that warehouse, I would've been cured right away. Big Kev wouldn't even be here."

"I don't know," Calvin said. "If I hadn't gone to investigate and gotten infected by that damn beaver, that Harmon would've never tried to infect you to start."

Realene looked at Nate. "See? This is actually all Calvin's fault. He never should've gone up to Canada."

"Hey, that's not what I meant." Calvin scowled.

"It's a joke, Calvin. None of us is to blame," she said, and finally believed it. "Do you know who is?"

"Harmon," Calvin said proudly, as if he'd just guessed a trivia question correctly. "I tried to warn ya. I knew he was up to no good."

She rolled her eyes. "We get it, you were right. Now we need a real plan. Trish is still across the hall. I think we should see if we can get her to help. Harmon still trusts her a little, and she might know what's happening with Kev."

"Dream team back in action," Calvin said.

Realene didn't chastise him for being excited about what was likely their imminent deaths. He deserved a little happiness after being kept prisoner. She cracked the door and checked the hallway. Still empty. "Come on."

They hustled across the hall and through the other door, closing it softly behind them.

Trish stood with her back to them, facing the cage that held her sister. Not noticing she had company, she gripped the bars and swung the metal cage door open.

Mindy emitted a growl and lurched from the cage, wobbling like a colt learning to walk. A shackle had been clasped around her ankle, but her stripped foot slipped out of it, leaving the chain behind. Her legs showed exposed bone and muscle, and she wore a tattered, red velvet dress. A holiday dress.

Trish opened her arms wide, welcoming her little sister into a hug. "Mindy, it's me. It's your big sister."

Mindy took another step, reached out with hands curled into claws. Behind her, the two others in the cage tugged against their shackles, straining for the open door.

"I came back for you," Trish said. "I came back."

"No!" Realene yelled. Trout whined and backed away, tugging on the leash.

Trish turned, her expression confused. "What are you doing? Get out of here." She saw Nate and her brow furrowed, "Nate. Your mom… I didn't—"

"I know." He beckoned her toward him. "Come here, come over here."

Mindy paused, attention still focused on Trish. When her sister took a step away, Mindy leapt, moving faster than should have been possible with her damaged body. She landed on Trish's back, tackling her to the ground atop Birdie's corpse. Mindy reared back, jaws wide as a viper.

Nate covered the distance between them in a flash and grabbed Mindy by the arm before she could take a chunk out of her sister, then flung the little girl to the side. She smacked the wall and fell to the floor with a gurgling moan.

"Leave her alone!" Trish cried, her shirt and hands streaked with Birdie's blood. "Don't you hurt her."

Realene dropped Trout's leash, letting him cower against the wall, and rushed over to the dazed little girl. She pulled the stun gun from her pocket, flipped it on with a flick of her thumb, and pressed the prongs to Mindy's arm. Electricity tensed the girl's body, and she went limp.

Nate bent to help Trish to her feet, but she pushed him away, crawling over to her sister. "Mindy?" Trish tugged on her sister, propping her up against the wall in a sitting position. The girl's head lolled to rest on her shoulder. "Mindy, wake up. Just wake up, please."

Realene got up from her crouched position, her throat tight with grief.

"We, uh, might want to keep the racket down," Calvin said, his face pinched.

Trish shoved Realene, who stumbled back into Nate. "You killed her."

Realene raised her hands. "You said you wanted her cured. The stun gun killed the worms." Guilt twisted her stomach, but she had no choice. If they hadn't stopped the little girl, she would have infected Trish, and maybe the rest of them, too.

Trish scooped Birdie's discarded weapon from beside his body and pointed it at Realene. "You. Killed. Her."

"Whoa." Realene took a step back.

Nate stepped in front of Realene, letting the barrel of the gun touch his chest. "Her body was too weak to live without the infection. I think you know that."

That was exactly what that bastard Harmon had wanted, to test how long a dead person could be kept alive by the worms.

"I don't want to hurt you," Trish said, the gun wavering in her hand.

"Don't want to hurt me? You knew I was infected and let me spread those things. You watched them kill my mom, then helped Harmon capture us."

Trish let her arm fall to her side, gun now pointed at the floor. "I couldn't leave her."

"I'm sorry you weren't able to save Mindy, but that's not our fault," he said. "If you try to hurt Realene, I will kill you myself."

"Stop it." Realene dropped her hands and stepped up beside her friend. Even with all she'd done, he still loved Trish and killing her would destroy him. "No one needs to die here."

"Except Harmon," Calvin said. "That pecker definitely needs to die."

Trish sniffled, looking at her sister's body still propped against the wall like some macabre doll. "You're right. This, all of this, is his fault."

Still carrying the gun, she strode out the door.

"Where's she going?" Calvin asked.

Realene watched from the doorway, Calvin and Nate peeking out from behind her. Trish approached the blast door at the end of the hall, which was now cracked open.

"Let's go," Nate said.

"Wait," Realene said. "We can't just barge in there. We have no idea what we're getting into. We still need a plan."

But Nate didn't listen, just ran after Trish, followed by Calvin.

Realene grabbed Trout's leash and crept along the wall in pursuit.

Up ahead, Trish tucked the gun in her waistband and heaved the massive metal door open wide enough to slip inside. She gave her pursuers a feral grin, then disappeared through the gap.

Realene kept a tight grip on Trout's leash, but there was nothing she could do to stop Nate, who rushed after Trish into the lab.

"Put your hands up," Trish yelled from inside.

Realene strained to hear, prayed this wouldn't turn out like Birdie.

"Stay where you are Harmon," Nate said. "You too, doctor."

"You think I'm intimidated by you, young lady? Put that gun down before you hurt someone," Harmon said.

Trout growled at the sound of Harmon's voice, baring his teeth.

"*You* put *your* weapon down, Colonel," Nate demanded.

Shit. Harmon had drawn his gun. Realene would bet on him as a better shot than Trish. Had she ever even fired a gun?

"I don't think I will. I should shoot your little girlfriend here instead, teach you both a lesson about who's in charge."

Trout growled again and yanked free of Realene's hold on his leash, sprinting from behind the door and disappearing into the room.

# Twenty-Nine

**REALENE LUNGED FOR** the leash as it slipped around the door, her fingertips brushing the loop but failing to grasp it before it disappeared. She rounded the door in pursuit of Trout.

The room was narrow but long, with shelves holding small animal cages on one wall. A metal table in the center of the room held a large, clear Plexiglass box filled with at least a dozen bloodied rabbits attacking each other in a frenzy. Standing beside the box was the doctor in his lab coat and safety goggles.

Harmon was on the other side of the table, his gun raised and aimed at Trish, but then he saw Realene and frowned. He limped toward her, his gun arm lowering slightly. "Realene?"

A shot echoed through the room and Harmon jerked, a dot of red appearing on his right shoulder.

"Yeah, get 'em," Calvin said, barreling into the room behind Realene and knocking her forward. She caught herself on the edge of the metal table as Harmon swapped his gun to his other hand and raised it, pointing it again at Trish.

"No!" Nate cried, lunging toward Harmon.

At the same moment Trout leapt in the air and clamped his teeth around Harmon's gun arm. The weapon went off, but instead of hitting Trish, the shot hit Doctor Goggles. He cried out and fell backward into the animal cages, knocking several from the shelves.

Nate tackled Harmon to the floor, where Trout still had a grip on his arm and was shaking and tearing at it as the man screamed. Realene wrenched the gun from his hand and smacked him in the skull with the butt of the weapon.

He passed out, his head thumping on the tile floor.

Nate sat back on his knees, panting. "Whoa. I can't believe that worked."

Doctor Goggles moaned and clutched his side. Blood seeped through the white fabric of his lab coat.

Realene scanned the room for something to restrain Harmon with. She spotted Big Kev behind the table, strapped to a gurney. He shouted something unintelligible through his cloth gag. Realene handed the gun to Calvin, glad to be rid of it. "Get Kev."

Calvin edged around her, stopping to deliver a kick to Harmon's ribs before making his way back to his nephew. Tucking the gun in his waistband, he began unbuckling the restraints that held his nephew to the gurney, doing surprisingly well one-handed.

Realene rubbed Trout's back. "You can let go now, buddy."

He released his bite on Harmon's arm and sat back, thumping his tail. Trout gave a macabre doggy grin, blood coating his mouth and dripping down his fur to stain his collar.

His leash. She quickly unclipped it, then rolled Harmon closer to the metal table so he was lying on his side. She pulled his arms behind his back and bound his wrists to the table leg with the leash.

"I've been shot," Doctor Goggles cried. "I need medical attention."

"Stand up," Trish ordered, aiming her weapon at him. Her blonde hair had escaped its bun, and Realene couldn't help but think she now looked like one of those Stars 'N Stripes Barbies.

Nate stood behind her, acting as back-up. "What's the plan? Should we take them with us?"

Doctor Goggles clutched at the cages, pulling several more from their shelves before making it to his feet.

A familiar screeching sounded from inside the cages, one Realene knew well.

Too well.

Goddamn prairie dogs.

Realene's breath quickened at the memory of the infected hordes that had pursued them through Demise. "We need to get out of here."

Trish pointed her gun at Doctor Goggles. "You helped him do this."

Near the back of the room, Calvin helped Big Kev sit up, then removed his gag.

Big Kev winced. "Where am I? Who're you?" he asked, looking at Realene and Nate, then at Trish. His mouth gaped when he saw the gun.

"Dammit," Realene swore. "They must've infected him with the Beta strain."

"Did you?" Trish asked Doctor Goggles.

He raised his chin, strangely defiant for someone at the business end of a gun.

The amount of damage all depended on how long he'd been infected, so they had to cure him as quickly as possible. Every second was another memory stolen.

"Calvin, catch." Realene tossed her stun gun to him, which he caught and used to zap Big Kev in one smooth motion.

Big Kev stiffened, then slumped when the shock ended, rubbing his arm where the electrified prong had connected. "Jeez, Uncle Cal, what'd I ever do to you?"

Calvin grabbed his nephew's arm and pulled him from the table, supporting him. "Trust me, kid. I'll explain everything later."

Realene went over to help, supporting Big Kev's other arm as they guided him past the still unconscious Colonel Harmon.

"What is this place? How did I get here? I don't…" Big Kev looked at Calvin. "It's a memory wipe, isn't it? They got us. Where's my dad, is he okay?"

"He's okay. Above ground waiting for you," Realene said. If she could get him and Calvin out, it would be two less people to worry about getting hurt.

"Above ground?" Big Kev looked around the room, his chest rising and falling rapidly. "This is some kinda secret government facility, isn't it? Like from *The X-Files*. And you guys are breaking me out."

"Just call me Agent Scully." She caught sight of a tray on the table that had been obscured by the box of rabbits. A tray with a dozen small holes that held vials of black liquid.

She helped Calvin and Big Kev the rest of the way from the room and down the corridor, stopping to herd Trout out with them. "This is Trout. He helped with your rescue. Look after him."

"Yes, ma'am," he said, a title she didn't care for at all.

Realene inserted Birdie's key and pressed the only button: Up. The doors opened, and Calvin tried to stay, but she pushed him into the elevator. "Ana and Mac are up there waiting, and we'll be right behind you, okay?"

"Godspeed, Agent," Big Kev said, giving her a little salute.

She watched the doors slide closed, breathing a little easier. Now they had to decide what to do with Harmon and the doctor. There was no doubt they deserved to die after everyone they'd hurt, but she couldn't just kill them. She had to focus on stopping these disgusting experiments and getting justice for those who'd been hurt and killed.

Heaving a sigh, she ran back to the lab. Trish still had her gun trained on Doctor Goggles, who was leaning against the wall, blood dripping to pool at his feet.

More screeching came from the cages on the floor, and they rattled back and forth.

Realene pointed at the tray of vials, some with black caps and some with blue. "Are those the strains you've been developing? Beta and whatever the other one is?"

Doctor goggles didn't answer, and Nate jabbed the man in the side. He grimaced, then replied, "Beta and Omega."

"Is there any more?" Trish kept her weapon pointed at the man, bracing her gun arm with her other hand.

Face twisted with pain, he raised his chin toward the back of the room. "In the fridge. Please, I was just following orders."

"That's no excuse," Trish said. "I should kill you right now."

"Please, don't," he said, whimpering.

"We can't," Realene said, meeting Nate's eyes.

"You're right." He braced one hand on the table, looking more tired than she'd ever seen him, and glanced at the fallen cages. "But we could infect them."

"Yes." Trish grinned, looking more deranged than happy. "Lock them up like they did my sister. Starting with you." She herded Doctor Goggles into the hallway, gun pressed to his skull. "Go on, go."

Realene felt a dark satisfaction twist through her gut at the thought of the guy locked in that same cage where Mindy was kept. Justice.

Nate headed toward the cooler that sat against the rear wall, and she followed. Several Snapple-bottle-sized containers filled with black liquid lined one shelf, enough to make hundreds more doses. "We need to get rid of this stuff, too. All of it."

An empty cardboard box sat beside the cooler, and Realene grabbed it. "We'll take it with us for now, figure out how to destroy it later."

Nate started packing the bottles, said, "We can shock it, like before."

Realene spotted a small desk and several filing cabinets beside the coolers. A coat featuring a patch with Harmon's name hung over the desk chair. She took a step closer, remembering Mac's comment about proof.

She didn't care about evidence of alien life, but if the colonel kept details on the experiments, it would give them plenty of evidence to release to the media about what was really happening here. A quick look inside the drawer labeled "H-J" revealed a tab with Nate's name. The drawer was packed with files, some new and some with yellowing labels. They couldn't all be from the past couple of months.

If he'd kept records of all his past experiments, even those not using the worms, she could expose those, too. Get justice for what he did to her parents. She pulled open the drawer labeled "E-G." There they were: folders for Louie Gustafson and Marion Gustafson. She pulled out the files, noticed another one behind them.

*Realene Gustafson.*

Hand shaking, she reached for the folder and pulled it free. The file was fat, packed with loose pages. Pulse pounding in her ears, she flipped open the front cover, saw a page with a picture of her. Her school picture from first grade. The same one that sat on her ma and dad's dresser.

"Hey." A hand gripped her shoulder, and she started.

Nate.

He held the cardboard box full of the jars of solution. "I'll drop this by the elevator and then we'll lock up Harmon. Give him a dose of his own medicine." His mouth twisted into a sadistic sneer.

"Yeah, okay." She stacked the files and clasped them to her chest, her heart threatening to burst through.

What had Harmon done to her? And had her parents known?

Nate stopped by the table to grab the tray of small vials, then carried the box out of the room.

Realene started after him with the files but stopped at the sight of a photo on Harmon's desk: him holding a baby. She grabbed the frame, not believing what she was seeing. He stood next to a woman who smiled up at him. A banner in the background read "It's a Girl."

He had a daughter.

A *thunk* sounded, and she looked up to see Harmon yanking the blast door closed.

"No!" she screamed, dropping the files and the photo and rushing toward the door.

He turned the wheel that extended metal pins into the frame, locking the two of them in and everyone else out.

# Thirty

**HARMON WENT AROUND** the table, examined the piled cages, discarded files, and blood pooled on the floor. "What have you done?" He clutched his right arm to his chest, the gunshot wound in his shoulder rendering it useless.

Realene crept along the wall on the opposite side of the table, where Trout's leash lay on the floor.

"I've escaped much worse," he said.

At least it was just her trapped. "They're all free, your little plan didn't work."

"You're supposed to be at home. Safe." He kicked the file at his feet, sending the pages skittering toward her.

"You killed my parents." She pointed at the papers on the ground. "And you did something to me, too, didn't you?"

"I've always protected you."

A rattle sounded as one of the caged prairie dogs thumped against the bars, then a series of excited chirps sounded. A blur of fur darted across the floor and under the bottom shelf of the metal table, but Harmon didn't notice.

She moved along the side wall in the direction of the door. "I have a file. I saw I was part of your experiments. Did they even know?"

He looked down, not meeting her gaze, and shook his head.

She knew it. Ma and Dad would never have put her in danger. Everything they'd done was to give her a better life, and Harmon took advantage of them. "You bastard. Tell me what you did to me."

Would she get cancer like her dad? Or dementia like Ma? Or something different, something worse.

"I never wanted to hurt you. You're like a daughter to me." Wincing, he bent to tug up his pants leg, revealing an ankle holster. Another gun.

She had nowhere to run, nowhere to hide. "What about your actual daughter? Did you experiment on her, too?"

He stayed in that hunched-over position, took in a ragged breath. "I couldn't save her. I tried."

The chirping of prairie dogs crescendoed, filling the small space.

"Shut up!" he screamed. His left forearm was ravaged by the dog bite, and he groaned as he reached across his body for his right ankle. He pulled the weapon from the holster, but before he could stand up, a bundle of fur launched itself from beneath the lab table.

The escaped prairie dog clamped onto the colonel's wrist, and he howled in pain, dropping the gun.

Realene lunged and grabbed the weapon, then backed away.

Harmon flung his arm above his head, launching the prairie dog through the air. The rabid creature smacked into the cooler doors, cracking the glass and leaving a smear of blood before it plopped to the floor.

Blood marred Harmon's wrist. He'd been infected.

Realene guessed the prairie dogs carried the original strain, the one that started with memory loss and confusion. That might work to her advantage. If Harmon lost his recent memories, it might give her time to get away.

Tucking the gun behind her back, she edged toward the door.

"Stay where you are." He shuffled toward her.

"I'm going to get some help, okay?" She inched closer to the door. "I know you're confused, but you have to trust me."

He glanced back at the lifeless body of the prairie dog, then gave a humorless laugh. "I'm not confused."

She shook her head. "You were bitten."

"I had myself inoculated months ago. We have a cure now, too, you know. Simple anti-parasitic, no electricity required."

"Shit." She drew the gun from behind her back and aimed it at him.

Harmon took a careful step forward. "Give me the gun before you hurt yourself."

"Don't come any closer. I'll shoot you." The gun shook in her grip. She hoped it was as simple as just pulling the trigger.

Harmon took another limping step toward her.

"I *will* do it. You deserve to die after everything you've done." She jabbed the gun at Harmon, and he flinched, stopped advancing on her. "And once you're dead, I'm going to make sure everyone knows what a monster you were."

He lunged at her, shoving her back into the wall as he wrenched her gun arm over her head and banged her wrist into the wall. The gun slipped from her grip and hit the floor. But when he bent to retrieve the weapon, she punched him in the injured shoulder, right in his gunshot wound. He cried out, and his face twisted, becoming that of the monster hidden inside.

Harmon wrapped his blood-slicked hands around her throat. She clawed at his fingers, but even injured, he was too strong. He was going to kill her with his bare hands. And once he killed her, he'd go after her friends. He'd win.

"Stop," she croaked, her vision graying at the edges. She fumbled in her pocket, but the stun gun was gone. There was only the pepper spray. The tube had a safety, would need a little twist to allow it to work. She struggled to rotate the top one-handed with fingers going numb.

It finally notched into place. Pain built from her neck up through her face until she thought her eyeballs might explode.

Then the pressure eased, as Harmon's hands pulled away. She slumped to the floor on her knees, coughing.

Harmon backed away, looking at his bloodstained hands, then up at her. "This is your fault, you coming here. I didn't want to hurt you. I tried to save you."

Realene rose slowly, hand still in her pocket. Her chest rose and fell with panicked breaths.

"I can fix this. There's more Beta solution. You'll take it this time and forget. It'll be like none of this ever happened." He glanced toward the table, probably for the vials that were now gone.

She pulled out the pepper spray, unleashing the noxious spray in Harmon's face.

The pepper misted the air, stinging her eyes and throat, and she coughed, struggling to suck in a full breath.

Harmon had gotten a direct hit. He bellowed and swiped at his face, stumbling back into the metal table and tipping it slightly.

The box of rabbits slid across the polished metal surface and smashed on the floor. The Plexiglass cracked, and the animals hopped through the gaps.

Realene pressed her back to the wall, extremely glad she'd worn her dad's combat boots, laced up tight over the open legs of her scrubs. They wouldn't protect her for long, though. Eventually the rabbits would climb up her legs and bite.

Harmon coughed and rubbed at his eyes, which were now swollen and red.

Tears streaming down her face, Realene strode forward and shoved him. He tripped on the remains of the box and fell flat on his back among the rabbits. The creatures swarmed his body. A mass of bloodied, furry bodies.

Realene ran to the door, glimpsing Harmon's weapon on the floor. She picked it up, gripping it in one hand and turning the door's crank with the other. The metal bars retracted, and the door opened an inch, letting in a gust of relatively fresh air.

"Leave and you'll never know," Harmon yelled.

She looked back to see him half sitting up, his face and body marked with bloody bites. He snatched at the rabbits attacking him, flinging them away. "I'm the only one who knows what was done to you, how to help you."

"Tell me now then." A stray rabbit nipped at her toes, but she kicked it back toward Harmon. Though he'd already been bitten and infected, they kept attacking, meaning they had been infected with the Omega strain, designed for maximum aggression.

"Once we're out of here, I'll tell you everything." He struggled to his feet, rabbits clinging to him by teeth and claws, dangling from his arms and legs.

She knew he was manipulating her, doing everything possible to stay alive, but he was right. If she left him, he might die or, more likely, be rescued. She'd never find out what was done to her as a kid. Dozens of pages had filled that file while Nate's held only a few. How many years had whatever he did to her lasted?

Realene raised the gun, pointing it at him. She could take him with her. Make him talk.

Or she could shoot him and take the files.

The rabbits continued to attack him, scaling his legs to scratch and bite. "I promised your parents I'd help you. Let me help you."

Her eyes burned, not just from the pepper spray. Her parents had trusted him, never knowing how he'd betrayed them.

He shook his arm, hard, sending a rabbit flying into the wall, and took a lurching step toward her.

"Stay there." Realene aimed at Harmon's face, which oozed with open wounds. The gun shook in her hand.

He moved closer, crunching Plexiglass beneath his boot. "You won't shoot me. I remember how hard it was for you when you had to kill Brooke. Give me the gun, and we'll leave together." He took another step forward, this time crushing a screeching rabbit beneath his foot. An innocent rabbit that had done nothing to deserve its fate.

He raised his hands, showing he was unarmed. Defenseless. He was trying to manipulate her like he'd done to so many others, like he would keep doing.

Rage ignited in her gut, for Ma and Dad, who only wanted to build a family, a life. For Nate, who'd had to watch his mom die. For Trish, who wanted nothing more than to get her baby sister back. For that filing cabinet full of people who were no more than words on a page to him.

She squeezed the trigger but hardly heard the crack of the shot over the rush of blood filling her ears.

Harmon's mouth opened in a surprised gasp as the bullet hit his chest, dead center. His legs gave way, and he fell to the floor.

Shouting sounded behind her as she was pulled through the door.

**NATE PUT THE** box down by the elevator and braced himself against the wall. Exhaustion infused every inch of his body, but he had to make it a little longer. Part of him thought he was going to die down there, but another very small part had been convinced Realene would come through.

Because of her, Nate would be able to give Harmon the slow, painful death he deserved in that cage, gnawed on by his own creations. The image of his mom lying dead in the snow flashed through his mind, and he shook his head, trying to physically dislodge the memory from his brain.

Behind him, Realene cried, "No!"

He sprinted toward the lab and saw Harmon standing in the doorway for a split second before the door swung closed and there was a heavy thunk of the rods sliding into place.

Nate hit the blast door at full speed with one shoulder. He was thrown back by the solid obstacle and left clutching his arm. Struggling to calm his panicked breathing, he surveyed the door, but there were no levers or knobs or buttons. He felt along the border, trying to wedge his fingers into any gap, but there was none.

The blast door sat completely flush with the frame, was only meant to be opened from the inside.

Pressing his ear to the metal, he held his breath and closed his eyes, trying to pick up some sound, some clue to what was happening in there, but no sound came through the thick barrier.

He ran at the door again, banging into it with his shoulder, then pounding at it with his fists. "Realene!" he screamed.

Still no answer, no indication she was even still alive in there.

He turned and slid down to the floor, sitting with his head in his hands. She had come down here to save him, and now she was trapped with that bastard Harmon. He punched the cement floor, opening up the healing split across his knuckles and savoring the pain that flared through his hand.

A gunshot sounded and someone screamed from one of the other rooms. Trish.

He got up, running down the hall and into the room where they'd found Mindy.

Trish was pinned to the floor with that doctor on top of her. He had a hold of her hair and was bashing her head into the floor.

Nate barreled into them, doing a flying tackle to knock the doctor off of her. "Leave her alone!" he yelled—for Trish and for Realene, though he could only help one of them.

"The gun," Trish said, panting, and rolled to her hands and knees to search the floor.

The doctor managed to get up and delivered a kick to Nate's side. Something cracked, probably a rib, and Nate choked out a gasp. He managed to grab the guy's ankle and yank him down to the floor.

Nate forced the doctor over onto his stomach and pulled one arm behind his back, wrenching it up, wanting the asshole to feel pain.

Trish had found the gun and pointed it at the doctor. "Get him up."

The guy screamed, and Nate pulled harder, wanting to hear bones break and ligaments pop.

"Hey," Trish said, kicking Nate to get his attention.

He forced himself to ease up, but only a little.

Blood trickled down Trish's ear and neck.

"You okay?" he asked, the urge to protect her still there, even after everything she'd done to him.

Trish swayed a little, pressing her free hand to the back of her head. "I said get him up."

Nate yanked the guy to his feet, keeping a hold on his arm. "We've got to hurry. Realene's in trouble."

Trish's aim wavered a little. "Get him in the cage, then we'll help her."

"She's trapped in the lab. We've got to find a way in there," he said. The doctor struggled against Nate as he was pushed toward the cage but stopped when Trish tapped the gun against his temple.

There were two infected in the cage, a man and a woman, both shackled to the wall by their ankles. The man was huddled in the corner and had barely moved at their approach, just rocked a little in place and opened his mouth to give a gurgle. Most of the skin and muscle were gone from his face and neck, showing white swaths of bone. The woman wore what was once a colorful, floral mumu that was now stained with blood and who knew what else. She was missing clumps of hair, and her skin was torn open in places, but she was more animated than the man, standing and shuffling toward the bars.

When Trish swung open the door, the woman stepped forward, her jaw already opening and closing, wanting a bite.

Nate walked the doctor to the opening, ready to be done with this, to get back to Realene, but the doctor snapped his head back, bashing Nate in the nose with his skull. Pain exploded through Nate's face, and blood gushed from his nose. He loosened his grip.

The doctor flipped around, grabbing Nate's shoulders, and rotated to shove him into the cage.

Nate pushed against the doctor, trying to shove his way back out as the woman clawed at his shirt with fingers that were still tipped with sharp, manicured nails. He screamed, writhing, pushing forward, trying to get away.

Trish fired at the woman, and hit her shoulder, knocking her back against the wall, and the doctor stopped blocking Nate to make a grab for the gun.

Nate grabbed the doctor around the waist and yanked him away from Trish, turning to throw him into the cell.

The doctor stumbled back into the woman, carried by momentum, but he wasn't alone. He had looped one arm around Trish's neck, pulling her along with him.

Nate reached out for Trish, fingers grasping for her wrist, but she lashed out, kicking him square in the chest with one flat foot and sending him back outside the cell door. He landed on his back outside the cage, all the air whooshing from his lungs. Coughing, he forced himself to sit up.

In the cage, Trish, the doctor, and the infected woman were locked in a triple embrace. The infected woman had her arms wrapped around the doctor, and her teeth latched onto his shoulder. The doctor's arm fell from Trish's neck, and Nate crawled toward her. If he could get a hold of her ankle, he could pull her free.

"I've got you." Blood filled his mouth, and he coughed again, crawling toward the cage.

The infected woman's hand reached around the doctor, and her nails landed in the soft flesh of Trish's neck, tearing into her throat.

Trish opened her mouth as if to scream but only made a gurgling sound. Nate reached out to her, and she matched his pose, but instead of grabbing his hand, she wrapped her fingers around the cage door and pulled it closed.

"Trish!"

Nate covered the last foot between them, yanking on the door, but it had locked.

The infected woman's fingers clenched and pulled, yanking out Trish's trachea. Her head fell back against the doctor, who groaned and pushed Trish's body off of him. He moved toward the bars, focused on Nate through his blood-splattered goggles. The infected woman thumped ineffectively against the bars.

Nate hunched over, sobs wrecking his chest. He looked up to find Trish staring at him, dead-eyed, from her position on the floor, and gagged, spitting red-tinged bile onto the floor.

Realene. He could still save Realene.

He stumbled from the room and into the empty hallway, shoving that grotesque scene from his mind. Shuffling down the hall toward the lab, he scanned the door for some secret lock or latch. Maybe he could go back for the gun and shoot through the door or see if there were some kind of explosives somewhere.

But as he got closer, he realized the door was already cracked open. No longer flush with the wall. No longer locked.

Nate wedged his fingers into the crack and heaved the heavy door open. A gunshot sounded, and he screamed, "Realene!"

Not her, too. He couldn't lose her, too.

But it wasn't her that was shot. It was Harmon. He'd been facing the door with his hands raised, then fell to the floor. Realene had her back to Nate, gun raised.

"We've got to go," he said, grabbing her arm and hauling her backward into the hallway.

Blood-covered rabbits feasted on Harmon's corpse. Several stood on hind legs and turned their beady black eyes on Nate. They dropped to all fours and hopped toward the door, but he pushed it closed, trapping the animals inside.

# Thirty-One

**REALENE WATCHED NATE** close the lab door, that last image of Harmon seared into her mind. He was really dead.

Nate grabbed her shoulders, examining her face. "You're good. Not infected."

A high-pitched whine filled her ears, muting his voice.

"Give me that." Nate gestured at the gun, which she hadn't realized she was still holding.

Realene swallowed, tasted the sting of pepper spray in her damaged throat. "I killed him."

He pulled the gun from her hand and wiped it off with the bottom of his shirt. Getting rid of her prints.

Her hands started to shake. "He attacked me." She gestured to her neck, to the spot where Harmon's hands had wrapped tight. "He deserved it, after everything… He wouldn't have stopped coming for us. I had to."

"I know." Nate opened the door to the room where Mindy had been kept, turning his head away as if avoiding looking inside. Still holding the gun with the edge of his shirt, he tossed it in and closed the door.

The hallway was empty except for the two of them. "Where's Trish?" she asked.

Nate shook his head, blinking rapidly, and blocked the door.

Realene pushed past him, turned the knob, let the door swing open. She tried to register what she was seeing in that cage. The man and woman. Dr. Goggles. A body on the floor.

Trish.

She had no throat.

Realene gasped and stumbled back, slamming the door.

Harmon was dead. They were supposed to be okay now. Everyone was supposed to be okay.

"I tried to help her," Nate whispered. "I tried."

Realene wrapped her arms around him, and he hugged her back, so tight she felt every bruise on her damaged body.

Nate pulled away and picked up the box, wincing. "We should go."

Realene inserted the key into the elevator controls and pressed the button, listened to the clang of the car traveling back down to them. She'd only been down in this awful place for an hour at most, but she felt changed by it. By what she'd seen and done and now knew.

The elevator doors slid open, and she joined Nate inside, trying to figure out how to tell him what she'd found in those files. "Nate, I—"

"You can't tell anyone what happened. What you did. Okay?"

"Yeah." She stared at her feet. At her dad's boots. Was that a drop of blood on the toe? Harmon's blood?

*Do what's right,* her dad had said. *Be brave.*

But shooting an unarmed person wasn't brave.

It was murder.

She was a murderer.

"I got blood on my boots," she said, her voice cracking.

"Hey, listen to me." Nate bent to catch her eye, and she noticed how badly he was hurt. His nose was bent at an odd angle and blood covered his face. "This is our story: We took the worm solution and left Harmon tied up with that doctor and Trish. Went into that room where you found me. We tried to open those cryochamber things because you wanted to get Brooke out, bring her home. We heard gunshots and stayed hidden until we thought it was safe, then we found Trish and the doctor in that cage and ran. Okay?"

The elevator doors slid closed.

Realene held back the sob that wanted to tear from her throat. "I'm sorry."

"You have nothing to be sorry for." He gripped her shoulder. "You saved me."

She sniffed. "And you saved me. That's what biffs do."

"We're gonna be okay." He gave her a shake. "Say it back to me. Say what just happened. Our version."

"Harmon was tied up. Trish had a gun." She tried to take a full breath, couldn't. "We went to get Brooke. We heard gunshots and hid. We saw Trish and ran."

The elevator doors slid open in the above ground office, and Trout ran up to Realene, jumping on her.

"Hey, buddy," she said, but didn't stoop to pet him.

She and Nate exited the elevator and were immediately swarmed by Calvin, Big Kev, Ana, and Mac.

"Thank God you're okay," Ana said. She hugged Realene, squeezing her tight. "Uncle Cal told us about Birdie. I was so scared something had happened to you."

Big Kev joined them, stuck his hand out to Realene. "Uh, thanks for rescuing me. And sorry I didn't recognize you. Memory wipes, eh?"

"Where's Trish?" Calvin asked.

"Dead." Nate crossed the room and set the box of jars on the desk.

Calvin patted Nate on the back but said nothing.

"What's in these?" Mac pulled one of the jars from the box, swishing the black liquid around in the jar. Nate snatched it back from him, sliding it back into the box.

"Where's the proof?" Mac asked. "You said they were experimenting with an alien craft. Did you get a piece of it?"

"Dad," Ana snapped. "Let it go."

"We're so close." He paced the room, wringing his hands, twisting them together in a painful grip. "And it's right there. We can finally prove they've been covering it up. That I'm not crazy."

"I'm sorry," Realene said, and she was. Mac had clearly been broken by what happened to him, but nothing here would fix that. "I found some files, but I had to leave them behind."

"There must be something else." He looked at her, his expression so hopeful, so desperate. "We'll go back down, take one more look."

"There are infected—I mean, rabid animals down there. It's not safe."

Nate leaned against the desk, looking ready to collapse.

"Dad, we're lucky to be alive," Big Kev said. "I want to go home."

"Me too," Realene said.

"What's the plan? How're we getting out of here?" Calvin asked.

"We were *going* to hide everyone in the trunk." Ana shot a sidelong glance at her dad, who was still pacing the room. "But there's no way everyone will fit. And with Birdie gone, we're going to attract a lot more attention leaving."

Realene pulled Birdie's keys from her pocket. "You and I have badges. We'll sit in the front, fit as many people in the trunk as we can, hope the guards don't look too close at whoever's in the back." She opened the front door of the building and peeked outside. No one was waiting, so she led the others out to the car, making sure Mac was among them.

She opened the trunk, leaving the keys hanging in the lock.

"Gonna be a tight fit," Nate said, shoving the box of solution into the back corner.

"Whoa. This place is massive." Big Kev wandered away, looking at all the buildings and airstrips. A *whoosh* sounded as a plane took off in the distance.

Realene scooped up a handful of snow and scrubbed it over her face and neck, the arms of her jacket. Better if she didn't look like she'd been in a gun fight.

Calvin took a few steps toward the chain link fence that marked the rear perimeter of the base. "What the hell is that?"

Mac followed his brother, and Realene swallowed the urge to scream at them all to just get in the damn trunk. "What is what?"

"I swear I just saw one of them snowbanks move." Calvin pointed at a mound past the fence.

She scanned the snowy landscape. "Looks normal to me."

The *thump thump* of helicopter blades sounded, getting closer. No way would they overlook something as fishy as a bunch of people piling into the trunk of a car.

"Guys, come on, we've got to go," she yelled, but there was no time.

The helicopter headed straight for them. A Black Hawk. Realene's dad showed her one when she toured the base as a kid, and she recognized the guns and rockets affixed to the wings.

"What do we do?" Big Kev asked, coming to stand next to Ana.

"Try very hard not to get killed." Realene raised her hands in the universal sign of surrender.

They were screwed.

The others followed her example and raised their hands, except Mac. He grabbed the keys from the trunk of the car and bolted for the building's door, his limp barely noticeable.

"Dad!" Ana screamed, running after him, her hand barely missing his jacket sleeve.

He rushed inside and slammed the door.

Ana gripped the knob, twisted, but it wouldn't open. Locked. Big Kev joined her, pounding on the door so hard Realene thought he might actually bust it from the hinges. "Open up, Dad!"

"I'm not leaving without proof," he yelled.

"That asshole's going to get himself killed," Nate said.

Realene wanted to explain she hadn't willingly included him on the mission, but that would have to wait.

"Stay right where you are," a loudspeakered voice called from the helicopter.

Ana and Big Kev both turned around, raising their hands. He looked even more scared that he had down in the bunker.

"No way I'm letting these assholes kidnap me again," Calvin said, defiant. He dropped his arms and made a run for the back fence, which was topped with barbed wire and still electrified.

"Calvin, stop!" Nate called.

Trout barked but didn't try to follow.

Realene held her breath, gaze jumping from the chopper's weapons to Calvin.

He covered the distance, about thirty yards, faster than she thought possible at his age, and grabbed the electrified chain link. His body went rigid, seeming stuck to the fence as he vibrated in place, but he finally got his hands free and fell on his butt in the snow.

"Bastards," Calvin said, cradling his hands in his lap.

Several military vehicles sped down the road toward them as the helicopter continued to hover overhead. She thought back to the military's arrival at Lake Sauer, where Realene and Nate were heroes.

They wouldn't be treated like that here.

The vehicles pulled to a stop about a hundred yards away and several soldiers jumped out and pointed guns at them.

"They're gonna shoot us, aren't they?" Big Kev said. "This is it. This is how I die."

"Calm down. They're not going to shoot us," Realene said, though she thought there was about a fifty-fifty chance. Especially once they discovered what happened to Harmon.

Nate moved closer, clasping her raised hand in his. Whatever happened, they'd face it together.

"Next year we're definitely springing for Florida," she said.

"Damn the gators." The corner of his mouth ticked up.

"Look!" Calvin shouted. "I told ya the snowbanks were moving." He pointed out at the field.

Letting go of Nate's hand, Realene turned to see several of the snowy mounds shifting and getting bigger. Standing. She initially thought of the abominable snowman, but they were actually people in white camouflage. One of them pulled out a bullhorn and said, "This is being filmed and transmitted live on the World Wide Web. I repeat, this is being broadcast live on the World Wide Web."

"Is that Flint?" Big Kev said. "Hell yeah, man. What a legend."

Realene had to agree. Flint really had been watching out for them. She held back a relieved grin, not wanting to antagonize their armed visitors.

Flint and his friends rushed the fence, standing close but not touching the electrified links. They were all dressed like abominable snowmen, and two of them held television cameras.

"I present the Alien Alliance," Realene said to Nate.

Still speaking through the bullhorn, Flint recited Realene's full name, then Nate's, and on through all of them on this side of the fence. He then said his own name, and what she could only assume were those of the people with him. "If anything should happen to us, you'll know we were last seen at Steele Air Force Base and that the American military is responsible."

When Big Kev smiled and waved at the camera, Ana jabbed him with her elbow.

The soldiers looked at one another and stopped moving closer but didn't lower their weapons. She figured they wouldn't mind shooting a few trespassers, but doing so on a live broadcast wasn't ideal.

The chopper began to descend, and the wind whipped the surgical cap from Realene's head. She squinted against the rush of wind from the rotors as the copter landed in the open space just ahead of them and beside the soldier's vehicles.

The rotors began to slow, and a man in a military uniform jumped from the open side door, followed by a man in a suit.

"Stand down, soldiers," the military man called, striding over to the men with guns.

Flint continued, "Colonel Harmon of the U.S. Air Force imprisoned both American and Canadian citizens and was experimenting on them using alien technology. This is a rescue mission of those prisoners."

Several vehicles pulled up behind the white-clothed men, and more soldiers hopped out to detain Flint and his friends.

"Don't hurt them!" Realene shouted.

The other man from the copter, the one in the suit, strode toward her and the others. His slicked-back hair was so solidly molded, the gust of wind from the slowing rotors didn't affect a single strand.

"Senator Schmidt?" When she sent him that message about the secret experiments going on, she never expected he'd come.

"Are you Ms. Gustafson?" he asked, reaching out a leather-gloved hand.

"Yeah, that's me." She shook his hand. "Figured you'd think I was some kind of crackpot."

"I've been concerned about Colonel Harmon's illicit activities recently. Your email reinforced those concerns." He scanned the area. "Where is he? Are the friends you mentioned okay?"

"Sir," Ana called. "My dad's down there in that bunker. Please don't hurt him."

The senator let the comment pass. "Anyone else still down there?"

Nate cleared his throat, said, "We heard gunshots. My girlfriend Trish, we saw her body. I don't know about the colonel, though." He swallowed heavily.

"There were animals, too. Like rabid animals. And blood." Realene didn't have to fake the fear on her face or in her voice. "We ran. We just ran."

"You're okay now. Stay here, and I'll see what I can find out about your dad." Schmidt jogged over to the man in the military uniform, and after they finished talking, several armed men entered the building.

Ana watched them, tears brimming in her eyes. She swiped at them with her hand. "If he gets himself killed, I'm going to be really pissed."

"He's tough," Realene said.

Ana went over to Big Kev and Calvin, and the three of them huddled together, staring at the building that held so many secrets beneath it. They may have already found Harmon's body.

The soldiers had fanned out to form a rough circle around Realene and her friends but didn't have their weapons raised. Still, they were surrounded.

"You okay?" Nate asked.

"Sure." Her heart pounded so hard she felt the thrum in her throat.

He hugged her, whispering in her ear, "We'll find out he's dead, killed by his own gun. Trish must've killed him because of what he did to her sister. Right?"

She pulled away. "Right." They were the only two who knew what really happened. So long as they stuck to their story, everything would fine.

"So, what's this email you sent?" Nate asked.

Realene told him about the evidence she'd sent Schmidt. "I figured it would be good to have a backup plan. Seems like I was right."

The senator walked back up to stand beside Realene and Nate, all of them watching the door now. She wanted to ask what they'd found but didn't.

"I have to say, I was doubtful when I saw your email," Schmidt said. "Secret experiments, super soldiers, prisoners. It's a bit unbelievable."

"But you still came." She didn't want to think about what would have happened if this hadn't gotten political, how the military would have handled things without the watchful eyes of the senator and the Alien Alliance.

"What's the saying? Better safe than sorry."

"Safe? You showed up in a chopper after receiving a crazy email." Nate cocked his head to the side. "Must've been some pretty serious concerns you had."

"Any excuse to ride in a helicopter, right?" He smacked Nate on the back. "You will need to go with these men and answer some questions."

He gestured toward a military van that pulled up. A soldier opened the rear doors, revealing bench seats on either side.

Though Realene definitely did not want to get into the back of another van, she said, "Okay."

"We won't let you cover this up," Nate said. "Not again."

Schmidt angled his chin toward the Alien Alliance people in the field. "I have a feeling we wouldn't be able to keep this quiet even if we wanted to."

The senator started to walk away, and Ana stopped him, asking if there was any update on her dad.

"You trust him?" Nate asked Realene, groaning as he sat down on the single step out front of the building.

"My dad used to say there was no such thing as an honest politician. Except Reagan. He loved that guy for some reason." Realene took a seat beside him, their shoulders touching. "I'm sure Schmidt has his own agenda, but he showed up when we needed help. That's worth something."

They watched as one of the soldiers pulled the box of solution from the trunk of the car.

"We're gonna be okay," she said, echoing his words from the elevator.

"We're alive, and we're not zombies," Nate said. "Probably the best we could've hoped for."

Trout trotted over and jumped onto Nate's lap, giving him literal puppy dog eyes. He hugged the animal close, burying his face in Trout's fur. Realene wrapped her arms around both of them, squeezed.

After a minute, Trout wiggled free. He trotted back over to Calvin, Big Kev, and Ana, as if checking on them. There was one person who hadn't made it out.

"I'm sorry about Trish," Realene said.

"Me too." Nate cleared his throat. "You think they'll give us anything to eat? I'm starving."

Realene pulled the Kit Kat from her pocket and opened it, broke off a section and handed it to him, then took one for herself. They ate side by side in silence.

The assembled soldiers watched the pair, as if expecting them to make a break for it at any moment.

"These are better than I remember," Nate said.

"'Cause they're Canadian. From Ana." She stuck the rest back in her pocket, wanting to save some.

He raised his eyebrows. "From Ana, huh?"

"Shut up."

A soldier approached, gesturing toward the van with his gun. The senator was with him. "Come with me, please."

Realene and Nate allowed themselves to be herded to the waiting vehicle, followed by their friends. In the field, Flint and his crew were being loaded into an identical van. Realene climbed inside, claiming the spot on the bench that was closest to the door.

Schmidt stood outside the doors, watching.

"Remember that a whole lot of people that were watching that footage know exactly where we are, Senator," she said. "And they saw you arrive, too."

He gave her an appraising look. "Cooperate fully, and I expect you'll be returned home within a few days."

The doors closed, leaving them in the shadowy interior of the van.

Nate sat beside her, and she grabbed his hand. Trout came up and laid his head on her knee. On the opposite bench, Big Kev, Calvin, and Ana sat huddled together.

"Mac'll be okay. He's tough," Calvin said, pulling his niece and nephew close.

Nate bumped Realene's shoulder. "I can't believe you pulled that off."

"I didn't." She looked around the van at the faces of her friends—her family, really. "We did."

Realene wasn't sure what would happen next, but today they'd won. Mostly. She'd gotten her friends free, and Harmon wouldn't be able to hurt anyone else. Maybe it was the calming effect of the chocolate, but she truly believed they were going to be okay, that they would make it home safe. And when they did, she was going to host a potluck supper for them all to put the church ladies to shame, featuring tater tot hotdish and Ma's famous lefsa.

# Thirty-Two

**NATE DROVE DOWN** Main Street, the acetylene torch tanks clanging against each other in his truck bed. He'd learned how to use one in junior year shop class, and Coach Buckley agreed to let him borrow it. More accurately, the man had grunted and said to have it back by Monday. Nate would finally be able to get into the bomb shelter and see what his dad had been hiding.

The gym came up on the right, and his throat tightened. Just a month ago, Trish had been so excited about applying to be an instructor. She would've gotten the job, too.

Inhaling a deep breath and blowing it out, he pulled up to the stop sign beside the cemetery. Trish was buried there now, next to her dad and Mindy. They still hadn't found Nate's mom's body, though, and likely never would. She was probably at the bottom of Lizard Lake or buried in some shallow grave in the Canadian wilderness by now.

Nate accelerated through the intersection, noticed a van was pulled over on the side of the road with a flat tire. He put on his blinker and started to slow to see if they needed help, then noticed the writing on the back of the vehicle.

*Judgment Day is Coming*

*Justice for Reverend Zebediah*

*Have you seen Irene?*

The Revelation cult was like a cockroach, just wouldn't die.

If it hadn't been for them, his mom never would have been in Canada, would still be alive. He knew it had been tough for Realene, but he was glad Irene got what she deserved. The only consolation in all of this was the fact that she and Harmon were both dead.

The car in front of him slowed. Someone shouted out the passenger window and chucked a fountain drink at the cult member standing beside the van, plastering them with soda. Nate drove past. The unwritten rule of North Dakota was you always stopped to help those in trouble, but not this time.

Nate crested the overpass and continued past the edge of town, turning off before the trailer park. He pulled into the driveway of his mom's house—his house now. The pavement was dry and most of the snow had melted, just random little piles of icy dirt left on the lawn.

The nativity scene was gone from the porch, packed up and donated to Goodwill along with much of his parents' stuff. Nate opened the front door, and Trout was lying on the floor in the hallway. He raised his head but didn't get up. He'd been through a lot, first losing Walt then Nate's mom, but it was getting better.

"Hey, bud." Nate patted Trout's back and pulled a treat from his pocket, one of the homemade ones from Trish.

Trout snatched the treat and chomped it down, his tail thumping the floor. They were the dog's favorite, but there were only a few left.

Nate walked down the hall, past the wall that had held the shrine to his dad. Those pictures were gone. In their place, he'd tacked up a photo booth strip of him and Realene in junior high and a picture of him and his mom from one of his first Christmases.

He tried to make the house his own, but the place still felt off, tainted with bad memories. Every once in a while, he'd get a whiff of peanuts or liquor or gun oil. He'd never been much of a believer in ghosts, but if anyone was able to live on out of spite, it was his dad. Realene suggested he get an exorcist, but he was pretty sure you had to be Catholic to qualify for one of those.

The phone rang in the kitchen, and Trout's head perked up, but Nate waited for the machine to pick it up.

The machine beeped and his mom's voice came on, saying "You've reached the Haugen residence, please leave a message."

A beep sounded.

"Hey, it's me," Realene said. "I know you're there, pick up."

A few moments of silence.

"Okay, fine. I'll be in Canada the next few days for the funeral. If you change your mind about coming, Kev said you can crash on the couch. Love you, biff."

She'd invited him to come with, but he told her he didn't want to cramp her new relationship. Ana was cool, and Realene deserved to find someone who appreciated her. Not wanting to be a third wheel wasn't the real reason he declined, though. He still hadn't found what he was looking for in his parents' house.

When he was tied up on that gurney in the bunker, the colonel revealed Nate's dad was aware of the old experiments and had been trying to blackmail Harmon and Realene's dad, but whatever evidence he possessed was never found. The colonel asked Nate about it and probably planned to find it himself after either killing Nate or wiping his memory.

Nate unloaded the torch from his truck and lugged it into the backyard, setting it down beside the cinder block structure that comprised the above-ground entrance to the bomb shelter his parents installed in their preparations for the end times. After searching every inch of the house and finding nothing, he was sure any proof of Harmon's experiments must be stored in the bomb shelter, which was locked with a combination Nate didn't know.

The acetylene torch cut through the bolts that secured the door in less than a minute, the fuel leaving the air smelling vaguely of garlic. Nate took off his welding goggles and pulled open the door to reveal a dark stairway descending below ground. He felt along the inside wall and found a light switch, flipping it on. One bare bulb lit the top of the stairs and another glowed from the bottom.

Sticking a flashlight in his pocket just in case, Nate took a deep breath and forced himself to trek down the steep decline. Concrete walls pressed in on him from both sides, and when he looked back at the doorway, a blinding rectangle of daylight, it seemed farther away than it should be.

He wished for a moment that Realene was there to back him up, but she deserved a break from government conspiracies and secret experiments, at least for little while.

The stairs opened into a single room. Two fold-down-style cot beds were attached to the wall to his left, a small couch and table holding a television and radio sat against the back wall, and shelves lined the wall to his right. A damp mustiness filled the space, and Nate found himself trying not to breathe too deeply. The bulb overhead flickered, creating a strobing effect that made him feel like he'd entered a horror movie.

It was too quiet, the sounds of a normal, spring afternoon not permeating the buried, concrete box.

Nate crossed the room in just a few strides and flipped on the small, boxy TV.

To his surprise, it worked, and apparently his dad had sprung for cable, which wouldn't have been a cheap addition. On the screen, televangelist Jerry Falwell cried out, "Judge not lest you be judged." It was always the most sinful who preached of not judging, of the importance of forgiveness.

Screw that. He flipped the television dial until it landed on *MTV News* and turned up the volume.

The spinning satellite dish filled the screen. "I'm Kurt Loder with an MTV news brief. Just months after the tragedy of the Meteor Murders, evidence of government corruption is emerging from Demise, North Dakota. An international group calling themselves the Alien Alliance livestreamed footage to their website of a government cover-up of human testing with what they state was alien technology."

The screen flashed a still shot of the footage that showed Nate, Realene, and the others at the air base, soldiers in the background with weapons raised. He'd seen the video many times. Everyone had. It had been rebroadcast across the world. Realene was convinced they could use it to make sure the truth came out about the alien worms, that it was the only way to prevent them getting into the wrong hands again.

"While the Air Force has not issued an official statement, republican Senator Schmidt of North Dakota has stated that a single military official was engaging in questionable conduct, and a senate committee hearing will be commencing shortly. That's the news for now, stay tuned for more throughout the day on MTV."

Nate turned down the TV. The senate hearings would be a joke. They'd reveal just enough to satisfy the public while brushing everything else under the rug. The military still hadn't admitted to any kind of operation in Canada, though that was a good thing for Nate. He'd been patient zero in an infection that had killed at least three people.

He pulled out his flashlight and swept it over the shelves. The first set was packed with cans and boxes of nonperishable foods, the second held dishes, toilet paper, and other supplies, and the third was packed with bankers boxes.

The boxes were labeled with ranges of years, and Nate grabbed the one with the lowest range—1975–1980. He sat on the floor, pulling the box close and removing the lid. Legal-sized file folders lined the box, each labeled with a single year. He pulled one out, found it packed with pages that looked to have been poorly photocopied—the type off-center or crooked, the edges shadowed black as if the original hadn't been placed correctly on the copier glass.

Nate flipped through the pages, stopping when he saw a particular name: Gustafson.

He scanned the print, wondering if it included more detail about whatever was done to Realene and her parents. Two words jumped out at him.

*In Utero.*

**REALENE STOOD NEXT** to Ana at her father's graveside, hands clasped, as they listened to Mac's friends speak. Sun shone down from a cloudless sky, glinting off the remnants of unmelted snow peppering the ground between the headstones. Prior to this cemetery burial, Mac's family held the customary three-day wake at the Lakota reserve where he and Calvin grew up, which featured chanting, sharing of memories, and playing of the funeral drum. Realene attended the final day and was particularly moved when Ana, Big Kev, and Calvin placed locks of their hair in the casket to accompany Mac on his journey.

This burial today was more familiar to Realene, and yet so different from Ma's. There were no bleachers, no mass funeral, no impersonal remarks. He was being honored and mourned by everyone who loved him.

Realene wished Nate was here. He said he wanted to give her and Ana some space, that he'd feel like he was crashing an event meant for family and close friends, but Realene wondered if he just wasn't ready for a funeral, *any* funeral, given he'd likely never get to give his mom the one she deserved.

Harmon had covered his tracks to the point that no one acknowledged the mission into Canada, though that was probably also to avoid an international incident. Realene hadn't pushed the issue on that part of the story, only really cared about the details of the colonel's experiments being revealed so they could never come to fruition. The senate hearing meant the truth would finally come out.

Not about what she'd done, though. Everyone believed Trish killed Harmon, and Realene had forgiven herself. She was glad he was dead, glad he wouldn't be able to destroy anyone else like he had her family. If her dad was alive, she thought he would be proud of her.

She knew what he meant now about regret, about not being able to find a way out. Because of her, Harmon wouldn't be able to do that to anyone else. If there was a hell, she hoped he was burning there.

"Mac lived and died knowing one thing for certain. The truth is out there," Flint said, and a cheer went up from the crowd. The people Realene had met before their infiltration of Steele Air Force Base were there, along with many others, but they weren't wearing black as she'd expected. While their outfits were subdued colors, they also wore UFO paraphernalia, alien masks, and elaborate tinfoil hats in honor of their friend. Mac's friends from the Alien Alliance had come from across Canada and America to celebrate the man they called a hero.

Ana smiled, tears staining her cheeks, and Realene pulled her close. Beside her, Big Kev and Calvin joined in the cheers, the latter brandishing his now healed hand, minus one pinky.

Mac had been telling everyone for a decade that UFOs were real, met all of these people at conventions and in online chat rooms to share stories and join in the quest to prove alien life, and the footage from the base caught Mac's mad dash back into the building in the ultimate confrontation against those who would keep the truth of alien life a secret.

He made it out of the building alive that day. The soldiers who raided the bunker found him in the room with the cages, screaming about what he thought were alien-human hybrids. Not exactly right, but not far off.

After returning to Canada, he collapsed and was admitted to the hospital. Turns out, he'd been diagnosed with terminal cancer months before and kept it hidden from Ana and Big Kev. Realene wondered if his diagnosis contributed to him risking his life to discover the truth.

She also wondered who or what might've given him cancer. Those things weren't always natural occurrences.

Anxiety churned in her gut, that familiar worry about what Harmon did to her. Nate was the only one who knew what she'd found, and she wondered every day if she'd be the next one struck by an unnatural illness.

"Today we mourn the passing of a hero and a friend," Flint said. "Mac taught us to fight against impossible odds and never give up. And to remember, we are not alone."

That last comment got the biggest cheer of all and brought Realene to tears. Again. While they'd been brought together under terrible circumstances, she felt extremely lucky to have these people in her life. She'd lost her parents and been betrayed by the closest thing she'd had to a father, but she'd gained friends she would have for life.

Realene hung back as the family made the rounds to thank everyone for coming and remind them of the reception. Ana walked up, her eyes rimmed red. "How you holding up?"

Ana shrugged. "Kind of hoped my mom might show." No one knew where their mom was, or if she'd even heard about Mac's passing. "Dumb, huh?"

"Not at all." Realene squeezed Ana's arm, thinking it was best their mom hadn't come, or she might have been tempted to scream at the woman for abandoning her kids when things got tough.

Big Kev found the two of them, clasping first his sister and then Realene in a bear hug to rival those given by his dad. "Ready to head to the hotel?"

"I can't believe you talked the Holidome into hosting the reception," Realene said.

"Ever since that gas leak, they've been lacking business for some reason." He gave a sly grin, as if he had any actual memory of that night. He'd lost about two months, which included all his time in Demise investigating the meteor site.

Calvin sidled up, wearing his ridiculous prairie dog fur hat. "And my dear brother loved mini golf. Though he never could beat me."

Ana linked arms with Realene. "Uh-huh, the way I heard it you never beat him." She led the group to the car, which was parked on the road that cut through the cemetery.

"Tell me again about how I saved everyone from attacking zombies at the cabin," Big Kev said, opening the door to let Realene in the front passenger seat.

She grabbed the most recent issue of *The Winnipeg Sun* from the front seat and handed it to Big Kev, who'd picked up the tabloid at a gas station after seeing the headline, "Mysterious Mountie Amnesia. Virus or Alien Abduction Cover Up?"

He slid into the back seat beside Calvin.

"Your backwards driving ability was top notch, a real sight to see. And I, personally, would have lost it when the bison began to attack. But you kept your cool," she said. He didn't know he'd betrayed them by planting trackers on their cars, since it was information Realene decided to keep to herself.

She flipped on the radio, which played "My Hero" by the Foo Fighters.

Ana got in the driver's side. "I have a feeling this is like those hunting stories, where the size of the buck increases with each retelling."

"We're going up to Pine Bluff tomorrow to look into a Sasquatch sighting. Official business," Big Kev said, taking the chance to remind them all he was now an officer of the Alien Alliance. "You guys want to come?"

"There's word this fella is particularly aggressive, might be a sign of them worms," Calvin said.

"No thanks," Ana said. "I'm taking Realene out for a pancake breakfast with real maple syrup. None of that Mrs. Butterworth's crap she insists on buying."

"Come on, it's not that bad." Realene reached out and took her girlfriend's hand. Still felt weird calling her that. But life was too short to be careful, to hesitate, to not go for what you want. She had to grab every moment of happiness she could.

**SENATOR SCHMIDT WALKED** into the conference room, closing and locking the door behind him. He took the head chair, greeting the others that sat around the oval table—an assortment of military officers, government officials, and private interests.

He pressed a button on the box near his seat that lowered a screen on the wall at the opposite end of the table. Another location across the country with a similar setup appeared on the screen.

"Should we get started, ladies and gentlemen?" he asked, opening his folio, which contained a stack of papers he was already familiar with.

"This mess with Harmon is unfortunate," a woman in a blue suit on the screen said.

"He exceeded his authority." Though they'd approved the colonel's tests after the events in Demise, no one had authorized the mission in Canada or the experiments that followed there.

"And you've exceeded yours with this senate hearing nonsense."

He scoffed. "A public incident requires a public flogging…of the colonel, of course. It will allow us to put full responsibility on him. And don't worry, we'll only reveal what we choose." It was unfortunate that the incident at the base was televised by those UFO nut jobs, but they hadn't truly seen anything of concern. The girl and her friends insisted they wouldn't keep quiet about what they knew, but it was very easy to make people look crazy when they said crazy things.

"I must say, I'm impressed with the results of Harmon's studies, whatever his methods," a man in a lab coat said.

The senator flipped the first page over, reviewing the details on the reinfection of Nathan Haugen and Calvin Belanger. "As am I. He made a discovery that will protect our soldiers from long term side effects."

"You're endorsing inoculation through infection?" the man beside him asked.

"We need to confirm the results with further testing, but yes, it would appear so. Once infected and cured, we can keep our soldiers infected longer, perhaps indefinitely."

Those infected just once with the Alpha strain and left infected had turned into virtual zombies, but he suspected being infected and cured before reinfection would result in soldiers who were, for all intents, normal. Aside from being highly contagious. And infecting them with either the Omega or Beta strains would allow targeting of what they wanted the soldiers to spread.

"What about the girl? Number 173."

"Yes, Realene Gustafson." He flipped another page. "I've included her information on page three. She was the product of another of Harmon's early experiments, Operation Juno."

"She knows too much, could be a liability."

"Potentially. I suggest we do nothing for now, monitor her. For all his faults, Harmon seems to have had a knack for uncovering hidden potential in his subjects. Perhaps this Realene may prove useful."

And best of all, she trusted him, which may prove very useful indeed.

KMFDeMise 97.5 "The Rock" Presents:

# Spring Broke '98

Sunshine is overrated anyway.

1. **Wynona's Big Brown Beaver**
   Primus
2. **Everybody Hurts**
   R. E. M.
3. **Wave of Mutilation (UK Surf)**
   Pixies
4. **Fantasy**
   Mariah Carey
5. **Jesus Built My Hotrod**
   Ministry
6. **Everybody (Backstreet's Back)**
   Backstreet Boys
7. **Sour Times**
   Portishead
8. **Sunday Morning**
   No Doubt
9. **Unbelievable**
   EMF
10. **Satan is My Motor**
    CAKE
11. **Smells Like Teen Spirit**
    Nirvana
12. **Intergalactic**
    Beastie Boys
13. **Tubthumping**
    Chumbawamba
14. **Gin and Juice**
    Snoop Dogg
15. **Closing Time**
    Semisonic
16. **Personal Jesus**
    Depeche Mode
17. **Hitchin' a Ride**
    Green Day
18. **Hurt**
    Nine Inch Nails
19. **Know Your Enemy**
    Rage Against the Machine
20. **Poison**
    Bell Biv DeVoe
21. **Who's the Man**
    House of Pain
22. **Volcano Girls**
    Veruca Salt
23. **Army of Me**
    Björk
24. **I've Got a Miniature Secret Camera**
    Peter Murphy
25. **Everybody Knows**
    Concrete Blonde
26. **My Hero**
    Foo Fighters

# Acknowledgments

**THIS BOOK, LIKE** the prequel *Frost Bite,* was inspired by my formative years growing up in the '80s and '90s in Grand Forks, North Dakota, which was only about an hour and twenty minutes from Canada. We really did cross the border to drink, since the legal age was eighteen there, and back then you didn't even need a passport. I have a soft spot in my heart for Winnipeg and periodically calculate if I could pull off a move to Canada. I think my NoDak accent would blend in pretty well, but I'm not sure I could go back to those brutal winters.

You may have surmised that I'm a big fan of *The X-Files.* My sweetie and I watched religiously in college, recording every episode onto VHS tapes. We ended up with boxes of those tapes, each meticulously labeled with the episode number and name. *The X-Files* and *Unsolved Mysteries* (I can still hear Robert Stack saying, "For every mystery, there is someone, somewhere, who knows the truth), inspired me to delve into UFO conspiracies in this book. Big Kev is a tribute to a few college friends of mine who loved nothing more than to stay up into the wee hours of the morning discussing what really is out there. I also consulted an excellent book titled *More Encounters With Star People: Urban Indians Tell Their Stories* by Ardy Sixkiller Clarke in an effort to capture the perspective of urban indigenous people toward UFOs and alien encounters.

*Cold Snap* wouldn't exist without the support of so many incredible people. Thank you to my sweetie, Zach. I'm the luckiest person in the world to get to spend every day with my best friend. I also appreciate you saying, "Shouldn't you be writing?" Yes, I should ☺. Thank you to my editor Rob

Carroll for believing in this series and helping me discover what it could become. Thank you to Eric Hibbeler, whose incredible cover art continues to wow me and inspires countless readers to pick up the books.

Thank you to Zach, Alexis, Saytchyn, Chelsea, Meagan, and Brian for your insightful beta reads. You helped make this book better than I ever could have alone. Thank you to all my many writer friends in Nervous Drivers, HWA, RMFW, and WHADS for your friendship, support, and encouragement. And thank you to my family, who are my biggest cheerleaders and fans. I am so lucky to have all of you wonderful people in my life!

Lastly, thank you to my readers! I wasn't sure how my wacky '90s sci-fi horror comedy would be received, and I am so thankful *Frost Bite* found readers who love it as much as I do. Because of you, I got to write a sequel, which is pretty damn cool! I hope you enjoyed spending more time with these characters as much as I did. As we would have said in the '90s: You da bomb.

—Angela Sylvaine

# About the Author

**ANGELA SYLVAINE** is a Bram Stoker Award-nominated author and self-proclaimed cheerful goth. Her horror comedy novels, *Frost Bite* and *Cold Snap,* and her slasher novella, *Chopping Spree,* embody her cheerful side, while her short story collection, *The Dead Spot: Stories of Lost Girls,* is fully goth. Angela's short fiction and poetry have appeared in over sixty anthologies, magazines, and podcasts. A North Dakota girl transplanted to Colorado, she lives with her sweetheart and creepy cats on the front range of the Rockies. For updates on the *Frost Bite Series* and everything else Angela writes, visit angelasylvaine.com or scan the QR code below for newsletter and social media links.

the CHEERFUL GOTH

# About the Cover Artist

**ERIC HIBBELER** is a freelance illustrator and animator living and working in Kansas City, Missouri. He has done work for major motion pictures, comics, videogames, film posters, board games, children's books and editorial publications. Visit his website at erichibbeler.com.

www.ingramcontent.com/pod-product-compliance
Lightning Source LLC
LaVergne TN
LVHW032008070526
838202LV00059B/6350
*9781958598559*